By:
J.R. Carrel

Cover design by: Matthew Alan Bon

Printed in the United States of America

Chapter 1

We used to dance. Oh, how we danced. We danced through the banquet halls of the Palais Cardinal the night it opened. We danced through all of the great halls and small taverns of Europe. We danced for fifty-seven years, and she was as beautiful as the day I met her. Some people just say that. The difference is that, for us, it's true. We don't age; our kind never does from the day we are turned. We have been called many things: Draugr, Gang-shi, Ekimmu, but most know us as "vampires". I knew the moment I laid eyes on her, that she was it for me. Like magnetism, I was drawn to her. Each step felt like a moment closer to destiny. She wore a beautiful green, silk, sleeveless dress that matched her emerald eyes. It made her stand out. The ladies of the time preferred long sleeves with their evening attire. I went with my standard silver and black doublet.

The room smelled of expensive wine and a multitude of different perfumes. It overwhelmed me as I entered the main room. I'm not much for these types of parties. I mean, the musicians were great. The violins and cellos were echoing through the room brilliantly. I get a little claustrophobic with so many people walking around each other. The best part was the hors d'oeuvre, tiny little sausages in between sweet bread.

I began to walk towards her. I like to think I'm a pretty suave gentleman, but when faced with such radiance the only thing that I could come up with was “Hello there”.

“Yes?” She couldn’t have answered with a more disinterested statement.

“Would you like to dance?” I had to recompose myself and get my words together.

“Why don’t you go find another girl with whom to fornicate with,” she responded.

I stopped thinking about what to say and let my instincts take over.

“All of these girls are just prey. I want a woman who knows how to hunt.”

“Are you of the night?”

She looked up at me and smiled a bit as she spoke the code of our kind to identify themselves to one another.

“I am one with the night,” I nodded slightly with my traditional response.

“So, my name is Lina. Who might you be?" she asked as she let out a small laugh, looking me over with a grin. I had to curb my giddiness.

“My name is Simon.”

“I am of the Maat Cabal, and you are?” Lina asked me with a curious look.

“I am of the Ecne Cabal,” I replied.

Chapter 2

I guess I should explain a little about our culture and history. No one knows when the first vampires appeared. It's said that most of the so-called "supernatural entities" came into existence because humans exited the food chain. I guess mother nature didn't like that. So, mutations and viruses occurred to produce what we now call ourselves: super-predators.

All vampires can trace our origins back to a single vampire, known as Lord Dracula. I'm sure you've heard some stories, but ninety percent of them are bullshit. He was turned about six thousand years ago. At that time, there may have been around one thousand vampires in the world. He lived in Samaria, and back then, vampires had no structure. It was survival of the fittest. Sure, there were some small clans, but nothing like what we have today. Dracula, as it's told, was no one special at the time. He was living day to day and trying not to get killed by his kind as well as other super-predators, not to mention humans.

He was one of the first to get into the science of what made us what we were. He was possibly the first vampire to study at what would've been the equivalent of a university. This was pretty impressive considering we don't get along with sunlight. We don't burst into flames or melt into a puddle, but it does feel like a thousand fiery needles are stabbing our skin. It drains some of our life force reserves to hold the pain at bay. This is why most of our activity is at night. Dracula would dress in a full cloak to protect himself from the sun. He studied under masters for years. He tested and experimented on himself and other vampires. Doing this, he was able to find out some very useful things about us. Some of his theories are starting to prove true with the recent discovery of cells.

Things that cannot be seen fascinated him even more. Like why when we feed on a creature, it will die before we take more blood than they need to live. He speculated that when we feed, we are taking a creature's very life force—possibly the electricity stored within. The more we feed, or the stronger the host we feed on, it's like the flow of energy is shut off from us after we take a certain amount of it from them. Especially if we are feeding on something stronger than us. That's one of the two ways we get stronger. We get stronger over time and by feeding on strong creatures, and that includes other vampires. When Dracula realized this, he formulated a plan to reshape the vampire world in his image.

Dracula started small-snagging young vampires. Since there wasn't any hierarchy or governing body to keep track of the vampire population, no one noticed if one of us went missing, or if a new vampire came into the area. He knew he needed more power to take on the elders, so he started draining livestock as an easy power boost. Soon he had cleared an area of a thousand miles. By now, almost all the vampires knew something was hunting them. The rest of the predator communities were wary of such an apex predator as well. Dracula moved out of Mesopotamia to continue the mass killings. He went north first, where fewer vampires resided. It wasn't hard to find them with fewer food sources available; he knew where they'd be.

After disposing of the last Northern vampires, he trekked southward. Vampires started to band together for protection. Dracula's power had grown exponentially; he was easily able to overpower multiple vampires at once. His increased speed and strength were facilitating the acceleration of his plan. He finished off the last of the vampires on the African continent with ruthless aggression. He set his eyes on the East. At this point, it was fair to say he was probably the most powerful vampire, if only because of his blood consumption. Asia and Australia fell like the others. It took him three hundred and three years to complete his annihilation of the vampire race.

He moved to the second stage of his plan. He would continue to feed and increase his strength for one thousand years. Then, he went on to the third phase. He had put enough distance between himself and any new vampires he had made. He believed no one would be able to make up the power gap he created. Within his structure, he would turn four humans in the four corners of the world. He settled in Egypt, which now had a booming culture and their power was beginning to grow. He spent a lot of time around Saqqara, watching the pharaoh Djoser build his pyramid.

He was very interested in Imhotep. He got close to him and tried to learn from him. That did not sit well with Ra, and he forced Dracula to back away from his high priest. Dracula stood face-to-face with Ra.

Dracula was unshaken as Ra spoke, "Imhotep is mine. You will back down." Dracula never broke eye contact. "This land will not always be yours, and when it is no longer yours, you will remember me."

You can imagine Dracula does not take threats well, but

he's not going to take a god head-on. Although Ra was not necessarily that much older than Dracula, there is a different scale of power for beings that are brought about and powered by worship. Not all gods are true gods in that sense. Some are simply beings that are beyond human understanding and convince other people that they are gods. A lot of ancient gods are powerful predators that sometimes happen to be immortal. Dracula began his search for a worthy candidate to turn and resurrect the vampire race in Africa and the Middle East. He wanted someone with exceptional intelligence and who knew the culture of the gods.

Roaming around ancient Memphis, he spotted a perfume shop that was teeming with business. As he walked in, he saw two women collecting coins and passing out bottles. He also saw a young woman with exquisite garments and beautifully done makeup. She was signing and stamping a seal. He found out that she was the main supplier for the pharaohs and nobles when it came to perfumes and elixirs. Dracula then began showing up frequently and building a relationship with her. He eventually revealed what he was to her. He told her that he could make her immortal and could transform her into a goddess, but she had always had a shaky relationship with the gods. He taught her how to convince those around her into believing she was indeed a goddess. Dracula had her persuaded and she let him turn her. She was commanded not to turn anyone until his return. He left her, but first, he bestowed the name Maat upon her. She would go on to become a lower goddess of ancient Egypt and Dracula got his revenge on Ra.

Dracula had always wondered if the northern people had made any strides toward a larger civilization. So, he

ventured forth in search of an heir to the north. He traveled over the Alps and through France until he made it to the isles of Briton. There
weren't large cities to behold, only some small villages. In the south, not terribly far from the coast, he found a village that would later be known as Amesbury.

Just a couple of miles away, he found the people of the village erecting tremendous stones. They had started putting together a massive henge. Dracula could see that they had been adding onto a wooden henge. He felt the power radiating from the monument and knew that there had to be a god, or even gods, in the area. He mingled with the people for a time. He got to know one of the builders. This man talked about exploration and how he knew he would never see the henge finished in his lifetime. Dracula told him that there was a way he could see the construction through to the end and beyond, but he would have to swear allegiance to him. The man didn't hesitate for a moment and took Dracula up on his offer. Dracula turned him. Dracula told him he would return and wanted the man to finish the henge. Before he left, he bestowed the name of Ecne upon him. Dracula moved east through Europe.

He sought a Far East influence, so he pushed toward the Pacific. Walking the northern tundra, Dracula looked at the barren wasteland and thought about the new world he would build, how this world would be vastly different from what he was brought into. His journey began to move south from the frozen lands of Siberia. He moved in the blistering desert of the Gobi region. It reminded him of Egypt during the summer. He was shocked when he saw a small herd of cattle and a handful of nomads. He stayed the night with them. In the morning, they pointed him in the southern direction where he could find civilization.

After another day's travel, he found himself following a large river, which was a great sight to behold. He drank of the water and thought that with such a great water source, there must be cities or villages somewhere. As he was about to change courses, he saw people in the distance. When he got to the village, he was surprised to find that the people were extremely polite and respectful. He met a philosopher who spoke to him of the ways of his people. They spoke of destiny and structure. Dracula knew he had to have this man. When Dracula made the offer to the philosopher, he refused. He told Dracula that everything has its time: a time to flourish, and a time to live and die. Who was he to deny nature's course? Dracula told him that nature made him and fate brought them together. Their destinies have become entangled, and the man who least wants the power and responsibility should be the one carrying it. After much meditation, he agreed to the transformation. Dracula told him that he would return and when he does, the man should be prepared to travel. He told the philosopher that his people should call him Wendi. His name is spoken, to this day, among common Chinese folk.

Dracula looked out at the expanse of the ocean and wondered what was out there. He followed the coast and ran into many settlements but never found what he felt he needed. He reached the southern tip of Asia, still in search of his last heir. He had heard a legend of a group who left a small island off of the coast of China and had been raiding villages and islands all over the ocean. Dracula got his hands on a ship and paid a small crew of three people to help him find the legendary raiders. They sailed east, hitting island after island. The people told the same stories of a race of giants whose bloodlust and strength was unmatched. Dracula pushed his men to work harder and sail faster. They stopped on a small island where they rested and spent the night.

In the morning, they woke to a terrible sound. Loud, rhythmic yelling. Dracula walked to the other side of the island, where he ran into a group of large men. They had tribal tattoos on their face, chest, arms, and legs. Dracula's crew caught up to him and asked what was going on. He instructed the men to stay quiet. More of the tattooed warriors arrived on the beach. One of the warriors saw Dracula and his men. They formed a line and their leader, a giant of a man, started walking around them. He began to yell, "Ka Mate!" The men began to do a type of war dance, slapping their chests and legs. The leader started walking toward Dracula. He was nearly half a foot taller than Dracula and maybe two hundred pounds heavier. He was carrying a teardrop-shaped jade piece in his left hand. He got right in Dracula's face and stared at him, his eyes almost bulging out of his head. Dracula's facial expression did not change in the slightest. Then, in the blink of an eye, the man slammed the jade piece into the left temple of Dracula. Dracula limply fell to the ground. The two crewmen ran, attacking the warrior. The warrior kicked the first crew member in the stomach, and as he bent over to grab his abdomen, the warrior smashed the jade piece down into the back of his head. The other crewman threw a wild punch at him. He leaned back out of the way of the punch. Then, he grabbed the man by his shirt and head-butted him twice.

"That is quite enough!" a voice from behind the warrior bellowed as the crewman fell unconscious.

The warrior turned. A shocked look engulfed his face. Dracula stood there, relaxed in posture, with not a single mark on him. The warrior motioned to his men to attack. They ran full speed at Dracula. They were carrying clubs with sharks' teeth along the edges. They swung at Dracula, but he blocked the first swing with his left forearm. He pushed the warrior with his right palm causing the warrior to fly back twenty feet. The next swung down like an axe. Dracula sidestepped. When the club hit the sand, Dracula stomped on it and shattered it into a thousand pieces. He grabbed the warrior by the right arm and threw him into the next warrior. The only one left standing was the leader. He moved toward Dracula with intent; every step was calculated. He stopped ten feet from Dracula. He looked him over and swayed back and forth on the balls of his feet, ready to strike at any moment. Dracula stares deep into his eyes. A small smirk starts to spread across his mouth.

"You are exactly what I need: fearless and ruthless," Dracula declared, his voice booming across the beach.

As Dracula heaped praise upon the warrior, his demeanor did not change until Dracula asked him if he wanted to be the greatest conqueror the world has ever known. The warrior told Dracula that he wanted to be a legend to his people. He wanted his name to live on forever. Dracula stopped him and said that *he* could live forever. The warrior's eyes shot open, but a flare of skepticism arose. Dracula told him that he walked the earth before the warrior's ancestors left the first island. The warrior asked how it was possible that he didn't die and how he survived the blow he dealt him earlier. Dracula explained what he was and how he wanted the warrior to join his family. The warrior agreed, as long as he could continue to travel the seas. Dracula told him that he wanted him to conquer the seas, but he would have to take a trip with him first. After that, he could return to his people. That night, Dracula turned the warrior.

In the morning, before they set off, Dracula spoke to the islanders and told them that when the warrior returned, his name would be Tūmatauenga. He announced that they will travel and conquer all of the islands of the ocean, but that they must wait for his return. They pushed off and headed toward the continent of Asia.

Chapter 3

Tū asked Dracula where they were heading. Dracula told him that they were going to pick up another one of his children. Tū asked if he, too, was a great warrior. Dracula said he uses his mind more than a sword. Tū scoffed. Dracula looked at him and told him not to underestimate him, that he chose him for a reason. Tū looked out to sea with a focused look on his face.

The trip took them two weeks. The people of the village had never seen someone like Tū. He was the largest person they had ever seen. They couldn't take their eyes off of him. Tū scowled as he walked beside Dracula and told him that he didn't trust these people. He thought they should leave quickly. Dracula explained to him that these people were perfectly fine and there was nothing to be afraid of.

When they arrived at Wendi's house, he had supper cooking and welcomed them in. Tū listened to Wendi and Dracula talk, sizing up Wendi. He was trying to figure out what made him worthy of Dracula's loyalty. Wendi genuinely took an interest in Tū and his life. He asked about his family, goals, and plans for the future. Tū realized that Wendi did not possess the same tools that he did. He lacked the tools of a warrior, but he did have the tools of a great thinker: persuasion and strategy. He could see all of the effects of a possible enemy. Tū embraced Wendi and accepted him as a brother. He looked forward to their journey. Wendi saw that Tū was more than what he appeared to be at the surface. Not a mindless killing machine, but a thinker as well. He knew he was going to be a great asset to Dracula.

In the morning, they pushed off after Wendi said his goodbyes. They planned on going through the Indian Ocean and up through the Red Sea. As they talked through what the best plan was, the sea started to turn on them. Tū told them that he believed Tangaroa was not pleased with them. They were blown off course and landed on the subcontinent of India. Dracula knew instantly where they were and once they moved onto land.

"Do not speak. This is not our land. This is the land of the gods," Dracula commanded. Tū gripped his shark-tooth club while Wendi skeptically looked around. Dracula began walking down the shore while Tū and Wendi fell in behind him.

They arrived in a small city. Dracula tried to move them silently through. As they made their way out of the city, a group of five women came out of the woods, carrying water pails from the nearby stream. They nearly ran into Dracula. They all put their pails down and walked around the men. The women began speaking loudly, looking over the men. Tū started telling them to get back, but the women didn't understand his words. Dracula told him not to engage with them, but the women began to touch Wendi and Tū. Tū pushed one of them to the ground. Dracula's eyes widened and he pulled Tū away.

"I told you not to interact with them," Dracula scolded Tū, glaring into his eyes.

The women ran into the city, screaming. Dracula looked at Tū and Wendi and told them whatever happens next, to not say a word. Just then, they saw a form coming from around a building at the edge of the city. It looked like a human, but much larger than average. The figure had eight arms and two legs. The figure was crawling towards the men. As the creature drew closer, it was apparent that it was a woman with swords, spears, and a shield in her multiple hands. All three men were still, but Dracula stood in front of them, unwaveringly. The woman was about a hundred yards away. She locked eyes with Dracula and began speeding up. She was on the men in a matter of seconds. She stood up, towering over them, and took a couple of deep breaths. The woman leaned over and got a few inches from Wendi's face, but Wendi kept his eyes forward.

"You reek of fear," she spoke with a bold, yet feminine voice. She leaned over to Tū; he didn't budge. She mocked Tū, saying, "But you are a fool. Fear is the correct response." Then she snapped her neck toward Dracula with her eyes wide, almost bulging out of her head. "And you, Dracula!"

It surprised Dracula that she knew him by sight. Dracula was acquainted with many gods, but not in this part of the world. She stood with her back straight.

"You are not wise to bring your offspring through these lands." She stood towering over the men, her red lips and bronzed skin nearly glowing in the sun. The lean muscles of her body rippled, showing that she was ready to strike at any moment. She was unaware that Dracula had some information about her as well.

Dracula lifted his head and said in a confident voice, "Hello, Durga." Laced inside his words was a small conscious bit of worship in them. As she stood upright, she felt it. She arched her back slightly and bit the side of her bottom lip. For a being at the level of Dracula, sensing even a small amount of worship must have been exhilarating for her. She let out a small sigh and looked down at Dracula.

Durga gushed, “I love the way you speak my name, but I was unaware that you knew me.”

“Your beauty and power are known far and wide, and couldn't be mistaken.”

Dracula’s compliments seemed to cool the bloodthirsty tone in her voice, and the murderous look in her eyes, if only ever so slightly.

“Leave these lands at once. You, or any of your offspring, must never return.” She looked at Tū and Wendi, cautioning sternly, “Next time you enter my lands and touch one of my worshippers, I will rip the flesh from your bones.”

Dracula spoke up, “And you should also remember that gods can die too.” There was a long silence. Tension weighed heavily in the air.

Durga sneered, “But not so easily.”

Afterward, Dracula, Tū, and Wendi made their way north, through the jungle and over mountains. They had two more places to go.

They finally arrived in a small village in the northern region. Even with his enhanced immunity, Tū showed disdain for the cold northern winter. He had never seen snow before and found it very unpleasant to the touch. Dracula asked some villagers where he could find Ecne. They told him he would find him at the Henge.

They made their way to the monument. Ecne was on top of one of the giant stones. He leaped down when he saw Dracula, landing on his feet with ease.

Dracula greeted him with a handshake and said, “I see you've been busy.”

Ecne nodded to him and confirmed, “Thanks to you, my lord, not only will I live to see it completed, but I will be the one to see it concluded.” Ecne introduced himself to Tū and Wendi. He invited them into his home.

It was a nice, round stone structure with a thatched roof. The stones seemed to reflect a blue color and were unlike anything the men had seen before. The interior was well-decorated with animal hides and some gold trinkets hanging from the walls. They ate a meal of boar and potatoes. Tū seemed to get along with Ecne, while Wendi seemed to be more silent.

In the evening, Dracula went to Wendi and asked him what he thought of Ecne. Sitting beside the fireplace in the guest hut, Wendi and Dracula conversed. Wendi told Dracula that he liked Ecne, but Dracula might want to keep an eye on him. Wendi sensed great ambition in him.

The following morning, they set off for Egypt. They walked along the main roads, which were no more than dirt and mud trails that animals and some merchants used. They entered Central Europe, where the forests dominated the landscape. After covering a fair distance, Dracula decided they would stop so that they could feed. They were nearly starving. Tū, Wendi, and Ecne all fed on deer while Dracula walked around their small camp. The men never saw Dracula feed, not once since the journey began. Not letting them see him feed may have been a way for him to show them that he had near limitless reserves. As they fed, the forest was mostly quiet, with the sound of a nearby stream running and some birds chirping in the distance.

Suddenly, Tū looked up and said, “We are being watched.”

Ecne reached down and grabbed his sword while

Wendi grabbed his dagger. Tū sat calmly with his shark-toothed club no more than an arm's length away.

Tū asked, "Is it a god?"

Dracula replied loud enough for him to be heard throughout the area, "More like a god's mistake."

No sooner had he got the last word out when they heard a grunt, then smashing through the limbs of the canopy. Before they could even attempt a guess at what it was, the figure was sliding down the side of a nearby giant fir tree. It tried to slow its descent by gouging its long claws through the bark and into the meat of the tree. Its claws cut through the tree like it was a block of cheese: there was very little resistance. It hit the ground without throwing much debris up. The ground was a mostly moist brush. The figure was right under seven feet tall, with its arms reaching down to its knees. They were slender, yet muscular, along with the rest of its body. The creature had a large chest and a small waist. It had very short, black fur all over its body, but you could see its muscles wanting to rip out of the skin. It had long, powerful-looking fingers with claw-like nails at the end, the same as its feet. Its most prominent feature, which gave away its identity, was its head. It could not be mistaken for anything other than a wolf, but its eyes were all too human.

Wendi immediately exclaimed, "Shapeshifter!"

Ecne corrected him, stating he was a lycanthrope. Dracula stood between the men and the lycanthrope and told him to declare his business.

"You hunt game on my family's land and insult my people? And you ask for me to state my business?" The lycanthrope leaned his head to the side, and as he spoke, his chest heaved up and down. His voice sounded like a man trying to catch his breath.

Dracula replied, “I hunt wherever I please, and it was not an insult but a factual statement. Zeus should not have been so careless. He should have stomped Lycaon underneath his foot. Then your kind would never have propagated itself as far as it has.”

The lycanthrope spoke with venom in his voice, “You are not the only one with knowledge. Our elders kept many scents for us to recognize,” he continued with great satisfaction. “And you are among them, Dracula.”

“It's good that you know of me. You should know to give my children and I a wide berth.”

The lycanthrope bolstered his voice and warned, “If one of your children is caught trespassing on my family's land, they will be made an example for all of the others.”

Dracula instantly blurred and was nearly chest to chest with the lycanthrope. He tilted his head ever so slightly and stared directly into the lycanthrope's eyes. “If one of your kind ever threatens one of my children, I will walk through the front doors of your father's Great Hall, and I will drain your entire clan for all of their strength. I will not be hindered in the slightest.” Dracula leaned in and whispered, “Make sure every creature knows because my thirst is unquenchable.”

A short time later, they arrived in Egypt to retrieve the final member. They met with two women at night in Memphis who were followers of Maat. They told Dracula that Maat had instructed them to guide them to her. They weaved back and forth through side streets and down alleyways and markets. Finally, they stopped in front of a perfume stand, which the women lifted and pulled away, revealing a secret door to the underground. They walked down about twenty stairs, at the end of which they came upon a long corridor lined with torches. After about a hundred feet, it opened up into a vast cathedral-like room.

Maat sat upon a throne carved out of black granite. She stood up and commanded her followers to leave. They dashed out as fast as they could. As soon as they were out of sight, she took a knee.

"Lord, you have returned."

Dracula told her that he was proud of her and that she had done well for herself in his absence. Dracula introduced each of the men. Maat took stock of the men. She could tell that Tū was a warrior, which was plain to see. By Wendi's dress and mannerisms, she could tell he was a scholar. But when it came to Ecne, she could not find what made him unique. Dracula told them to mingle for the day and meet back here at night. Then, he would show them the future. The group shared stories of their homelands and accomplishments. It all seemed cordial until Ecne boasted about the henge he had built. Maat said it must not have been that impressive if she hadn't heard about it, whereas everyone for thousands of miles knows of the pyramids. Ecne stated that he would build the greatest empire the world had ever seen.

That night, Dracula brought them all together and they feasted on the blood of humans. Dracula told them that their job was to go back to their homelands and convert the locals into worshippers. They were not to turn anyone for at least one hundred years, and they were not to turn any family members. Each new vampire would not be allowed to turn a new vampire unless they were at least one hundred years old. They could only turn three people, each of those people being approved by one of the four. Any vampires breaking this law were to be executed immediately. They were to expand their empires as far as they possibly could while keeping complete control. There were to be no wars between supernatural or other predator factions without consent from Dracula first. When their empires expanded far enough that they met Dracula, they would draw the lines.

So it was for the next several millennia. Tū dominated the seas, conquering nearly all of the islands of the world. Wendi would go on, taking almost all of Asia. Maat controlled the Middle East and Africa, while Ecne reigned over Europe. Since Ecne and Maat were the closest, they were at odds with each other the most over land and resources.

This brings us all the way to today. This is the world I find myself in the middle of.

Chapter 4

The Maat and Ecne cabals haven't got along for as long as anyone can remember. Especially right now, as we are going through a restructuring phase ever since Christopher Columbus sailed the ocean in 1492, one hundred and forty seven years ago. That arrogant prick brought a lot of attention to the "New World". Of course, we've known about it for at least five hundred years before he found it. We've been slow playing and arguing back and forth about who should lay claim to it.

Around the turn of the century, a deal had been struck. Maat would give Tū Madagascar, and she would give the Turkish area over to Wendi. Wendi gave Tū Sri Lanka and the islands off the coast of China. Tū also was given access to all shipping ports, and Wendi got to keep Japan. After all that shifting, Ecne got all of the New World. In exchange, he has to give Maat all of Europe. It was a gamble with Europe. Ecne has more wealth than any other cabal leader. He believes he can build an even larger Empire, but it has to start from scratch. They set a fifty-year timetable for Ecne to have Europe vacated. He is pulling all of his resources out and has to leave his framework behind for Maat.

I'm not a big fan of the idea. I like Europe. I like my home. I'm not that big on exploring. I've decided to be on the last crew out of here. We have eleven more years before we all have to be out of here, and Maat takes over everything. That's why when I told Lina I was from the Ecne cabal, it raised her eyebrows a little. Which, by the way, I thought was adorable, but if I had ever told her that, she would have probably ripped my throat out. No, scratch that. She really would have ripped my throat out.

In a confident voice, she asked, “So what are you still doing here? Shouldn't you be headed over to explore the New World?” She had a very sarcastic tone to “New World”.

“I'm part of the clean-up crew, just trying to make it all nice and shiny for you. Plus, I thought I'd stick around for a while. I might find something interesting,” I replied.

She smirked and countered, “Well, Mr. Simon, have you found anything interesting?”

I didn't think any words would do, so I held my hand out for a dance. She was quite the dancer, I must say. I'm no slouch at moving my feet, but she was a better dancer than I. Her hair was darker than ink, yet it reflected the candlelight of the hall: a perfect contrast to her pale skin.

After we finished our dance, the party concluded. I asked her if she would mind going for a midnight stroll. I told her that I had never seen a member of the Maat cabal that looked like her. She explained to me that she's actually from Eastern Europe and that her parents were wealthy merchants. They go on a trip to Egypt every year for supplies and relaxation.

When she was at one of Maat's perfume and potion shops in Alexandria, she saw a man pickpocketing a woman. She called him out. The woman turned out to be Maat. She knew the man took the object from her pocket. He was quickly dragged away and was drained and burned. Maat was satisfied with Lina. Maat told her she could pick any perfume in the entire store. Lina then began coming back every day while they were in Alexandria to talk with Maat and the other women of the shop. As her parents were packing up to head back to Europe, Maat came to them and offered them a large sum of gold to have Lina stay with her. She promised them that Lina would get the best education from Alexandrian scholars. The offer was so generous, her parents could not refuse. Lina said she started working in the shop. Then as they taught her more and more, she ended up running the shop. She was good at it; it became Maat's most profitable shop. Maat began to reveal more and more to her. After a couple of years, she offered to turn her. By this point, Maat was like a second mother to her. Lina accepted eagerly. She went from being a shop runner for about fifty years to, with this transition, becoming a sort of liaison to Europe since she was familiar with the area.

Lina looked down at my hand. She saw the scars on my knuckles and the big scar on the top of my right hand.

She ran her finger across the rough skin and asked me, "How did you get this?"

The thing about us vampires is that after you have turned, any scar tissue you have stays with you. From there on, you will never produce another scar. I told her it happened the day I was turned. She gave me a look that told me to tell her more.

"My story is not as warm as yours. It's colder." *It's much colder*, I thought. When I was a young child, my parents died. They left me in the care of a knight who had a roaming sportsman tournament business. He would set up tournaments all over Europe: jousting, swordsmanship, archery, and horseback riding. He taught me everything he knew about the business and the art of swordsmanship. We all have some god-given ability. The sun rises, fish swim, and I handle the sword. It must have also helped that I thought it was fun. Therefore, I always wanted to practice. I was never happier than when I was a child, and I had a sword in the palm of my hand. My master was more than happy to oblige. I got so good that before I even had hair on my face, he put me in his show. I was called "The Boy Wonder". You could place a bet on yourself to go against me with practice swords. He would match anyone that I would go up against, even men three times my age. I would defeat them all.

As I got older, I wanted to enter the official tournament for myself. At first, he let me, and I began winning tournament after tournament. The participants started to complain that there must be something nefarious going on. My master told me that I could continue doing the sideshow and placing bets, but I could no longer be in the tournament. I quickly became bored and wanted to do something more fulfilling. While the show was down, I would travel to local villages that had a bear or wolf problem, or were threatened by bandits. Sometimes I would go to a village, walk into the tavern, and there would be four marauders trying to extort them. Those were the kinds of challenges I loved; they would always be overconfident. My master said to fight to the best of your abilities. It's better to try your hardest and make it look easy than to make it hard on yourself and die. I was always a straightforward swordsman. If you cannot take a person out in three moves, you shouldn't be fighting them. I don't do any of those pirouetting or twirling techniques. They leave you far too open. If you ever catch me doing that, you can be certain that I am outclassed, and I have no other option. This went on for several years.

My master was getting up there in age. One day, he

took me aside and told me he wanted me to take over the business. I was too young to want to settle down into that type of lifestyle. The day it happened, we set up outside of Montpellier. It was nearly a hundred and eighty years ago, but I remember it vividly.

It was midday. Most of the workers and knights had gone into the city for lunch. I remember the day being extra bright, or maybe it was just me hyper-focusing. It started with the screaming. Then came two calls for help. What happened, I learned later, was that a young, freshly-turned vampire had lost his mind in thirst. When you first turn, it feels like hell. They keep you locked away and feed you heavily for a few days. That will typically keep you calm. Then they can begin to reason with you and tell you the rules of how to be a vampire, but he broke loose of his containment. For a few weeks, he ran around the countryside, randomly turning folks in the area. Since they didn't know any better, they got lost in a combination of thirst, confusion, and being caught in the sunlight. It sent them into a frenzy, and we just happened to be the first thing they ran into. There were fifteen of those vicious little animals.

I jumped up after the first scream and grabbed my sword. I ran out to the middle of our camp. Two women were lying there with their throats ripped out a few feet from me. They were choking on their blood that was still pumping from their necks. The first vampire came at me in a blind rage. I speared my sword clear through its abdomen. To my shock, it kept coming. I kicked it in the chest, pulling my blade free and whipping it from the ground upward, cutting off its left arm at the shoulder. That just seemed to piss it off. It looked down at the blood squirting, then looked back up at me and came for my throat again. I swiped my sword upwards, spiking it through the bottom of its jaw, and up through the top of its skull. That seemed to do the trick. It instantly dropped. I pulled my sword free and began running towards the screams. I saw more people on the ground this time. Some of the knights still had their swords in their hands but were lifeless.

I came upon two more vampires. They were out of their minds. Their eyes were completely bloodshot, their fangs drawn. I remember thinking that they were horrifying to look at, and their speed was as fast as any knight I had ever dueled with. They had no technique. They were running at me, slashing their hands, and trying to bite any part of my body I left exposed. I parried the first one that rushed me head on and I slashed the second one across the chest and shoulder. He backhanded me behind the right ear and it wobbled me. I spun, keeping my sword out in front of me. The one that first missed me came back recklessly, and I speared him through the right eye. The other one was on me quickly. All I had time to do after pulling the sword out of the first one's head, was to swing it down like a battle-axe. It struck halfway through his skull. That was enough to stop him cold.

The next thing I could think of was to get to my master's tent. I knew he was in rough shape, but I also knew that the man's pride would not allow him to hide. I was right. He was standing outside his tent with his broadsword in hand.

“Simon, what in the bloody hell is going on?”

I told him there were crazed lunatics ripping people's throats out. Four more of the bastards came at us. Without hesitation, my master took the lead. He did not have the speed and strength he once did, but he could still get off an amazing first strike. Not knowing what I had learned a few minutes earlier, that you have to go for the head, he stabbed the first one through the heart. In the same motion, he removed the blade, and swung it down toward the collarbone of the second. The blade bit down through to his right lung. I was already moving to intercept the other two when he leaped into action. It was a small woman and another man. They were so thirsty that they ran into each other trying to get to me which made it simple for me to swing a horizontal strike that cut her head off at the top of the neck. I had to pull the blade upwards to strike the man in the face, cutting his head off at the lower jaw. Those two blows sent blood spewing through the air.

As I turned to assist my master, I found his lack of knowledge was his undoing. Those strikes would have laid waste to any human. The problem is it only slows these newborns down. They had jumped him immediately after the strike, which he paused after for half a second, believing it to be a deathblow. They were ripping and tearing at his shoulders and neck. I can still see the look of shock and fear in his eyes as these vicious animals began to drain him. They didn't even hear me coming as I released both of their heads from their bodies in two quick strokes. I knelt down to comfort him, but he was already gone. These newborns weren't turning anyone; they had zero knowledge of what was going on within them; they were simply out for blood.

As I moved my way through the camp, I ran into a couple of dead vampires. It looked like they had been hacked dozens of times. The handful of knights that were still in the camp must have kept hitting them until they stopped moving. A few steps further, I started to find the bodies of those knights. You can tell they fought until the very second their souls left their bodies. They had rip marks all over them where they struggled. Another female vampire was on her knees sucking the blood from a bicep of one of the knights. I swung my blade from the ground upward, like I had seen people do when playing the new game of golf. It took her head off just below the chin.

I made my way towards the front of our camp. I bumped into two more vampires, a woman and a man. I later found out that he was the one turning everyone. I must have startled him because his first reaction was to grab her and throw her at me. I had more stamina than most when it came to swordplay because I was used to taking bets and fighting for hours, but that was when I was well-rested and one hundred percent prepared to do battle. This was a different scenario. I was losing steam quickly, but I still had enough in the tank to easily dodge her and put my sword straight through her forehead.

I ran after the man as I came to the front gates of our encampment. I saw our cook. She was a sweet lady. I remember the master telling me that she had come down from Scotland with him twenty years ago. She had long, red hair that was almost orange. She was a stocky woman. I never saw her get pushed around by anyone, but there she was on the ground, crying and backpedaling away from this vermin.

"Hey, you piece of shit! Get away from her!" I called out.

He turned to look at me and uttered in a stuttering motion the only words I heard any of them say: "Your blood will do too."

He came at me head on. I was tired, and his slightly enhanced speed over the others meant I missed on my first strike. He slashed at my face. I lifted my sword and blocked it but he caught the back of my hand, ripping a gash open. It hurt beyond belief but I was trained to get my hands hit over and over again with a wooden sword. It became muscle memory to never lose grip on your sword. I brought my sword down and added an arc towards his knee. He was able to move fast enough that it barely grazed his thigh. Then, before I could raise it again, he kicked me in the stomach, which slammed me back into the jousting cart. I went down hard. Whether he thought I was dead, or assumed that I was incapacitated enough for him to turn away, he went back to the cook. I tried to get up as fast as I could. The pain was shooting down from my lower back, making my feet wobbly. I heard her screams and I saw him tearing her open. I lost it. I grabbed a lance from the cart and ran at him in a blind rage. Anyone nearby must have heard me screaming. He turned around and I speared him through the chest into the ground as hard as I could. The lance must have dug deep into the ground because he couldn't pull himself free. It gave me a second to reach down and grab a sword that had been dropped. I took it in both hands and with all the force I could generate, I cut off his left arm at the shoulder, then his right. My emotions were completely controlling me. I began to hammer him with my fist over and over again until there was nothing left of his head. I happened to look up, and there were three more vampires, about twenty yards away, staring directly at me. I stood up slowly and grabbed my sword. I had very little energy left.

Three riders on horseback rode in quickly and stopped about ten yards from me. They were completely covered in black, flexible leather armor. They had three eyes that were barely visible. The one in the middle jumped off of his horse and landed on the ground. He made three leaps towards the vampires so quickly, I could barely comprehend it. Half a second later he was standing there with a rag in his hand, wiping the blade of his weapon, and behind him, the heads of the three vampires tumbled off. The two men that were still mounted sat with their arms crossed over the horn of their saddles. I could hear them discussing what they should do with me.

The one on the ground walked up to them and said, "He took out ten of them by himself. For a vanilla human, that is pretty impressive. I say we take him back and let the local magistrate decide what to do with him."

One of the men on horseback looked around and said, "The cleaners can deal with this."

I probably would have resisted if I had any strength left. One of them walked up to me and merely took the sword out of my hand and tied my hands together. They threw me on the horse and took me back with them. The magistrate decided I could be of some use. They decided I would be turned by one of the local leaders. I know a lot of people react differently to the change. There is usually no ceremony to it; they normally bite you near an artery and inject the virus, after which you will normally be chained in a room. They wait for you to change, which can take anywhere from an hour up to half a day. Then they'll put someone in the room with you, typically a homeless person or a criminal from the local jail. If they think you have taken hard to the thirst, they'll give you a second. Once you have drank enough to focus and you start to calm down, they will tell you what is going on and how it is going to be. This is very similar to how it went down for me. I can still remember my first. He was a middle-aged man who was caught stealing grain from another family's stocks. I remember him being very dirty and smelling of piss. I grabbed him by the top of his head, got a handful of his shaggy hair, pulled his head to the side, and ripped his throat out with my teeth. I drank his blood until my stomach was full.

The next thing I hear is Lina saying, "Well, you're right. It wasn't as warm as my story. I won."

I snapped back to reality, and asked, "You win?"

In an amused voice, she replied, "Obviously the nicer story always wins, Simon."

"Obviously," I mumbled, mockingly.

She looked out at the night and said, "These old stories have made me famished. Do you want to grab a bite to eat?"

I couldn't help but laugh. "Oh you're funny. How could I resist your charm?"

"I know I am, and you couldn't if you tried," Lina replied.

Chapter 5

We were walking down De La Harpe Street when she stopped at a carriage. It was an immaculate carriage drawn by two large, black draft horses. The carriages were also ash black and had a lantern on all four corners. With a carriage like this, you could tell Lina was not some lowly servant of Maat. On the door of the carriage, there was a depiction of Maat in an ancient Egyptian manner, a beautiful woman with bird feathers going down both arms. She opened the door to the carriage and lifted a hem around her waist that I assumed was for decoration. It concealed buttons all the way around which she had promptly undone in a second or two. Underneath she had on tight-fitting black silk pants. She saw the curious look on my face.

With a nonchalant look, she said in a pouty voice, "A girl never knows when she will have to make a quick escape." She smiled and bobbed eyebrows at me. She threw the bottom half of her dress into the carriage and we were on our way down the streets of Paris in search of dinner.

Cobblestone streets were virtually empty aside from vagrants or drunks stumbling through them. Lina was scanning the buildings, side to side, with her eyes. I knew she had found what she was looking for when all of a sudden, she said: "Got you." I asked her if she had found what she was looking for. She responded, "These rich humans make it too easy, leaving their balcony doors open."

I looked up and sure enough, the second story balcony door above us was wide open, probably trying to take in the cool evening summer air. Lina took one more look up, bent her knees ever so slightly, and launched herself upward. She cleared the balcony twenty feet above with ease. I followed right along with the same motions. That sort of jump isn't a problem for vampires our age. We have some built-in biological mechanisms that help us get close to humans. For one, we secrete a pheromone that is very similar to the pollen of the lavender plant, but on a more extreme level. It relaxes the majority of humans subconsciously, telling their body and mind that we are no threat. Its effects are even greater when humans sleep. For thousands of years, humans have put lavender in their baths to relax them and get them ready for sleep. This is why if we do not have a human that is willing to give us their blood, we tend to go after humans while they sleep. It is against our protocols to go around ripping the throats out of humans. Sure, it's a quick and easy way to get a meal, but it's also the quickest way to get discovered.

Once we entered the bedroom, we saw that it belonged to a wealthy family. The bed was enormous. It had ornately carved bed posts and a canopy covering it. Our second asset to keep us from being detected while feeding is our venom. It's very similar to that of a conotoxin used by sea snails. A sea snail is slow and needs to immobilize its victim very quickly. Its venom drops the blood-sugar level in its victim, rapidly putting it in a state of paralysis, and shuts off the nerve endings. That is precisely what our venom does. Simply biting someone does not turn them into a vampire. Our fangs have two small holes in them, one above the other. The first hole is for the injection of our venom. The second hole is above, hidden inside our gums and we have to force our fangs down like a snake. That is what releases the virus that turns humans.

We crept to opposite sides of the bed and pulled back the ornate curtain. The couple had expensive tastes and they had a large purple comforter with flower designs on them. Purple was a hard color to get in the fabric at the time, making it very costly. Lina was on the husband's side while I was on the wife's side of the bed. He was lying flat on his back with his mouth gaping open, while his wife laid on her side. Drool was dripping from her mouth and onto her pillow. They both looked as dopey as most people do while they sleep. This is especially why most people refrain from sleeping in public, even more so once you get into middle age, such as this couple. It's not a refined look. Lina looked over at me and I thought she was about to burst out laughing. I gave her a look that conveyed whether we are going to do this or not. She returned a pouty face that said *you're no fun*. She put her hair back into a ponytail and gently lowered her mouth down to the man's throat, revealing her fangs a half an inch before she bit into his neck. Her pupils completely dilated and I can tell at that very moment that the surge had hit her. I followed suit and sunk my fangs into the woman's neck.

To describe the feeling that you get when the blood first starts rushing into your mouth, it's like the coldest water you've ever drank on the hottest day that you've ever felt. It was refreshing to the point of being orgasmic. Then, after the initial wave, it feels like a low electric pulse entering your whole body. The whole experience is euphoric. As you get older, you learn to control it better. That's why most of the human deaths during feeding are from vampires under the age of fifty. If you're not planning on draining them to death and you do it properly, it only takes about a minute to feed. We never worried about the risk of being discovered because the venom would give them the deepest and best sleep they'd ever had in their life. The bite marks would go away in a couple of hours. Our fangs are as sharp as obsidian, and our saliva contains enzymes in it that allow the wound to heal far more rapidly than it would naturally.

We both came up at the same time. Lina was breathing heavily and I could tell that the experience had been quite pleasurable. She had intense, wild-looking eyes that made her even more alluring to look at. She had more control than I did because while I was daydreaming about the extraordinary things we could be doing in this bedroom right now, she had made her way around the bed, leaned over and whispered in my ear, "Quit drooling and let's get out of here." I snapped to attention and we walked to the balcony.

As we stood on the balcony, there was a cool breeze blowing. It lifted her hair ever so slightly off her shoulders, and in the clear night sky, the moonlight lit up her eyes. She looked out to the city and said, "I do like this view." She turned her head slightly towards me and continued, "You know Paris will be the new capital for Maat."

I had no idea that she was planning that. I asked, "Isn't that going to piss off the vampires of Africa?"

Lina shrugged. "Maat is telling all of the leadership that it is imperative that we show the rest of the predator and supernatural nations that there will be no power vacuum, but it's really because she likes Paris and wants a change of scenery," she chuckled. "Maat has been sneaking into Europe outside of official business for several hundred years now. Maat especially likes Italy and France and that's where she plans to spend most of her time once she takes over Europe."

"Ecne is making the city that had recently popped up, called New Amsterdam, his new capital," I mentioned.

"What is your job within the cabal?"

"I am part of the Nigrum Gladio." It translates from Latin, meaning "black sword". We are called that because the handle of all of our swords are black and we ride in all-black, tactical gear.

"Why would you be part of them?" she asked.

I shrugged and said, "They were the ones that saved me. They kind of pushed me to join them. Honestly, I don't mind it because I get to stop what happened to me from happening to others.

She perked up and said, "You are the guys that go out and kill rogue vampires, right?" Before I could answer her, she had another question: "And you're the ones that have the stupid nicknames, right? What's the stupid name that you call yourself?"

I said, "Well, first off, yes. We kill rogue vampires, among other things, and we do not get to pick our nickname. If we did, they wouldn't be stupid. The other members pick your name."

With an eager face, she demanded, "What is it?"

It's a tradition within our club, if you want to call it that, that each member gets their nickname chosen by the group. I told her with an embarrassed face, "Blood Vain, and it's not the type of vein in your body. It's the type of vain like when I go on a mission, and I'm out for blood, but I'm also out to be the best dressed while I'm doing it." She slapped the railing of the balcony, laughing, and waved her right hand in the air. I waited for her to regain composure. “Are you finished yet?”

Holding back a laugh, she said, “Almost.” Then she bailed out a few more peeps of laughter in my direction before she recomposed herself and said, “Well, you are a pretty boy, no mistaking that.”

“What is your role in this transition time?” I asked.

“To usher in a smooth transition, as well as making sure Ecne’s people do not destroy the infrastructure.”

I told her I hadn't seen anything to that effect. The middle-tier vampires are taking it as a challenge. The older vampires don't care much about what happens. The only ones that are making a fuss about it are the ones under the age of a hundred. Vampires of that age sometimes still have family members walking around, some that they even knew before the change. Over time, as you age, your family members start to die off. Which, in itself, distances you from your previous life. The cabal kind of pushes you away from everyone you knew before the change. That's why the rules say you cannot change a family member. This would lock you into what you were before you were reborn. There had been some small pockets of resistance. I think this was simply because we had been in a cold war with Maat for as long as most can remember. I couldn't care less. I do my job and I try to stay to myself. I don't do anything that would label me disloyal, but I'm not trying to climb the ranks either. The elders look down upon Nigrum Gladio. They see us mostly as mindless swords. They understand that we're necessary, but I think it has more to do with them thinking they are so sophisticated.

Once a vampire reaches five hundred, they are considered an elder because there are many ways for you to die before you reach that age, including breaking a law that will get you executed. It's considered an accomplishment to make it there. I wouldn't say that it is exceedingly rare though. I have personally met a handful of vampires that are above one thousand or better. Once they reach that age, their power is immense. You can feel it just being in their presence. It would take a very powerful creature to take down a millennial.

Another reason it is so rare to reach such a great age is that the ancient ones start thinking that they might be coming for them, even the cabal leaders. It is not unheard of for ancient vampires that are getting close to the top of the ladder to disappear. The only explanation you'll ever get is that they left. No one ever questions or says anything about it. Whether they're scared of asking any questions, or they are that stupid. Yes, people disappear without notice. For example, husbands may leave because they no longer want a family. One thousand-year-old immensely powerful vampires do not just vanish. I can't even think that without sarcasm. I asked if she had some of Maat's troops with her after investigating.

"I am in charge of a dozen soldiers."

I held back a laugh as I said, "Oh, I bet they loved that."

"No. No, they do not. They loathe me," she explained in a deadpan voice. "It doesn't matter if they think I have gotten preferential treatment, which I probably have, but I am more than competent in my role. No other could do a more exemplary job than I am doing right now."

I chuckled, "I mean, as soon as they hear you talk, they should understand your brilliance."

She jumped right in with, "Oh, you would think that, but you underestimate how dumb their ape brains are." She went into an imitation of a caveman's voice and began to do the motion of swinging a sword up and down.

"Me big strong man. Club him in head with sword, problems go away." She continued doing both sides of the conversation, back and forth from the caveman to her voice, "No, you big dumb-dumb. You club him in the head, his friends and compatriots may get angry, they come back and slap you on the head with a sword."

"These types never seem to learn no offense," she said as she laughed.

It was my turn to do a caveman impression, "No offense, me have been known to go clubbing. I club bad man, then I club bad man's friend who try club me. I have best club." I proceeded to bang on my chest for emphasis. Lina burst out laughing. She fell forward and put her hands and forehead on my chest. Now, I don't care if you're fifteen or two hundred and fifteen. When a woman of that magnitude that you are interested in does something like that, it sets off a fire inside your soul.

She looked up at me, and through her laughter, she said, "Simon, you may be the cutest man I've ever met."

I puffed my chest out and said, "I'm not cute. I'm rugged and manly, manly as hell." I faked a stutter and continued, "I-I kill stuff and things, a-and I do other manly stuff." I turned my head back and forth, acting like I was looking around making sure if anyone was listening, they heard me. There was no one in the area but it made for a good effect. In a sarcastic tone, I questioned Lina. "Have you ran into any resistance? Has anyone given you any problems? Cause if they have, I will club them to death."

She smiled and said, "I've only had a few idiots to deal with, dear Simon. I can take care of myself. You should see the last man who put his hands on me without my permission." I put my hands up to my sides in surrender and took a couple of steps back. "That's right. That's right, fear me!" she exclaimed, playfully.

We laughed a little together for the next few minutes. Then, she nodded her head back towards the ground. I nodded in the affirmative. We both got off the railing and landed silently on the ground. She told me she was staying at a very nice home that Maat bought from a noble here in town which didn't surprise me. All the cabal leaders had homes or nice offices in every major city. Even if it's out of their region of control, kind of like embassies, if you will. As we walk through the streets of Paris, the lantern bearers walk their patrons around. No doubt that they are wealthy men coming back from their mistresses residence.

One of our many advantages is our night vision. It has been speculated that we have more light receptors in our eyes. Somewhere on the order of magnitudes up two or three times. This helps us see much clearer at night time, but it's not as though everything looks the same as day-time. From what I remember when I was human, at night time, your eyes would continuously search for any light it could grab. Most of the time, in a city like Paris at night, if you don't have a lantern, you can make out the big shapes and that was about it. You would be lucky to make it a block without tripping over something. As a vampire, you don't get to see the vibrant colors. Everything is muted grayer but it is as clear as day.

We walked along the banks of the Seine River, walking so close to each other that we would occasionally bump. This time, she acted as though she might fall into the river and she grabbed my hand. I knew it was all a ruse, but I wasn't going to say anything. Finally, we made it to an extravagant home. Lina waved her hand at the door and said, "This is my humble abode."

I smiled and replied, “A very meager living situation you find yourself in.”

“Well, a girl's got to have a place to lay her head, Simon.”

We both chuckled and I told her that I was staying in a chateau outside of town. There was a cast-iron lantern hanging beside the door. She looked beautiful in its flickering light. I grabbed the tip of her middle finger that was hanging by her right side. She interlocked her fingers with mine and I knew I had to go in for a kiss. I moved in slowly and I felt no resistance from her. I put my right hand on her cheek. Her skin was so smooth that noblewomen could bathe in their lotions and never come close to Lina. When our lips met, it may have been my imagination, but I could feel our energies meeting. Though it felt like a lifetime, the kiss probably only went on for ten seconds or so. When our lips released, I put my forehead to hers. We were both breathing heavily. I whispered, “May I come inside?”

She bit her bottom lip and let out a little whimper. “I want you to, but alas, you cannot. I have to get up in the morning. Tomorrow will be very busy.” I tried to stay composed. She said, “I know where to find you now, Simon.” She slipped inside the house. Before the door closed, I heard her say, “See you soon, Simon the vain.” As I said before, no matter what age a man is, at the end of the night, if the first date has gone well, it feels euphoric and that is exactly what I felt.

Chapter 6

My initial plan was to go to bed, then go visit Lina in the morning, but that changed. Instead, I planned to go and drop off a note, if she was not there, to let her know that I was being pulled away on a mission. Because my life sucks. At the crack of dawn, my fellows and I awakened to urgent pounding on our front door. It was a messenger sent with a word from our superior. There was a group of five vampires that were killing indiscriminately in northern France. The letter told us that we were supposed to meet at a Nigrum Gladio outpost closer to our destination. We would be filled in with the rest of the details once we got there. We all packed our bags with our supplies and the swords which we all carried. They were customized swords, similar to that of the crusaders, except they had black handles and hilts. Each member also had a weapon that they specialized in. Michael, who was the oldest of us, being just over three hundred years old, was packing away his spear that he had customized to be able to screw and unscrew into two different pieces, effectively making it two fighting sticks that he could carry easily. Olbrecht was nearly as old as me; I believe he is 175 years old. His weapon of choice was a mace. I once asked him what the advantage of that over his sword was. He had told me it's more satisfying to crush people than to chop them. It may have also been better for breaking through certain types of armor. Then there was Philip, the youngest of our crew at 109. He was close to the age limit. They don't even allow you to get on the waiting list until you're seventy, and they don't accept you into the program until you're one hundred. He likes to use the new flintlocks. He carried two of them with him; they were both double-barreled. Against an older vampire, they would be nearly useless as they would move faster than a bullet in all likelihood, but since we mostly went up against younger vampires, they were quite effective. Philip once told me that he put something special in each bullet that makes it effective against vampires. Whether that was true or not, I don't know. Rumors have circulated for as long as anyone can remember of a mysterious substance that hurts vampires.

When everyone was set to go, I made my way in town to say goodbye to Lina. As I had thought, she wasn't available, so I left a note. I won't bore you with the whole details of the note. I told her that I was sorry that I couldn't say goodbye, but duty had called, and to not weep too loudly at night when she thought about me. For I shall return to her once again. I figured she would get a chuckle out of that. I didn't expect to be gone long anyway. The men and I set off. It was a two-day ride to our rendezvous point for our briefing: a log cabin, just off the main road. It had flowers growing up all around. It reminded me of an herbalist shop. You see those from time to time in between cities. Sure enough, as I walked inside, it was a full-fledged functioning herbalist shop. I would later learn that the herbalist did run the shop out of there, and that he gets a kickback from the cabal in exchange for his blindness and deafness to anything going on in his basement. As we walked in, he treated us like any other customer: "Greetings, travelers. What can I do for you? Are you in need of a medical tonic?" He asked cheerfully.

Michael flatly responded, "Pretty dark around these parts."

The shopkeeper's face went from smiling to neutral. "Indeed it is." Then he flipped up his countertop door and ushered us to the back room. There in the corner, I saw the largest mortar and pestle I have ever seen. It was the size of a bathtub that could fit two full-grown men. He must do some major grinding in that thing. He looked down at the floor below it then walked away. We instantly knew that was where the door was. Seeing as how it was made out of granite, there's no way he could move that thing by himself. It would probably take three human men to do it. Olbrecht promptly stepped up, put his arms around as much of it as he could, and pulled it back to reveal the staircase down. All four of us made our way down and I closed it behind us. It was what you might expect the basement of a log cabin in the middle of nowhere to be. Cold, damp, and musty. The walls were lined with masonry brick and there were multiple candles hanging. They illuminated the room quite a bit. There was a table big enough to fit four people on each side of it in the middle of the room. All four of us sat down on one side, and our informant sat on the other. He told us that the five vampires were being led by a former Nigrum Gladio.

The leader's name was Reynaldo. He was 152 years old. The other four men are believed to be Nigrum Gladio in training, which puts them around seventy. That's why they had been armed with swords and crossbows. They had been on a constant, straight path from Moscow. Within the last couple of days, information has surfaced that they are headed to a small village west of here. Their target is likely the local sorcerer, but it is unknown why they are targeting him.

"What do we know about this sorcerer? Is there anything that could make him special?" I inquired.

Without hesitation, the informant replied to me, "He is an average sorcerer. Maybe 250 years old. He is not known to have any major connections or fought in any significant battles." He gave us a map that had the layout of the village and the last known whereabouts of the vampire group.

After he left, we all sat in silence, thinking about the situation. It was odd. I'm not sure what they would want with the sorcerer. All of the information given to us does not lead us to think he is anyone significant. I mean, for two hundred and fifty years he has kept his nose clean. If a sorcerer had learned the trick of slowing their aging process, it's not that abnormal for him to live several centuries. The cabal likes to keep track of most major sorcerers across the planet. The oldest known sorcerer lives in Spain; he's in the neighborhood of nine hundred years old. If the information is correct he's barely hanging on at this point, and won't live to see another fifty years. There are rumors that Merlin is still alive. If that is the case, well, he's more than two thousand years old. They say even if a wizard learns to extend their life, they start losing steam at around five hundred. Merlin was better than a thousand years old when he died, and he was still the strongest wizard on the planet. Now, this happened some five hundred years ago, well before my time. All that is just a rumor, and our sources say he is dead. So this wizard not having significant power, significant age, and no significant connection to the situation perplexes us.

I began standing and said, "Well, let's go take these pricks out before they can cause any more collateral damage. Then, maybe we can question the sorcerer."

Olbrecht waved his hand, "Not so fast. Reynaldo and his merry band are within a day of this sorcerer. Why don't we just let them kill each other? Maybe he takes out a couple of them. That's less for us to deal with. If he dies, oh well. He already knows about vampires. We're here to keep the general public from becoming aware." I could see Phillip nod his head in approval and Michael had a look on his face that said he was considering the option.

"Come on, guys. There's nothing to think about. This is our directive, this is what we do. We go kill these bastards before they do any more damage. We let the bureaucrats do the thinking," I said, trying to keep my voice down.

Michael looked up at me and said quietly, "I think Olbrecht may be right on this one, Simon. They are already nearly upon him. We owe the sorcerer nothing; he's not an ally of ours. If he takes even one of them out, it's less danger for us to incur."

I slammed my fist down on the table. "Are you afraid? Does Reynaldo and his pups make you quake with fear?"

Phillip stood up and raised his voice, "Simon, I hope you are not insinuating that I am a coward." He had his right hand on the hilt of a sword.

I yelled back, "Call it whatever you want, take it however you want. I'm going to do my job, you can all stay here if you'd like!"

Michael looked directly at me. "These are trained soldiers that you're going after. I'm not saying that you cannot take them, or that we would have a hard time with them, but it's not smart doing it alone."

I continued walking towards the door and declared, "Come with me or stay, it makes no difference."

I don't know if it was my drive for duty, or my hatred

for rogue vampires that pushed me to go. I made my way along the road since I knew it headed straight to the village where the sorcerer lived. I was going to make it there before them and question this sorcerer. Then maybe I could get some answers. The sun seemed extra bright that day. I hate being in the wrap. Not only is it uncomfortable, but you look like a leper covering everything on your body. There are times where I get frustrated and go out, and take the pain. Knowing I would have a fight ahead of myself in less than twenty-four hours, I didn't want to spend any extra reserves.

When I arrived at the village, I asked a couple of locals where I could find him. They told me to keep straight and that I couldn't miss it. I kept going through the village, down to the pond. The people of the village seemed nice. It was like any other village in the area, everything was covered in dust and dirt. The people tried to keep it clean but there's nothing you can do. I made my way down to the pond, and on the other side were the remnants of an old castle, now mostly laid in ruin. It looked as though he had renovated one of the towers and built up stonewalls about ten feet high around it. This wasn't going to be able to keep out vampires or any predators or supernatural entities unless he had some magical defenses, which I assumed he did. Rather than try to sneak in, I felt the safest course of action was to walk right up to the front door. At least this way he may not immediately perceive me as a threat.

To my surprise, the front door was immaculate and very ornate. I expected with the condition of the castle for the front door to hardly be hanging on. It looked brand new with iron studs and beautiful red oak. I took off my sun mask so I could make myself look less threatening and I knocked on the door.

A jovial, yet dismissive voice came seemingly out of nowhere all around me and said, “Please go away, thank you.” I looked up into the air with a look of complete confusion. My eyes were searching for a window, or where the man should be talking to me from. After a couple of seconds, I could tell that there was nothing.

I raised my voice and asserted, “You probably want to talk to me before you end up talking to the other vampires that are on their way.”

The disembodied voice came over again with the same tone, “What? Haven't you dealt with them yet? I thought you were one of the vampires who kill vampires. Are you not?” I was miffed. Not that he knew who I was, because my attire would give that away to anybody in the know, but because he already knew the situation. I'm not a fan of the people I am coming to help having more information about the situation than I do.

This time I looked at the door and spoke, “I give you my word, I am not here to harm you, but I do need to speak with you.”

Immediately, he responded with a slight chuckle, “Your word? Ha! Like that means anything. On second thought, I will speak to you, but if you try anything, I will send a message out that Ecne’s word is no longer good in these parts, how about that?” He sounded very pleased with himself.

“If that makes you feel better.”

“What are you waiting for? Get inside,” he urged. I was taken a little off guard seeing as how he didn't tell me to come inside, nor did the door open. I grabbed the door handle and sure enough, it was unlocked. The door was surprisingly heavy and very solid; you might even need a ram to break it down. As I stepped through the door, I could feel the magical energies flowing around the place. It was almost ridiculously neat inside compared to the outside. You would have thought there would be cobwebs and dirt everywhere. It was as clean as any palace I have ever been in. I thought he would have maids walking around cleaning it constantly. There were beautiful rugs on the floor and tapestries on the walls. It was illuminated by some of the brightest candles I had ever seen. The furniture was finely crafted. Beautiful wood and metal-working had been done to produce them. Then, on the center table of his living room, was a giant crystal ball. It must have been two or three feet in diameter. We sat down on his couch and he poured both of us a glass of tea.

"Did you know I was coming?" I asked.

In a proud voice, he answered, "Yes and no. I saw you coming from eight furlongs away, and no, I did not know you were coming before that." Before I could get my next question out he blurted, "But to answer your next question I did, however, know that the other vampires were coming."

"Do you know what they want with you?" I asked quickly so he didn't anticipate my question.

"Well being as how stupid they are like most other vampires, no offense, it may have something to do with my specialty."

"Which is?"

"I am a creator of complex structures and machines, somewhat of a magical engineer. Not only bending and cutting, but I can do intricate work," he said, puffing out his chest a little.

I let that information soak in my head for a few seconds before asking my next question. "What would they gain by getting to you?"

Dismissively, as though he's throwing away the comment, he proposed, "They may believe the old wives tale that if a vampire drinks the blood of a wizard, they will gain his powers or knowledge."

Slowly I murmured, "Well, that's not true."

He immediately yelled at me, "I sense a questionable tone in that statement, you fool! Of course it's not true. Yes, if a vampire were to drain a wizard, he would get much more power than from a normal human, but you're going to get whatever kind of power a vampire already has. You're not going to *magically* gain the powers of a wizard. You have to work for it!"

I sat there, looking at him with his scarlet robe and his wizard staff that twirled to the top. He couldn't have looked any more pompous. "Can you defend yourself against them?"

"Well that all depends on what you mean by 'defend'. I can keep them out of here for as long as I am alive. The problem lies in that I only have food and water for two to three weeks; they could wait me out," he pointed out with a smug look on his face.

I had to ask the next obvious question, "Could you kill them?"

"I do not hunt, I do not eat meat. I most certainly do not kill living beings," he scoffed.

I had to laugh. Not only for the fact that it is exceedingly rare to hear that somebody does not eat meat, but that he wouldn't even attempt to kill the people who are coming to kill him. I plainly said, "They will not have that same sentiment, I assure you."

Chapter 7

I stood up and walked over to one of the paintings, staring at it for a few seconds. It wasn't that I was interested in it, it was only a painting of a rowboat on a pond. I just needed some time to figure out what I was going to do. Without turning around, I addressed the sorcerer, "If I'm going to help you, I need to get a layout of this tower and the surrounding area. Will that be a problem?"

Keeping with his pompous tone, he said, "It shouldn't be, as long as you don't rifle through my drawers, not that you would know anything even if you saw it. Ha!" I could see why someone might want to kill this man. He urged me on, "Well get going, think up some dastardly plan to trounce our enemies!"

I raised one eyebrow as I thought to myself: *Yeah, our enemies. Right.*

I began walking the tower to see the most strategic places for an attack. The first floor was mainly a living space; it was all open with stone columns holding up the ceiling. The only walled-off portion was the kitchen in the back. It had one way in and one way out. Right in the middle was a staircase that ran the entire height of the tower. That is how you got from level to level.

The next story of the tower was a library. It had bookshelves running from one end to the other; it looked as though these bookshelves were integrated into the floor and ceiling to hold up the structure. I always knew that sorcerers stocked up on knowledge, but this guy had done some serious reading. Honestly, outside of the cabal headquarters, I don't think I've seen so many books in one location. He told me this level has an air vent built into the back wall to keep the humidity at the perfect temperature for the books. I could most definitely use this to my advantage. The third level was his laboratory.

“Are there any dangerous chemicals I need to be aware of?”

He laughed heavily from his chest, “It all depends on what you mean by dangerous. If you're asking me if there's anything in there that will go kaboom, then the answer is no. If you're asking me if there are chemicals that you probably don't want to get on you, then there might be a few but nothing, I think, would kill you.” This was not comforting to me. I made a mental note to not get any chemicals on myself. Again, this room was large but it only had minor ventilation tubes with no exit, except for the staircase. This level had a few walled-off rooms. The bedroom was enclosed with a door to the left of the staircase. The bathroom was off to the right, and within the bathroom, another room was used as a closet.

The fourth level was the roof, which had four-foot walls around it, but of course, was open on top. There were gaps every so often in the walls, probably for marksmen back when this was a fortress. We made our way back down to the first level.

“What type of defenses do you have?”

He ushered me to follow him. We went through the kitchen and out a door that led into the backyard. It was about a half-acre and it was completely walled in with the walls ending up against the tower.

He looked up towards the sky and said, “Let me show

you." He threw a rock up into the air. After twenty feet, it was smashed. It's an invisible wall of force. The shield let out with a greenish color and looked like a dome. He smiled as he saw the surprise on my face.

"Is that impenetrable?" I asked.

He smirked and replied, "It would not be broken by anything you could throw at it, let's just say that. The shield extends into the wall and the tower itself."

This certainly changes things, I thought, looking around at all the space.

"Why do you have all this space back here?" I asked him with a perplexed look.

A sort of embarrassed look came over his face as he said, "Yes. Well, about all my space back here, I normally keep livestock back here such as dairy cows, goats, and chickens, but it just so happens that whenever I earn enough money to buy more animals, I donate my current stock of animals to peasants in the nearby village."

I had to laugh. "Well, isn't that perfect timing."

He laughed alongside me, "You aren't lying there. The universe must have a shitty sense of humor sometimes." We went back inside and he sat down on his couch. I figured it was time for me to let him in on my plan.

I propped my fingers on the hilt of my sword, and said, "We've got two ways of going about this. Number one happens if they are stupid, and number two happens if they think they're smart." He scoffed at that notion, and I continued, "Let's hope they think they're smart. What I want you to do is bring down your defenses-"

He cut me off before I could continue, "You want me to let them walk in here and kill me?"

I put my left hand up and said, "If you would let me continue... I need you to let down the defenses in one small section, so that they believe that there is a gap. I want them to be confident when they come through and enter the tower. From there, I will ambush them."

He chimed back in, "And what if they are stupid, like they most certainly will be?"

I shook my head. "In that case, you will have to bring down your defenses after they pound on them for a moment and let them think they have beat them. The only problem with that is then they will know that you were on to them, but they still won't know I'm here." It didn't take long for the warning to come upon the sorcerer's crystal ball. It was fascinating to look into. It was like an aerial view as though you were looking down on them from the tops of a tree. This meant there were only a few minutes before they would be there at the speed they were moving.

The plan almost worked out as I hoped it would. I had the sorcerer go up into his bedroom and lock himself in. I had figured they would split up once they made their way into the tower so I wouldn't have to face them all at once. Luckily, they thought they were intelligent, so they went around checking for weaknesses. The sorcerer left one small spot in the back wall vulnerable. As they made their way through it, I went out the front door. I was going to give them a minute to run through the first level before I snuck back in behind them. Thankfully, the sorcerer maintains his home immaculately. So the door opened smoothly, without creaking. I moved pillar to pillar to stay out of sight. I got halfway around the room when I saw the first vampire. They must have left him on guard duty. He was going through the table drawers. I was able to sneak right behind him, and with one swift flick of my sword, his head fell from his shoulders. If the rest were as oblivious to their surroundings, this was going to be an easy day. I needed to make a distraction to get their attention away from the staircase. I pulled a rock from my pocket that I picked up while outside. I crept up to just before the opening to the next level and chucked the rock at an angle. As it hit the far wall of the library, I could hear two of the rogue vampires rush to investigate the sound. I took that time to hop up through the stairs. I hid at the end of one of the bookshelves, lying in wait. As one of the vampires turned the corner, I swung my sword down and at an angle, but he dodged it slightly. The strike still managed to sever his left arm off at the shoulder. He leaped to the side as the blood rushed from his body. I swung to finish him when the second vampire thrusted a spear through a row of books and stabbed me in the shoulder. These guys were starting to piss me off. I snapped the shaft of the spear with a downward swing of my elbow. He launched himself at me and we fell to the floor. I pushed him with both feet and he slammed into the injured vampire. I ripped the spearhead from my shoulder, and before they could get to their feet, I slid over and stabbed the vampire who was already bleeding out through his right eye. The rage that filled me from letting myself be injured by these pathetic vampires drove me to bite the other vampire in the side of his neck and rip to his spine. His blood tasted like burnt liquor. I had to fight my instincts to feed off of him, and let the pain fuel me.

I remembered the vent in the wall. I used it to get to the sorcerer's bed-chamber. The sorcerer leaped back and pointed his staff at me. I was in no mood for it.

“Stay here,” I commanded. I continued by opening his door to the stairs. I immediately saw the last two vampires in the lab. I couldn't help myself. I sprinted down to face them. Reynaldo clashed his sword with mine head-on. I pushed him back and attacked the other; he was nowhere near my level. He felt so slow. I deflected his first and second blows in rapid succession. Then, I stabbed him with an upward thrust. It went through his neck and out of the top of his skull. Reynaldo took the opportunity while I was distracted to stab me through my left thigh. It felt like my leg was on fire. I spun to attack him, but he turned to run upstairs after the sorcerer. I was digging into my reserves to keep up with him. As he dove into the door, it exploded into a thousand splinters. I came through, right on his heels. He ran toward the sorcerer but before he got to him, the sorcerer pointed his staff at the floor, muttered a word, and metal bars shot out of the floor. Reynaldo slammed into them and spun around as I swung my sword down at him. He deflected it. We circled each other, both of us were breathing heavily. I was burning the candle at both ends, using my reserves to heal and to keep fighting at a high level.

Reynaldo lifted his head and said, “Why are you defending this sorcerer?”

“Because if I don't, vampires like you will expose us all, with your foolish and reckless ways,” I retorted.

He laughed and replied, “You're nothing more than a tool for the leaders, a sheep.”

“And you're nothing more than a wannabe revolutionary.”

“If you knew half of what I knew, you'd be on my side,” the rogue sneered.

“Let's finish this,” I bellowed, rushing towards him. I knew now that we had time to size each other up. There were no surprises. One on one, he was no match for me, even in my current state. I knew exactly what he was going to do. He was going to use the last of his reserves in his first strike to try and catch me off guard. He knew he couldn't stand a prolonged battle. Even though his movement would have been a blur to most, I saw it coming quite easily. It was an upward diagonal slash aimed at my ribs. I parried with my sword, pushing his sword up and over my head. As soon as it cleared, I struck with a backward thrust that went straight through his heart. I immediately withdrew the sword and came down on the left side of his neck. It went halfway down his chest. He dropped his sword and stumbled forward. He coughed up blood and looked as if he was going to say something. So I finished him off with a horizontal cut of my blade. His head leaped from his body and the rest hit the floor. “Son of a bitch,” I mumbled as I used my sword to help me kneel to the ground. The sorcerer came over and helped me to my feet. He walked me to a chair next to his desk. I closed my eyes to focus on healing.

He sat on his bed and asked, “Are you going to fully heal?”

“Yes but it's going to take a little while. I normally don't take this much damage.” I grimaced in pain. He started going through a trunk that was underneath his bed. He pulled a necklace from it and smiled.

“This should help you heal faster. It's a gift that I received from a fellow wizard. I don't know exactly how much it will affect you, but it was designed to bring a powerful wizard back from the brink of death.”

“How does it work? Do I need to speak a spell or something like that?”

“Not for this one my friend, break it in your hand,” he told me. He handed the necklace to me; it was a glass teardrop-shaped pendant. I took a closer look at it and it seemed to be illuminated from the inside. I closed my hand into a fist and began to squeeze. The sorcerer stepped back, possibly thinking there might be an explosion or something. It burst in my hand and my fist began to glow yellow, then into my forearm. I began to be able to see through my arm. It crept over my entire body. It felt like a lightning bolt hit me, yet it wasn't painful. It was like being on the strongest opium you could imagine. I saw myself in the full-length mirror. My whole body was glowing, and you could see my bones and veins through my skin. I felt and saw my wounds healing in front of me. After a few seconds, there was a flash and it was over. The sorcerer ran over to me, looking at where I had been injured. He had a look of astonishment as everything was healed perfectly. “How do you feel?” he asked, still having that shocked look on his face. I flexed my arms and moved my legs.

Smiling, I replied, “I feel amazing, I feel better than that. I feel lighter but stronger at the same time.” I couldn't help but laugh.

He slapped me on the back and said, “Well I'm glad, my boy. Even still, I owe you one. You saved my hide.”

Standing at his front door, I asked him again, “Are you sure you don't need help cleaning up?”

“I think after what you did for me, I can handle the clean up.”

I was about to turn and walk away when I realized that I forgot to ask him something, “I didn't get your name.”

He laughed, “Well I guess you didn't get it. You can call me Agrippa.” I nodded and walked away.

I made my way back to the herbalist cottage to meet with the rest of my men. They were all outside and under a tree, drinking mead as I walked up. They stood and yelled, “About damn time!”

Philip slapped me on the shoulder and eagerly asked, “How'd it go?”

Olbrecht reached out to shake my hand and stated, “They didn't stand a chance did they? Easy there, Simon, don't break my hand.”

Michael looked at me with a questionable eye, “You were able to dispatch all of them? Were you wounded?”

“Yes, they are all dead, and I didn't sustain any injuries that lasted,” I retorted.

Michael looked at the rest of the men and announced, “Well boys, this is cause for celebration! Let's drink.”

We all lifted our glasses and drank our fill throughout the night. Before I laid my head down to sleep, I could only think about getting back to see Lina.

Chapter 8

I arrived back at my chateau outside of Paris. I had to document the encounter. I made sure to leave out a few details. I heard word that Lina had to leave Paris, but that she would return within the day. I couldn't wait to see her. I went out to the market and gathered some supplies that I would need to make this a perfect evening. I got a bottle of chardonnay that came from Château de Goulaine. I also got some cheese and berries. I preemptively went to a villa and paid the owner to allow me to use the open roof. I set up a giant umbrella for us to sit under and laid out all of the goodies that I had procured. I went back to Lina's residence to see if she had returned. When I knocked on the door, I was greeted by one of the guards.

"What do you need?" he interrogated me with a scowl on his face.

I tried to be polite, "I'm here to speak with Lina, my good man."

He looked me over.

"You've been here far too often. What is your business here?" These guys love to power trip, but I tried to take the high road.

"This is above your pay grade, my friend," I joked. He didn't seem to like that very much. He stepped close to me like he was going to try something.

Another of Maat's men walked up behind him and put his hand on his shoulder. "Gentlemen, let's not make a fuss. I heard you from upstairs. Let's all calm down." I could tell he was of higher standing because of the way he moved and his more regal clothing. He introduced himself. "My name is Samuel, and you must be Simon." I was already getting bored with this conversation.

I responded with what I felt was only fitting, "That's what they call me."

Samuel smiled, "What I think my friend was trying to say is, how can we help you?"

I responded, "You could let Lina know I'm here, and nothing more, my good sirs."

Samuel, visibly annoyed, said, "If you have business on these premises then I need to be informed, and trust me, my pay grade is higher than yours." This was about to be a full-on pissing match.

Just then, Lina walked downstairs and said, "Go ahead and measure them already, boys." She looked gorgeous. She wore a dress similar to the Portrait of a Lady in White painting. She slipped by them and said, "Simon, we have no time to waste." As I turned to walk out, Samuel went to grab my shoulder and I spun, grabbed his wrist, and twisted his arm backward. Lina interfered and pushed both of us backward, demanding, "Gentlemen, that is quite enough!"

"My apologies. In my line of work, we get a little jumpy if someone tries to sneak up on us," I said.

Samuel straightened his suit out, "That's quite alright. I could see how you could take it the wrong way being in the Nigrum Gladio." He still had that smug look on his face but I let it go.

As we walked down the street, Lina popped open her umbrella. It was silk black with ornate flowers laid in silver stitching. It helped her blend in as a noblewoman. We rarely move around during the day. There are so many more rules to follow while the sun and humans are out. We ran into one of those situations just before we got to the villa. In this part of Paris, only certain people were allowed to carry swords, and we ran into a do-gooder from the military. He stopped in front of us and asked, “Sir, do you have permission to carry around that weapon?” I can't go around disposing of every person that gets in my way. The body count would be way too high, trust me. Another trick we vampires have up our sleeves was about to be put to use.

I began speaking to him while I walked forward, “Good fellow, you don't remember me? I'm sir Simon.”

“Nah,” he replied as we started to lock eyes.

With a smooth tone, I whispered to him, “Of course you remember me. I'm free to roam these streets with whatever weapon I desire.”

“Yes, yes of course, Mr. Simon. Go ahead. Don't let me slow you down.”

Some people say our eyes look like cat eyes, but the truth is much stranger. Our pupils can change shape. Some vampires, like myself, have learned the ability to oscillate our pupils. If a human, and maybe even other species, stare into our eyes while we do that, it puts them in a state of hypnosis. I've practiced this trick a lot more than most so I've gotten quite good at it. I’ve even been able to have people completely forget our interactions.

I took Lina up to the roof. When she opened the door, there lied the walkway of foxgloves and lilies that I had made. I had a Persian rug laid out that was red and green. I made sure it was the softest rug in their inventory. The wine and cheese was set out on a bronze platter. As she walked the path, she kept looking around with surprise on her face.

She looked at me and said, "Simon, you shouldn't have. This is too much."

I cut her off, "Nothing is too much for you. I would lasso the moon for you."

"No one's ever done anything like this for me. Most vampire men think they're above such gestures," Lina spoke with tears in her eyes.

I bent down and took a knee, "You radiate such beauty. I'm lucky you grace me with your presence." I grabbed both of her hands and kissed them. I swear I saw her blush but she'd never admit it. I stood up and walked her over to the rug where I had our food displayed. She laughed as I poured her some wine. We ate an assortment of cheeses. She fed me a berry and I grabbed one to feed to her. As I went to put the berry in her mouth, she bit my finger ever so gently. I went in for a kiss, and our lips met softly for half a second. I rubbed my cheek across hers, breathed slowly next to her ear, and nibbled on her neck. She pulled her head backward, exposing her neck for me. I took it as a sign to keep going. I kissed and touched her throat ever so slightly with my tongue. I could feel the energy building in the air. She pushed me to my back and we kissed, our tongues rolling with the flow of passion. In the process, my shirt was thrown to the side and she kissed my chest and ran her hands over my body. I tried to open my mouth when she began to run her kisses down my torso, but she put a finger to my lips. Soon I was unable to speak. She was amazing. I couldn't be more ready for her. She stood up. Even with the canopy covering us, the sun was coming in behind her. She popped a few buttons and pulled a string. Her dress fell to the ground. With the sun Illuminating her, it was like the heavens were revealing what true beauty was to me. Her hair was like the night laying against her perfectly pale skin. She had modest breasts that pushed out ever so slightly from her body. Her nipples were the same pink shade as her lips, perfectly round. They told me she was ready too. She had a beautiful body. Not like a woman wearing a corset, but she curved naturally. She had a small beauty mark on the right side of her inner thigh. It told me she was real. I went to her. We kissed in the sunlight for a moment. With all the sensations, the sunlight didn't even register. I picked her up and she wrapped her legs around me. We laid back down on the rug. Now it was my turn to taste her. She grabbed at my hair with her right hand and the rug with her left hand. I could feel her stomach muscles tightening as she moaned. She gasped, “Now. I need you now!” When we intertwined, her eyes flew open and she kissed me with more passion than I ever thought possible. It felt like an eternity of blessing.

“Now?” I asked.

“Yes!” she screamed.

We laid there, me on my back and her with one leg over top of me. Instantly, I knew this is where I wanted to be, with her in my arms forever. But alas you can't live on hopes and dreams. There was work to be done.

We got dressed as we got to the door. I put my hands on her hips and gave her one more kiss. She smiled.

“Simon, as much as I would like to stay here and play with you some more, I have to go to work.” She booped me on the nose. I couldn't help but laugh.

“I know, I know,” I replied, giving her a pouty face as she left.

I made my way back to the chateau, but the perfect day couldn't stay perfect for long. Claude was there waiting for me. He's the head of the Nigrum Gladio.

"Simon, my dear boy," he said to me as soon as I stepped into the door. He put his hand out for me to shake and as soon as I did, he pulled me in for a hug. "How have you been? It's been too long since I've been to see you," he bellowed out.

"I've been doing alright, you know, slaying all those who dare defy me," I smirked.

"I bet you have. I heard about Reynaldo and his little group of misfits. Very impressive!"

"Nah, it wasn't that impressive. They all were low-level scum."

"Nevertheless, it was an excellent job. You brought no unwanted attention to us."

I tried to be a little humble, "That is our job, is it not?"

"Absolutely, my boy. Oh, have you been feeding more than usual? You feel stronger than normal."

"I'm only gathering back what I lost in the battle. You never know when the next one will come, you taught me that," I quickly explained.

"Good thinking. Things are coming to a close here. We need to make sure the transition is easy and without too much bloodshed." I nodded my head in agreement, but my thoughts wandered back. I had also been noticing that my strength had grown over the past few days. "Simon, this isn't a social call. You have a meeting with Ecne himself," Claude told me. That took me off guard. I've only met him a few times.

"Do you know why?"

"I'm not sure, but I assume it has something to do with the move overseas." I audibly sighed. "Simon, I know how you feel about it, but if Ecne says you go, then you go."

After I got my things packed for London, I snuck over

and told Lina what was going on. I explained to her that I would be gone for about two weeks. She kissed me and told me to be careful. All I could think about was that if this was about going over to the New World, I had to figure out a way to have him let me stay in Europe.

We arrived in London four days later at a large estate, just outside of town. It had guards at the front gates, as well as guards constantly walking the perimeter wall. These were not Nigrum Gladio. They were Ecne personnel guards, but a lot of them were former members. You had to be at least two hundred and fifty years old to even be considered. On top of that, you had to be the most disciplined, and you had to be in the elite of the elite at some form of weaponry. You could tell who they were by the patch they wore on their shoulders, it was a gold torch, symbolizing enlightenment. Claude told me that once I reached the age limit, I had a great shot at getting in. The perks of being in the guard were amazing. Your living quarters are extravagant, your meals are free, and cooked by the estate chef. The pay was quite good and, considering everything else was free, you basically could put that into a retirement fund for yourself. I believe you are contracted for fifty years at a time. I've even heard that there were a couple of millennials still doing the job. I knew even if I was offered the position, I wouldn't accept it if I didn't have to. I like the lifestyle I live in now. You're almost a prisoner when you are in the guard. You can't leave the premises, or Ecne's side when he leaves.

We went inside and were shown to our rooms. I unpacked and started running ideas over and over again in my head. It pretty much went down the way Claude said it would. We had dinner with Ecne and about a dozen other nobles and high-ranking officials. After everyone was done eating, we moved to the next room over which was more of a hall with no places to sit. It was big enough to have semi-private conversations. I'm mean, sure, you could be twenty feet from the next group, but if they focused, they could hear everything you say. Ecne gestured people over one at a time. I'm sure with how busy he was, he'd have to meet with multiple people almost every day. It was my turn after about four or five people had gone. I wouldn't say I was scared; it was more of a nervous thing. Once I got over to him, he waved his guard away. Ecne looked me over and said "Do you know why I've called you here?"

I respond directly, "I haven't the faintest idea, sir."

He put his hand on my shoulder and said, "Let me put your mind at ease, you are not in any kind of trouble if that's what you were thinking." I didn't let my body language change one bit, but I was relieved. He continued, "It's quite the opposite. I have been keeping my eye on you for several years now, and you have been one of the best of the Nigrum Gladio."

I quickly stated, "Thank you, sir."

Ecne went on, "As you know, in under eleven years, we all have to exit the continent. Well I'll cut to the chase, I would like to have you over there with me to help me keep New Amsterdam in line."

I had to think of something to say. One of the many responses I had been going over lept from my mouth, "Sir, I wasn't aware that you were having issues over there already."

Ecne answered without a pause, "We are not having any issues at the moment, but you know that cannot last. Someone is going to turn the wrong person or not watch their newborn close enough, and there will be trouble eventually."

I had to make him think that I was looking out for the cabal's best interest. "Well, sir, I know we're trying to have the smoothest transition possible, and there have been flare-ups, but I think my talents would best be served making sure we don't have anything slowing down that process here. Especially since it's going well over there."

I could see the calculations in his eyes before he started to speak, "I see your point, and I understand there may be some hesitancy about leaving your homeland, but this is the biggest opportunity in history. This land is filled with gold and coal and anything else you can imagine."

Meticulously, I responded, "Of course, we all must make sacrifices and I will go when I'm needed, but I feel for the cabal, we need to secure our exit."

Ecne laughed, "I like your independent thinking. I am surrounded by yes men. I'll give you until the exit date, but if I need you, you will come."

"Absolutely, no questions asked," I vowed.

The party went on for another couple of hours and then Ecne brought in some willing humans for us to feed on. I always find it kind of weird that they just sit or lay down and let us bite them. It doesn't feel natural, but most of the millennials feed this way. They have acquired enough resources and connections that they don't need to hunt anymore. I sat back and sighed in relief. I had bought myself another eleven years and I would make the most of it.

Chapter 9

I was excited when I arrived back in Paris, I couldn't wait to tell Lina the news. I had to be careful though. I now knew that I was on the shortlist to be called out. That meant that Ecne would want to be able to get in contact with me within a day. There would be some soft surveillance on me from time to time. When we met up later that evening, she was ecstatic, but she told me she had to go out east for a bit.

"What's going on out there?" I questioned.

"There is some dispute over funds and some equipment that Ecne's men want to take, but it should stay with the building," she revealed with an annoyed look.

"I could come along, or just happen to be there," I suggested as I threw a wink at her. "I have a little more room to move and I can always say I'm helping with the transition."

Lina put her hands on her hips and tilted her head sideways. "Now, Simon, I can't have you stalking me all over Europe."

"It's only stalking if I get caught."

She shook her head, laughing.

She left the next day. I was going to have to take a less direct path as to not make it so obvious. I could say it was within my powers if there happened to be a violent episode over there. It's an interesting area. She's headed over to Bulgaria. Sofia is a city that has the presence of Ecne, Maat, and Wendi's cabals. Wendi's area goes through Constantinople, Maat has always had a presence in the Mediterranean and the Black Sea, and it's within Ecne's borders. There were some issues in Constanța. I could head out there and then, once I finished, I could go down to Sofia. I went to talk with Claude and see what info I could gather about the situation there.

When I found Claude, he was buried underneath a mountain of paperwork, which was his least favorite part of his job. I could see the frustration and anguish in his eyes. I knocked on the door frame before slowly walking in. He looked up at me.

"Yes, Simon? What can I do for you?" He quickly paused and said, "I apologize, I hate paperwork."

"I'm the same way, no need to explain."

"I know they want me to have these done as soon as possible, but I'm glad that you are here. Now I have a reason to take at least one minute away from it all before I long for the sweet embrace of death," Claude chuckled.

I smacked my hand on the bookcase and laughed, "I've been there too, trust me. I'm stopping by to see if you know anything about the situation over in Constanța."

He was already on top of it. "Well, at first, I thought it was nothing until Áed and Ahit got involved." My jaw nearly hit the floor.

Each of the cabal leaders has three people directly below them, like their right-hand men or women. A handful of them are the originals, the first three to be turned by the cabal leaders. Áed and Ahit are originals that make them around four thousand years old. Áed is one of Ecne's most powerful and trusted men. While Ahit is Maat's oldest child. She is not known for her kindness toward anything having to do with Ecne or his men.

"Why would they possibly be involved, unless it was something major or something we would have heard about?"

Claude quickly threw it in my lap. "I'm glad you're interested in it. You can deal with that shit show. With your meeting with Ecne, you may have clout with them."

Once I got out to Constanța, I looked up one of my old contacts. Joan is as tough as they come, and smart too. I met her at a little hole-in-the-wall tavern; it was one of our normal meet-up points. I spent a year or two traveling up and down the Mediterranean, and this was one of my stopping points. She was a big woman, nearly six feet tall. Some might even say she was stocky, but she had a charm to her. She thought she was one of the best-looking women around, especially after she had a few drinks in her.

As soon as she saw me, she yelled, "Simon, you bastard, what brings you back here?"

I couldn't help myself. I had to mess around with her. "Well you know I missed your pretty face."

Joan got even louder, "Shut your mouth, you're prettier than I am." We both laughed and gave each other a big hug. "What brings you in?" Joan asked.

"There's an issue and Áed and Ahit are both here. I was hoping you've heard something."

Joan took a swig of ale, shook her head, and said, "Well you get straight to the point, don't ya?"

"You know me," I quipped back.

She leaned in and said, "The word is that an artifact was found on an archeology site, right outside of the city." I knew that this area had been occupied by vampires, even before Lord Dracula's time.

"Who's running the show at the site, do you know?"

"More like who *was* running it. As soon as Elizabeth uncovered either a door or a tomb, Áed swooped in to take over the site. He probably realized that they only have ten years; they can't spend two decades uncovering it."

"So, what's the issue?"

"Ahit has been going over to different buildings and facilities, making sure that Ecne leaves enough behind. She is arguing that since the site has not been opened, and in any ordinary time it would take more than ten years to get through, it should rightfully be Maat's property," she explained.

I bought Joan another round, then went to get settled in. Afterward, I was going to find Elizabeth and see if she could tell me what the artifact was.

I found her the next day, in the city library. She was covered in dust like a true archeologist. She had books strung out all over the table. When I sat down, she didn't even look up at me. "Simon, please go away," she begged.

Two can play at this game. "Now Elizabeth, don't be like that."

Still staring into her books she said, "I do not have time to deal with you."

I was not to be outdone. "But you don't even know what I'm going to waste your time with."

She finally looked up from her books. She had the bluest eyes you've ever seen, and even though the dirt on her face, you could tell she was gorgeous. "Oh Simon, let me drop everything, what can I help you with?"

Elizabeth and I have a bit of history. I wouldn't say we were ever an item but we were together on and off for the time that I was out in the region. There's a possibility that she thought it was more than I did. Let's just say she didn't take it so well when I reposted back to northern

Europe.

"Well since you asked so nicely, I was going to ask you what was going on with the dig you got kicked off of?"

"It's a pissing contest between Áed and Ahit. One of the fools on my team leaked information out, and then they both came running."

I sat down across from her. "So what's so special about this site?"

She looked up at me like I was an idiot. "It's a tomb. From what I've discerned, it might be the resting place of Erisvorsh, the Slavic god of the sea." That piqued my interest.

"That's an amazing find, but what's worth such commotion?"

She spun a book around and pointed to a picture depicting the god. "They think his staff was entombed with him. They believe the staff itself has power over the seas, at least in your general vicinity. So if you are traveling with precious cargo, you can guarantee smooth sailing, or you could destroy an enemy's fleet." She nodded as she saw the realization come over my eyes.

"This is a battle over a superweapon; this is going to get ugly. I need all the information you have about this."

Elizabeth looked at me sideways, "Simon, what are you going to do?"

I sighed, "Whatever I can."

I went back to the Ecne house to start researching. I lucked out. Áed wasn't there. I was hoping I wouldn't run into him just yet. There were some new faces as well as some old acquaintances at the house. I pour over her notes and the lore behind this god. I needed to find out if there was any truth to the theory of his staff having power. This wouldn't be the first time that a fight has broken out over an artifact. Old gods and religious artifacts pop up every so often. Some are duds. Either they were a lie, or the power was within the god himself. On the rare occasion that a genuine artifact is found, it attracts the attention of all major factions, not only the vampires. You can bet that if there are any Lycan packs in the area, they will try to get their hands on it, as well as any number of others. Not to mention if that god had any family members or any gods that were close to him, they may come after it. What we don't need during the transition is a small-scale war.

I woke up early the next morning. I had arranged to meet up with Joan close to the site. I found her kneeling beside a boulder. Áed was standing at the entrance in front of three of Maat's men. If he chooses, this won't go well for the three of them.

I looked at Joan and asked, "Well, what do you have?"

She didn't take her eyes off the tomb. "From what I've gathered, they haven't opened it yet. That's what Áed is freaking out about."

I stared over at the tomb as well. "They're trying to stall him."

Joan, who normally had a jolly expression, was stonefaced. "That's not going to work. If he wants in, he'll get in, and what would normally take years, he will rip through in minutes if he thinks there is a genuine artifact in there," she stated matter-of-factly.

I pulled out a sheet of paper that looked like a blueprint for construction. "Elizabeth said that this is the type of tomb they would've constructed for people of this status. It looks like about a hundred yards beyond the entrance of the tomb is an air shaft."

Joan stared at me blankly. "So, there's an air shaft. First

off, if you're trying to gain entrance, neither one of us is going to fit down an air shaft. Secondly, I'm not even sure what you're planning on doing down there."

I smiled and said, "I think I lucked out this time. There's a man in town who's perfect for this job."

"You're not talking about who I think you're talking about, are you?" I bounced my eyebrows. She knew exactly who I was talking about.

We arrived at the most upscale brothel in the city. You could smell the scent of candles and perfume from outside the door. Joan worked her magic on the doorman, and we made our way inside. It wasn't hard to find our man. He was sitting in a corner on the couch. He was wearing his usual multicolored clothing, and he had his feet propped up on the table, while twirling his wooden flute. He played a few notes off of it and the waitress began dancing on the table.

We walked up to his table and I greeted him, "Hey Rattenfänger, how's it going?"

He looked over at me with a shocked look.

"Simon, is that you? How long has it been?"

I gripped his shoulder and confirmed, "Too long my friend."

He looked over at Joan and queried, "And who might this lovely lady be?"

Joan was all too quick with her jab, "Don't even try it, fairy."

Rattenfänger quipped back, putting on a pouty face, "Now, that hurts."

I waved her off and she went over to the bar to get a drink. "Rattenfänger, what have you been up to?"

He took a swig of his ale, responding, "You know me. A little of this, a little of that."

“I bet you have. I hope you've been staying out of trouble. We wouldn't want another Hamelin incident.”

He laughed, “Hey, that only happened once. Plus that bastard of a mayor reneged on our deal, and I don't like deal-breakers.”

I leaned in and whispered, “Do I have a deal for you.” As I started going through my plan with him, he stopped me.

“So, wait. You want me to help you get into a tomb that Áed and Ahit are watching? Is that what I'm hearing you say?”

I was sitting with my arms propped on the back of the couch. I looked at him nonchalantly and contended, “Well when you say it like that, it sounds bad. It sounds much better when I say we're going to walk up to the back of the tomb unseen and withdraw an object.”

He started spinning his flute. “I'm going to need my fee for this one. I can't give you a discount for this kind of risk.” We shook hands and planned to meet the next day at noon.

Joan and I left, and she showed me an easy house to get into. We fed for a few minutes. Afterward, we hashed out the plans for tomorrow. We went our separate ways. When I got back to my room, I sat on the bed and let the gravity of the situation hit me. I had pushed my way into staying here against Ecne’s initial judgment. If a war broke out, especially with my involvement in it, that would be the end of me.

Chapter 10

I woke up the next morning, put on all my gear, and headed out. It finally started to dawn on me that I was going to try and steal an object underneath the noses of two of the most powerful beings I've ever met. Joan met me on the street, and, faithful to his word, Rattenfänger was at our meeting point: right outside of where the air shaft should be. When we got there, it wasn't apparent that there was an air shaft but I knew Elizabeth's knowledge was good.

We started pulling up rocks and rummaging around when I heard Joan say, “I found it over here.” We began pulling back the rest of the rocks around it to reveal a rectangular hole in the ground carved through the stone. I was hoping the debris hadn't clogged it. I took a twig and used a piece of string to tie it to a circular rock. I set the twig on fire and let the rock roll down the shaft. It was a small enough twig that it would burn out quickly and not harm anything in the tomb if it made it to the end. Our luck held out. You could see it travel down about a hundred feet before the light dropped away. We knew it was clear.

I looked over at Rattenfänger and said, “You're up.” He pulled out his flute and began to play a high-pitched melody. Then, out of seemingly nowhere, rats started to spring up. There were probably about a dozen of them in total. They stood in front of him on their hind legs, mesmerized by his song. I was about to ask him a question when he held up his left index finger, a signal telling me to wait, while he continued to play with his right hand. He stopped playing for about two seconds and then played one final five second note. Immediately afterward, the rats sprang into action, jumping and running down the air shaft.

"Is this going to work? Do they know what they need to do?"

He tapped the flute on his shoulder. Looking over at me, he said, "Oh ye of little faith, if it's down there, they'll find it." I've never really understood how he does it or whether the magic is solely in his flute or not, but it amazes me every time.

We had been waiting for about five minutes and Joan was getting antsy. "Rattenfänger, what is going on with your friends? This is taking too long."

Rattenfänger continued to stare at the air shaft. "They've never been down there before. Give them time." Less than thirty seconds after that, we could hear scratching coming up the shaft. Three rats came out backward. Low and behold they, along with the other rats, were dragging a scepter out of the ground. It was about two and a half feet long, and was made from what appeared to be iron plated in gold with an ornate bulb on top made with rows of gold wires and a blue gem in the middle. When I picked the scepter up, I could instantly feel its power. It was like an invisible weight pushing on you ever so slightly. We all looked at the gem. It looked like the inside was made of liquid, as though it was moving. Rattenfänger tapped us both on the shoulders and said, "It's time to go." I wrapped the scepter in a plain brown cloth and we made our way to Elizabeth's.

I knocked on her door. When she saw the three of us standing there, she had a suspicious look on her face. "What are guys doing here?"

"No time, we need to come in," I interjected. She stepped aside and we shuffled in. Elizabeth closed the door behind us.

"What in the hell is going on here?" she demanded. I pulled up a chair for her. When I unwrapped the scepter and laid it on the table in front of her, she knocked the chair backward, popping up. "Are you guys crazy?" she yelled.

I put my hands out, trying to calm her, "Let me explain —"

She quickly interrupted, "You are going to get us all killed, Simon."

I raised my voice. I hated being interrupted. "Shut up and listen for one moment, no one knows it's gone. The tomb is still closed. I used your research, and Rattenfänger here used his little friends to get it out. Can you make a model of this or something?" She looked at the scepter and ran her fingers across it.

"A model? For what?"

"If you can make a model, we can put that one back in the tomb and when they find it, they'll realize it's useless. We can prevent a war."

Elizabeth looked at the three of us and instructed, "Give me some space." She poured over research papers and went over the scepter with some of her tools. A few hours later, she smacks the table and says, "I think I have it." We all ran over to see what she was talking about. Elizabeth was holding the scepter out and pointing at the blue stone. "All of the power comes from the stone, the scepter is meaningless."

"And?"

"Well, Simon, what we could do is remove the stone, and substitute it for another. They shouldn't know the difference."

Joan chimed in, "Do you have a stone that would be believable considering it belonged to a god?"

Elizabeth smiled and pulled out a tray from her desk. The tray was covered in precious stones.

"Holy shit," Rattenfänger gawked, his eyes wide open.

Elizabeth laughed, "I don't only find old pottery." She brushes aside a few rubies and picks up a big sapphire. "It's not a perfect match but they won't be able to tell the difference once I'm done with it." A few hours later, she had finished removing the gem and replacing it with the replica. She had put the original with the rest of her precious stones.

Joan, Rattenfänger, and I made our way back to the air shaft with the replica. Rattenfänger played a few notes of his flute and his rat friends drug the scepter back down into the tomb. We covered up the air shaft, like it had been when we found it.

The following day I made my way to the entrance of the tomb. Both Áed and Ahit were there, but I strolled right up to them like I owned the place. I had to be sure not to show any fear, even though I knew if I pissed them off, they could rip me apart without breaking a sweat. Áed was the first to acknowledge me.

"Simon, what are you doing here?"

Keeping my cool, I responded, "I'm here on behalf of Ecne. I heard that there was an issue, so I came to help facilitate compromise."

Áed looked like I just said something about his mother. "I don't need someone looking over my shoulder. Ecne doesn't think I can handle this?"

I put my hands up at my side. "Not at all, we didn't know you were involved at first."

Ahit jumped into the conversation, retorting, "We don't need a low-level messenger boy telling us what we should be doing!"

"Ecne wants the Tomb opened immediately," I bluffed. I thought that Ahit was going to rip me apart. "So, unless Maat wants to come up here herself, this tomb is being opened."

I walked away and hoped that Áed being there and getting what he wanted would stop Ahit from attacking me as I left. The archaeology crew led by Elizabeth walked up to the tomb door and began working on it. As soon as they opened the covering stone, Áed ordered men inside. There was another stone blocking the way into the burial chamber.

Elizabeth walked out and said, "We need to get our tools to remove this stone, it'll only take a few hours."

Áed said, "Out of the way."

He walked into the tomb and saw the stone. It was six feet tall by three feet wide and was thought to be five feet deep. Áed stood still for a moment. Then, with a blinding speed, he punched the middle of the stone. The impact reverberated through the entire chamber. It was like an earthquake. His next strike sent spider web cracks through the entire stone, and the concussive blast sounded like an explosion. He kicked through the stone and rubble. The rest of the crew moved the remaining small stone. I don't think I could've managed that feat no matter how many times I hit the rock. That shows how strong a multi-millennial vampire is. They brought the scepter out to Áed. As soon as he grabbed it, he took a look, then threw it to Ahit. She looked it over and threw it to Elizabeth. Ahit had a disgusted look on her face.

"Useless piece of junk. You can keep your dig site." She walked away with the rest of her people. Áed walked up to me and said, "From now on, you stay out of my way. I don't care who directs you, even if it's Ecne himself."

I leaned back a bit and in a relaxed tone said, "Don't shoot the messenger." One of Áed's men went to grab me by the arm. I grabbed him by the wrist and twisted his arm behind him. I yelled, "Keep your hands to yourself." I pushed him away. He went to spin back at me, but I had already drawn my sword and had it pointed at his throat. He looked over at Áed. He motioned with a move of his head, and the man backed away. Áed nodded to me and I bowed to him in turn.

I returned to Elizabeth's place with Rattenfänger. He was in a glorious mood.

"Simon, that was one of the most entertaining things I've seen in awhile. Did you see the look on Áed's face when he realized the scepter was junk?" He continued to laugh with his arm around my shoulder. Elizabeth opened the door, looked around and pulled us in. She looked none too happy.

"Do you guys think this is a game?"

"I don't, but I think Rattenfänger might," I countered as he was wiping tears from his eyes.

He looked at her and retaliated, "Well everything is a bit of a game, if only a cat and mouse game, but there is the quite serious matter of my fee." I looked at Elizabeth.

"You keep the gem, but I'm gonna need you to help me with Rattenfänger's payment." She looked at me like I was crazy.

"First off, I don't want the gem. If I get caught with it, I am dead. So no thank you. And why should I help you?"

"Well I did save your dig site. Without me and my merry crew, you'd be moving around looking for another find, and it probably wouldn't be as good as what's still in there." Rattenfänger gave her a look that said *you know it's true*.

She looked back at me and said, "Dammit." She pulled out her stash of jewels and put them in front of Rattenfänger.

He picked out about five stones and announced, "Well it was nice doing business with you all, but I must be on my way. I'll be at the Björngårdsteatern. It's this new comedy club that recently opened in Stockholm, if you want to look me up." Elizabeth and I both waved goodbye as he shut the door behind him. She smacked me as soon as he left.

"Damn! What was that for?" I yelped while rubbing my cheek.

"Simon, you walked right back in here like you didn't leave me high and dry. You didn't even consider me before you left, and now you nearly bring death to my doorstep." I didn't plan on the day going this way, but she was right. I owed her an apology.

"Elizabeth, I know it wasn't right just leaving, but we weren't compatible. You have a career and goals and you want a life. I'll never be that guy for you, but you are a great person and I want you to know that you can always call on me if you need anything."

She crossed her arms and looked away from me. "I still hate you," she commented. I slid up next to her and hugged her. She laid her head on my shoulder and said, "I'm still mad though."

"I know," I replied, laying my head on hers.

The next day, I went and told Joan that I appreciated her help and if she needed anything, to get a message to me. Then, I met Elizabeth at the edge of town.

"I hope you find all kinds of artifacts in your new dig site, and don't be flaunting around your new magical stone too much," I joked.

She laughed. "I do appreciate you helping me get back my site. I believe we will learn a lot, but that stone will be tucked away for many years before I look at it. I'll have to wait for the heat to die down from this. One of the two may get the idea that they were being played and come back for a second look."

I hugged her and said, "Well, keep it safe, and you stay safe too. I'll see you around." *I don't know how I keep getting myself in these situations*, I thought to myself as I began the trek down to Sofia to see how Lina was doing.

Chapter 11

Things have changed in the area between Sofia and Constantinople since the Ottomans took over. I'm old enough to remember the great city when the Romans still held it. I was a teenager when it was sacked. It's still a nice enough place but there's a lot more volatility in the surrounding areas. It's thought that Constantinople is the largest city in the world. There's always travelers and merchants on the road from Sophia to Constantinople. It's only a two-day journey. I stopped to buy some wine from a merchant on the side of the road. He had his two sons with him. They were learning the craft. The merchant had a very low bass tone. It definitely would have helped him, when he made it to the city, to distinguish him from all the other merchants standing around.

“What can I help you with today, young man? Food? Drink? Would you like a look at my wares?” The quality of the man's goods was quite nice, actually.

“Do you have some quality wine?”

He began to look through his cart. As he disappeared into the covered wagon, I heard him yell from within, “It must be your lucky day!” He hopped down with a bottle in his hand. “When I travel the roads, I don't normally have good wine with me. It typically gets sold before I leave the city limits, but I do have one mid-tier bottle left. It's not going to impress the king, but you can drink a couple of cups without it ripping your stomach to pieces.”

"I'll take it." I winked at his oldest son. "And since your son is such a good salesman, I'll take that sharpening stone that he was showing me while you were in the cart." I figured I'd help the kid out and make his dad feel good at the same time. Plus, I needed a new sharpening stone, and this one did look good. A nice black stone, smooth on the bottom where I could sharpen, and a nice rounded edge on top where I can keep it in my palm.

In total, it took me about two days to get to Sofia. I could have made it in one, but I didn't want to break down my horse. As I entered the city, I saw what we called "messenger men", sometimes they were even young boys. For a coin, they could tell you any rumors that were going around. They were normally reliable, seeing as how, on a busy day, they can make a decent living. The messenger I talked to was probably a few years younger than me before I was turned.

I tossed him a coin and questioned him, "Anything interesting going on in the city over the last week or so?"

He rubbed the coin on his dirty shirt. "Well, I don't know nothing about anything, but what I do hear is a group from Constantinople, who looks even more Far Eastern than normal, is making trouble with two other groups in town. I don't know what about, but I'd stay away from the North End if I was you."

I nodded my head and told him, "Thank you. Stay safe out here."

I made my way to the Ecne safe house downtown. We have had dealings with Wendi's people before, coming over from Constantinople. There were two men at the house. One was a passer-through that I didn't know. Then, there was the keeper who was a permanent resident, Andheri. He was a good man and he knew everything about his city, and most about his country. He's been here for over three hundred years, after all. As soon as he saw me walk through the door, he jumped up and embraced me with a giant bear hug which was fitting, because that's exactly what he looked like, a bear. He was around six and a half feet tall with a barrel of a chest and a gut to match, and a giant, black beard.

As he squeezed me, I squeaked out "You trying to crush me, Andheri?" He let me go and slapped me on the shoulder.

"Don't be a wimp. Good to see you, friend. What brings you back?"

We sat down and I began to tell him, "Well, I talked my way into staying until the last day, so I'm doing clean up. I heard there's some stuff going on in the area." He took a swig of whatever he was drinking. I'm guessing it was some kind of ale and from the smell of it, a strong one.

"Well then, you've heard correctly. You have Ecne's, Wendi's, and Maat's people in town making waves. I'm not sure that Wendi's men that are in the area like the way Maat's people are operating."

I shook my head in disbelief. "Well, wait until they take over officially."

I spent the night devising a strategy on how to approach this issue. I want to help Lina, but I can't make it obvious, and I'm not trying to hurt my people as well. Wendi's people really shouldn't be active in the area at all. Other than diplomatic relations, there's no reason for them to have a force here.

The next day, I went out and hit up all the messengers in the city that I could find. I was trying to see if I could snag any new information, but it was all pretty much the same. Most of the activities were going down in the north end of town. The only thing I knew about the north end was that it was heavy industry: steel, clothing, that sort of thing. So, my next stop was going to be some of the businesses in the north. I went to the textile workshop first, as I knew it would close first. I left as the sun was going down. I assume no one ever really expected anybody to want to break into this place; there wasn't any security. I was able to sneak through a window in the back of the building.

The place was exactly what you would expect from a textile factory. There were large slabs of cloth waiting to be cut, or laying in organized stocks. Spinning wheels were in the centre of the floor. But I didn't come here to look for a new wardrobe. I quickly made my way to the office. It was the only room in the building, at least that I could tell, that had a lock on it. One of the skills I have acquired over the years is lock picking, and this was a rather simple lock. Again, probably because nobody would ever want to break into this place. It took me less than thirty seconds to pop it. I made my way inside. Whoever ran this place was pretty organized. I had an easy time finding the log and who everything was registered to. I memorized the major names, but none of them were familiar to me. I locked the door and made my way out the same way I came in, making sure not to move anything and leave no trace to reveal that I was there.

My next stop was the foundry. It was a few blocks away from a much larger facility. It produced the most steel of any foundry within a few hundred miles. It is mainly exported to Constantinople. I was going to use the same method as I did in the last factory. I found the least visible entrance to make my way inside. As soon as I turned the corner to go down the back alley, I saw someone trying to enter. They were shorter than average, wearing a black cloak with the hood up. Your standard bad guy attire, of course. I stayed out of sight and made my way closer and closer, coming from behind them. They were not an expert burglar. I would have been in the building ten seconds ago. I decided to go with the direct approach and maybe scare them off. I walked right up behind them.

"What do you think you're doing?"

Yeah...that didn't work out as well as I'd hoped. They spun around way faster than I had expected. Maybe a year ago, they would have caught me but I've been putting on supernatural muscle. What they slashed at my throat, I believe they call them Karambit knives. Small, semicircular knives. I could see them as they passed an inch from my face. I could tell they were very sharp. I ducked under the blows, then kicked them in the back. Once again, I tried to reason, "Stop before you get hurt." I'm not even one hundred percent sure they could see me with the hood halfway down their face. They came at me again, this time trying upward slashes to throw me off. I used shoulder motion and my footwork to dodge every slash they threw at me. I was not wanting to seriously injure or kill this person, but they were getting close to slashing or stabbing me and I can't have that. I decided to go on the offense. They tried a double stabbing motion with both hands. I grabbed them at their highest point, held their arms out straight, and shoved my knee into their stomach. As they gasped for breath for half a second, I ripped their cloak back, figuring once they knew I saw their face, they would run.

When we looked upon each other's faces, we both said "Shit."

"Simon? What the hell are you doing here?" Lina prodded.

"I could ask you the same thing," I stammered back to her.

She looked around real quick, explaining quietly, "I'm doing my job."

"I didn't know breaking and entering was in your job description."

"I'm investigating something big. I think this foundry, along with a few other businesses in the city are owned by Ecne, and his men are trying to sell it to Wendi's cabal without cutting Maat in on it."

I put my hands up in surrender and shook my head, "That's way above my pay grade, I'm simply a pee-on."

She looked at me with a joking face, saying, "That's not what I've been hearing recently."

"That's stuff I was thrown into, and if you think about it, it's your fault," I protested.

"My fault?"

"Yes. If you weren't so beautifully mesmerizing and so sweet, I would be able to resist you, but alas, I cannot."

She let out a laugh. "Shut up, let's get in there."

While I was good at breaking into places, she was good at knowing where stuff should be. I would have been walking around for ten minutes, trying to find the office, but she knew exactly where it was. It was probably all of those years of running businesses herself, and not my lack of knowledge. Again, I popped the door to the office and she went to town, looking through all the paperwork. She found the names she was looking for.

"Just as I suspected," she proclaimed as she pointed to a few names on the paperwork that she showed me.

This situation got a lot more complicated, I thought. We exited the building making sure we didn't disturb anything. Before I could turn around from relocking the door, she yelled, “Simon!” I turned around to see four masked figures running at us. I could definitely tell by their speed and their stride that they were supernatural beings of some sort. I drew my sword and prepared to fight when, out of my peripheral vision, I saw an object flying past me. It smashed into one of the runners and exploded into a greenish mist. The person stopped dead in their tracks and began to flail as their clothing started to tear away from them. I looked over at Lina as she spun her knives into place in a backward grip. She nodded to me and we took off after them.

The first of them swung a horizontal strike. They were using a short sword, similar to that of a yatagan. Lina slid underneath the strike, slashing with her right arm, her blade cutting deep into their thigh. I drew the other two towards me. They thought they were being smart. The first struck down at me vertically, hoping that I would come up to catch his sword with mine so that the other could either stab me with a thrust, or hit me with a horizontal strike into my stomach. I was having none of that. I decided to test my speed. I was able to kick the first in their knee before they could come down upon me simultaneously, throwing a lunging strike at the other. The kick landed perfectly but the thrust, they were able to dodge by falling backward which gave me enough time to set up my second blow before the first one could recoup. Just as they were lifting their sword back up, I struck with a slash across their chest and their right bicep in their sword hand. I rolled out of the way as the second person tried to decapitate me from behind. I did a 180 degree spin on my knee, then lunged at them again. They parried my blade right before it hit home. I side kicked them in the chest with my right foot. It threw them off balance, and I followed that up with a downward strike of my own. They were so off-balance that they could barely lift their sword to defend. I knew they didn't have a good grip on it as I hit it. It released from their grip. I pushed into them with an upward lunge that went straight through their sternum, most certainly piercing a lung and I kept pushing, running them into the nearest wall. I turned just in time to see the previous one that I had injured coming at me through the air with a sword in his good hand. I took one quick side step and stabbed him in the side. I felt his ribs breaking as I impaled him. I turned to go help Lina. It was fairly even between her and the other one. She was blocking their repeated blows with her small blades. I knew it couldn't last forever. They finally caught her on the left shoulder but just barely. I watched her wince in pain. She jumped backward and threw a small, rounded, glass flask. As it smashed into the person's head, it had a different effect than the last one. It ate right into the top of their head like acid. I grabbed Lina and we ran like hell out of there.

Once I felt like we had gotten far enough away, I stopped.

“What in God's name was that?” Lina gasped, breathing heavily.

“If I had to guess, I would say that it was a crew of Wendi's men by the looks of their weapons. What's with the daggers and the chemicals?”

“I told you I could take care of myself. I am far from defenseless, and I learned a thing or two working in Maat's potion shops.”

“How is your arm?” The bleeding had lessened from what I could tell.

“I'll live. It should be healed up by tomorrow, it wasn't that deep. I see you managed to avoid any damage.”

“Well it was two on one. The odds weren't very good in their favor.” I didn't want to take the chance of them possibly attacking again, so I walked her to around the corner from where she was staying.

She took one last look around and said, “I will see you tomorrow. We can meet at Maria's café and talk about all this craziness.”

“Sure thing,” I replied. I ran the back of my hand across her cheek. She kissed me and put a piece of cloth over her wound to conceal it as she went inside. I made my way back to the house, using some erratic and varied pathways to make sure I wasn't followed. As I laid my head down on my pillow, I thought about how I needed to stop getting myself into these situations.

Chapter 12

The next morning, I met Lina at the café. I had been looking forward to this all night. Not only because I wanted to spend some quality time with her, but because I love coffee. As I walked up to the table, she had a waitress bring me a cup of coffee and then Lina poured in some milk and sugar.

"I think I'm in love," I sighed.

She looked up at me and raised one eyebrow, "You think?"

I took a sip of my coffee, "Nope, I'm pretty sure now." She laughed before I continued, "So, can you bring me up to speed on the politics of this situation? I know it's shady to sell the businesses to Wendi's people, but is it illegal?"

"It's not unheard of for one cabal to sell a business to another, and it isn't illegal to own things in other cabal areas. During the transition, Maat should get to match any offer, but they are trying to sell it before Maat even knows it was available"

"So, what's the move?"

"Well, Simon...I was thinking you could walk right up to Wendi's headquarters and ask them." I knew I wasn't going to like this plan from the very beginning. I'm not a trained spy. I'm a soldier. I'm more of a "point me at the problem and I'll go slash it to pieces" kind of guy. This was going to take subtlety and a bit of confidence.

A few hours later, I found myself dressed in my most

official clothes, walking straight to the front door of Wendi's consulate. As I got ready to knock, I ran the names Lina had made me memorize through my mind. I had met very few of the Wendi cabal in my lifetime. I knew it was going to be very unlikely that I would know anyone here.

When I knocked, a woman opened the door, and with a pleasant look on her face, she asked, “How may I help you?”

With my best card playing face, I said, “I'm here to speak with Hüma.”

“Who may I tell her wants to speak with her?”

“Tell her it’s Simon. I'm here to finish up for Ecne.”

“One moment,” she said. As she walked away, I started second-guessing myself. I couldn't have more than blinked before she was standing back in front of me again. “She will see you now.” I nodded and followed her upstairs.

The hallways were decorated with beautiful paintings and calligraphy. It had such a different feel from Ecne, or even Maat’s offices. They were much darker and muted than this color and texture. She stopped at the end of the hall, stood sideways, and with an open palm, ushered me to open the door. As soon as I walked in, I noticed there were flowers and a painting, but they were perfectly organized. It looked more like an upscale human office than a vampire’s. The woman sitting at the desk was of East Asian descent. She matched the room to a T. She was wearing beautiful silk clothes that conveyed importance and class, though they were more European attire rather than Asian.

Hüma looked up from her paperwork and chimed, “Simon, I didn't know Ecne has started using warriors as diplomats."

"I'm trying to broaden my horizons. I'm a man of many talents."

"So, you're here to expedite our process of acquisition?"

"Yes, you've been dealing with Ivan, correct?" I was hoping to get more information out of her. She took the bait perfectly.

"I have been working with Ivan, as well as Jonathan."

I was thinking of a Jonathan in the area that would be associated with Ivan and the only one I could think of was out of Chișinău. He had been trying to climb the political ladder. I wonder if this was one of his plays. I needed to find how far up the ladder this goes. I needed to leave here without tipping either of the men off, as well as not make myself look suspicious to Hüma.

"You are in good hands. Continue working with Ivan and Jonathan. Try not to speak of our interaction here. I'm kind of overseeing this thing out of their sight to see how they do. They may be in line for a promotion with how well they're doing." She gave me a look that said she was impressed.

"Absolutely, my lips are sealed. Glad to be working with a true professional." It has never been harder for me to keep a straight face than it was at that moment.

I made my way out of the building, and once I knew I was out of sight, I started to speed walk my way back to the restaurant where I was to meet Lina.

She started with the questions as soon as I sat down.

"Did they catch on to you? What did you find out?"

I took a bite of my pastry and said, "One thing at a time. I think she bought it. As far as she knows, I'm the overseer of the transaction. I'm supposed to lie low. She's not supposed to tell anyone anything about our meeting."

"That's good, did you find any new information?"

I smiled. "Well I did find out that one of our guys named Jonathan has been running this deal. I know of him. He's been trying to climb the ladder for about the last fifty years now. He's not a whole lot older than I am, just more ambitious I guess."

"Do you know how far up the food chain these guys are?" As I was going over it in my head, I knew I didn't keep up with our political situation probably as much as I should.

"The last time I heard of either of them, they were lower-middle-class management types. Certainly they weren't anyone for me to be afraid of. How do you think we should approach this? You're more politically connected than I am." She tapped her fingers on the table a few times. I could see the gears moving in her head.

"It all depends on how high this goes. Sure it's looking illegal, but if you go up the chain high enough, it doesn't matter."

"Truer words have never been spoken."

Lina took a sip of her tea. "Why don't you pay a visit to one of the men and I'll see what I can dig up on my end," Lina suggested.

I knew Ivan was in town so I decided to see if I could meet up with him and find out a little more dirt.

"Guess I'm headed to Ivan's place," I declared. I took the last bite of my food and kissed Lina on the cheek. Then I was off to go cause some trouble.

Ivan had a nice place on the edge of town and I knew he'd liked to throw parties this time of the week. I had been to one of his parties several years back when I was in the area. I and the rest of my crew dropped in for some fun, so I knew it wouldn't look suspicious for me to simply walk up in there. As the sun began to set, I strolled up to the front door. The party had already started. I knew the doorman from years ago, and he instantly recognized me.

"Simon, you old hound! What brings you around?"

"I'm passing through town and I know this is the spot to let loose."

He gave me a big handshake and a pat on the back, then let me through. It wasn't too hard to find Ivan. He was at the bar, chatting up everyone, and pouring drinks for his friends.

"Hey, you rascal, pour an old friend a drink," I bellowed, making my way towards him. I could see him going through the files of his mind, trying to find my name.

"Simon, my man. How long has it been?"

"Way too long. How have you been?"

"You know me, just moving and shaking things up."

That's how the next few hours went. Bantering back and forth with him like we were old friends. I was biding my time and letting him get drunker and drunker. One thing I did find out, however, is that he managed to move up later enough to get blood donors, which I was a little surprised at. As everyone started to settle into their own spaces, I got Ivan into our own little private space. It was time for me to work my magic.

While he was relaxed and had both arms on the back of his couch, I said, "Hey, you know, Johnathan sent me down here to help you out." Ivan had a confused look on his face.

"Why would he do that?" I knew I had him where I wanted him.

"I think maybe he thought you couldn't handle this on your own," I bluffed.

"Well...that little shit. This was my idea from the get-go."

"That's not the way he made it sound."

"I'm the one who convinced the manager to sell and who to sell to. The only reason I brought Jonathan in was because he has connections with Wendi's men. This is my deal. I'm bringing him along for the ride. He better believe that when this is finalized, it will be noticed by Bill. I will be the one getting the credit for it." That was all I needed to know. He had done this from underneath the nose of his superiors. That puts Ivan and Jonathan within my jurisdiction now. I need to find out what's going on with the other two sides of this.

I went back to my place. I wanted to collect my thoughts before getting back with Lina. I got to my room and went to light the lamps so that I wouldn't have to sit in the muted colors of darkness.

As I lit the second lamp, I heard a sultry female voice behind me say, "We meet again, Simon."

I tried to say, "What?" For a split second, I saw the woman, and what appeared to be a flowing nightgown of sorts, sitting in the corner chair, covered by shadows. The next moment she was upon me, tackling me and we landed on the bed. Laying on top of me was the most beautiful woman I had ever laid eyes on. "Lina?"

"Who snuck up on whom this time?"

I looked her over. "You're lucky I didn't pull out my sword."

She smirked and said, "Well Simon, what do you think I came here for?"

I smiled and egged her on, "Let's see who wins this battle."

She bit her bottom lip and whispered, "Let's see."

It was an epic battle. Both sides fought valiantly until they were both exhausted. We both lay there, her having one arm and leg across me while we both recouped our strength. She picked up her nightgown off of the floor, put it on, and walked over to my writing desk which had a decanter of gin. She opened it and poured two glasses for us. That is a sight that I wish I got to see more often. I could see her hips swaying beneath the silk fabric of the nightgown, and on her way back, every step revealed a perfectly smooth pale leg. She sat down on the bed and then gave me one of the glasses. She proceeded to push my mouth closed. Once I realized my jaw had been picked up off of the floor, I made a gesture like I was wiping away drool from my mouth. I swear there wasn't actually drool on my chin. We clinked glasses and we both took a sip.

I let the flavors settle for a moment before I asked, "So, what have you found out on your side of the fence."

She took another sip and then sighed, "No one on Maat's side knows anything aside from me, and as far as Wendi is concerned, I think it's solely a Hüma deal, but if it goes through I'll have to report it. Even if I don't, Maat will find out."

"With that information, I can take action against them."

"Are you going to call in the rest of the Nigrum Gladio?"

"No, I don't want Ivan or Jonathan to get spooked. I'm going to play them against each other."

Over the next few days, Lina found out when the deal was supposed to get brokered. Hüma was sending a representative with the coin, and Ivan and Jonathan were supposed to provide the paperwork and the owner's seal. My part was going to be the guy at the party who drinks way too much and ruins everyone's fun. The deal was going down oddly in the middle of the day. I got to the spot about forty minutes before the deal was to go down. I also wore my full Nigrum Gladio outfit so they would know I was there on official business. Earlier, I paid off a few messengers to spread rumors to only Ivan and Jonathan's closest men, ones that I knew would be in on the deal and that would alert them right away. I told them your standard, "each one of them plans to kill you. Take the coin and get all the credit". These were not complicated men. I knew that it would be enough to set them over the edge. To their credit, they arrived right on time. Hüma had sent three representatives, one Turkish looking woman and two warriors in the same outfits that Lina and I battled in earlier. Ivan and Jonathan must have been feeling very confident because they were the only ones attending the deal. I would have thought they would have at least brought one man apiece. Ivan was the one who had the paperwork and the seals in his hands. They had a minute of pleasantries, introducing each other. Ivan then patted the files with his hand, showing he was ready to make the trade. Hüma's representative took off the satchel she was wearing and unbuckled it, leaning it a little forward so Ivan and Jonathan could see that it was filled with what appears to be silver coins, probably akçe. A lot of these shady backdoor deals were made in silver coins instead of gold. It's easier to spend and move even though there's more of it. No one questions silver because everyone uses it daily.

Ivan moved forward to make the trade when Jonathan put his right hand up towards Ivan and moved forward, signaling he would take possession of the satchel of coins. *Here we go, time for the fireworks*. Ivan was clutching the paperwork underneath his left arm and trying to push

Jonathan back with his right. The representative and her men began to look at each other. They could sense the deal was about to go south. The two bodyguards drew their swords and began to walk backward with the representative. Ivan tried to explain to her that it was a mere misunderstanding and that everything was alright. She threw the satchel back across her shoulder and waved her hand across her body, signaling that the deal was off. The two bodyguards escorted her out of the courtyard.

Ivan and Jonathan became belligerent with each other. Ivan shoved Jonathan with his right hand. Jonathan returned the favor, pushing him with as much force as he could muster with both hands. Ivan went flying across the courtyard, falling down. The papers went scattering. He jumped to his feet and drew his sword. Jonathan drew his in kind. I knew they were both of similar age. Ivan's a little bit older than I, but as far as I knew, he wasn't well versed with the sword. I didn't know Jonathan as well but, I could tell by his stance that he at least practices occasionally. Ivan swung a powerful horizontal strike from his right side. Jonathan easily parried to the side and stabbed Ivan in the left shoulder with a thrust. Jonathan removed the blade quickly and was back to his stance. Jonathan's movements were mechanical in nature, but they were technical. Ivan's movements were erratic, trying to land one big strike to finish the fight. Ivan came with a vertical strike straight down. Jonathan dodged it to the right and then came down with a strike across Ivan's back, cutting about a foot-long gash. This time, Ivan audibly screamed and spun his sword around like a windmill, but he didn't catch Jonathan off guard. Jonathan simply ducked under and slid his blade across Ivan's torso. Ivan stumbled forward before falling to his knees.

That was my cue.

I silently started to come down from my perch above the courtyard. Jonathan was walking around Ivan and you could see the fury in his face. A look of pure disgust.

Jonathan began to scream at Ivan, "You piece of garbage! I handed you this deal on a silver platter and this is how you thank me?"

Ivan was still on the ground clutching his stomach, but he managed to speak through the pain, muttering, "I knew you were going to double-cross me as soon as you could; you'd never just share in the spoils."

"Shut your mouth. I already know what you had planned, begging wouldn't even help you now."

This really couldn't have worked out any better for me. As I crept up behind them, Ivan's eyes widened as he noticed me walking up. That was enough to alert Jonathan.

He spun around and as soon as he saw me, he yelled at Ivan, "You snake!" and kicked him in the side of the head. I'm pretty sure I heard vertebrae snapping. Ivan fell over to the ground. Jonathan looked at me and with confidence said, "You have nothing on me."

"Jonathan, Jonathan. I've been here the whole time. I saw the whole thing. That is all I need."

He knew that there was no reason to keep talking. I wouldn't change my mind. He brought his sword to guard, then he used all the speed that he could gather and lunged at me. He tried to thrust from the right side, which isn't typically a bad maneuver but I was too well-trained and quick. I knocked the sword off to my left side and kneed him in the side of the head as his momentum carried him forward. We reset and he shook his head back and forth to try and clear the cobwebs. He came at me once again, this time trying to slash at my left leg. I like this tactic but his movement was far too mechanical, with no fluidity to it at all. I could tell what his next move was going to be every time. I used my left hand to take my sword to the ground, blocking his strike while he was off-balance. I used my right elbow to shatter his left orbital bone. His face instantly began to swell. He backed away. I was having as easy a time with him as he had with Ivan. Now he knew what it felt like to be outclassed. It was time to end this, no more games. I made sure I stayed off to his left side where his visibility was diminished. I leaped in as fast as I could and with an upward thrust, I drove the sword under his sternum and through his heart and out through his shoulder blade. The look on his face was that of surprise and shock, having realized he was moments from death. Then he did something I did not expect. In an act of a desperate animal, he bit me right above my left bicep as hard as he could. That made something inside of me break loose, my inner beast. I drew my fangs and I bit down on his exposed throat. I ripped a giant chunk out of his neck. Then I bit down again and began to feed on him uncontrollably. I could feel his power entering me. I had never felt anything like it before. I had never fed on a fellow vampire. I didn't stop. I kept going until I felt the last of the essence leave his body. I was crazed with the thirst. I looked down and saw Ivan still breathing. The only thing I could think was why let him go to waste, and I sunk my fangs into him and drained him completely. I sat there on my knees between the two for several minutes until I came back to my senses. Then I realized what I had done.

In a court of law, I would have gotten away with it simply for the position that I am in. Secondly, it was in self-defense, which would have gotten me away with it as well. When you're in a fight to the death, anything goes. The higher-ups would have seen this as them getting what they deserved. In vampire circles, especially the middling of us, you are looked at as an outcast, a monster, if you feed upon another vampire. I knew a guy who runs an operation in all the major cities of this area. For a fee, he will make anyone, or anything, disappear. I cut Ivan and Jonathan's heads off above the bite marks. Two men came, and with no questions asked, I gave them a coin pouch and the bodies vanished. I had to take the heads back to the headquarters of the Nigrum Gladio for Claude to catalog.

I went back to my room and took one of the longest baths of my life. I felt like I couldn't get clean. I could still feel their blood on my face, and I could feel their energy within me. Some people on the outside believe that we are undead. That myth still persists to this day. That's simply not true. It is more accurate to say that we are reborn. The vampiric virus has taken over our body. We are slightly cold to the touch but we are not corpses. We can feel pain in a certain fashion. Our bodies do get damaged, but we heal far faster than humans. As you live longer, you learn to control your emotions. That doesn't mean that we don't have any.

I rode out to the edge of the city, where I met Lina. I told her that we were successful, and that I had to take the proof back to my superiors. She gave me a kiss and told me to be careful. It was going to be a long trip back to headquarters, mentally as well as physically.

Chapter 13

This is how the next decade went:

Lina and I would find a plot or a rouge band of vampires. We would take them down and report it to our superiors. We would have secret rendezvous sometimes, during a mission or just for fun. Lina already enjoyed a good position within her organization. As far as my position goes, I was starting to get recognized for taking down so many people by myself, as far as they were concerned. The rest of the Nigrum Gladio were getting quite peeved that I wasn't bringing them in. We were all over Europe, but it seemed most of the issues were around the Mediterranean area. It probably had something to do with the fact that most of the higher-ups that were still in Europe were in France and Britain, while the younger vampires tended to be on the outskirts of the continent.

Time flew by so fast for us, year after year passed. We grew closer and closer together. I tried not to be away from her for more than a week if I could help it. Time snuck up on us when we both got separate letters. It was December 18 when we got them. The letters stated we were to meet in Paris. The ceremony for the handing over of Europe from the Ecne cabal to Maat's cabal would be there. It was going to be a giant, lavish party. Attendance was necessary for those of Ecne's cabal left in Europe. The party was originally supposed to take place in London. That would have been the most natural place for it to be because that was the capital of Ecne's cabal. Maat felt with the English Parliament executing Charles I, there was too much unrest in England right now. It wasn't a big secret that she had planned to move the capital to Paris anyway.

My specific instructions were that I was to collaborate with the rest of the Nigrum Gladio as security for the event. I'd rather have that anyway so that I can stay out of the public eye. As a guard, you kind of go completely unnoticed, and blend into the background. Especially at one of these events where everyone is so self-absorbed, trying to make other people see how great they are. I had to figure out a way for Ecne to let me stay in Europe after the transition was over. My options we're going to be very limited. One way I could stay is by becoming a steward of an embassy. That seems like the least likely of all my options. I don't want to speak ill of embassy stewards, but they are not really considered assets in the way that I am considered right now. I doubt my superiors would want to take me off the board like that. Another option would be for me to become some form of politician. The most likely would be some form of liaison, either military, or like Lina, in intelligence. Becoming a military liaison, I definitely would say is a long shot. I am not qualified for that position. Especially over the last ten years, I have made more contacts and have had success in keeping operations quiet. I believe I could convince them to transfer me over to the Intelligence Division. The key was going to be for me to get sponsors. I know Claude would hate to see me go, but he liked me and I knew he would support me. Then I would need someone in the intelligence community to back me and get a politician, or the boss above Claude, to vouch for me. It really shouldn't raise any flags, because I'm getting to the age where most vampires start trying to go up the ladder. All these operations that I had been performing for the last ten years would make sense to them. They would see them as me trying to pad my resume. I hope that Maat wouldn't send Lina back to Africa. Either way, that would be a shorter trip than me trying to sneak back over here across the ocean from the Americas. It wasn't going to be too hard to contact Lina, as we were both in Italy at the moment. We had both been in the area more and more since the end of the Bohemian revolt two years ago. Lina was in Rome and I was in Naples. So it would be an easy two-day trip. I sent a messenger to inform Claude that I was on my way to Paris.

Two days later, I was in Rome at a cafe, walking with Lina. We were able to be a little bit more open because hundreds of vampires from every major city were leaving to go to Paris, so it wouldn't be out of the ordinary for us to be seen in public talking.

"Simon, I hadn't really been thinking about what to do when the time comes. It's sort of snuck up on me."

"It isn't your problem to come up with a plan for. You're staying here. My job is to figure out how I can do the same."

"Still, I despise sitting on my hands. What's your plan? You do have a plan right?"

"Do I have a plan? Do I have a plan? Of course I do." I put a playful, fake nervous look on and started tapping the table with my fingertips.

"Quit playing around Simon, this is serious. I wish I could help you."

"Well, now that you mention it, there is something you might be able to do."

"What's that?"

"If you could leak some information that would make

it appear that Maat's intelligent crews think that I'm a good source of information in Europe, it would be great."

"Simon, what are you aiming at?"

"With my success over the last ten years of stopping covert operations, I'm going to try and convince my superiors that they should move me into an intelligence position."

"Intelligence? I don't know if anyone would believe that," she snickered and took a drink of coffee.

"Oh, you're funny," I retorted with a not-so-amused look on my face.

She set her cup down, and with a fake smug look, she said, "Yes, I know I'm hilarious." She took a short sip of her coffee with her pinky up, then said with a mockingly fancy voice, "I'll see what I can do, sir."

I shook my fist at her and facetiously warned, "One of these days, I'll pop you right in the kisser."

She puckered her lips, raised an eyebrow and sassed, "Don't threaten me with a good time." We both laughed.

She knew of a friend's house that was empty in the city, so we spent the night there together. We knew, once we got to Paris, we would have to act as though we were barely acquainted with each other. I think we held each other extra tight that evening. In the back of our minds, we both knew this might be our last night together.

In the morning, we rode off separately. I left first because I had to get set up for my guard duty. I arrived with five days to go before the event. I met with Michael, Olbrecht, and Philip, as well as a dozen other Nigrum Gladio. Claude gave us our orders, the usual for these types of events. We each had our own area to control. For most of us, it was a hundred or two hundred foot area that we had to control, to not let anyone through without authorization. After Claude got done with the group as a whole, I waved him over.

"Can we speak in your office?"

"Of course, Simon. What can I do for you?"

"I have a favor to ask you, and I'm not sure if you're going to like it." He put his hand over my shoulder, opened his office door, and we walked inside. I don't think I'd ever seen one of his offices so clean. His desk was spotless, with no paperwork clutter on it, and there were only a few words and a painting on the wall. "Sir, you really tidied up the place."

He let out a big hearty laugh. "Even I have to impress my boss, Simon." I mean I knew he had bosses, but I never thought about him actually interacting with his boss. "So, what is it that you need me to do?"

"Well, sir, these last few years I have built up a network of connections, and I would like to apply for an intelligence position. I think I could be a great asset collecting information and performing any special operations that might need to be done in Europe."

He kept a straight face, I couldn't read him at all. He spoke after what seemed like an eternity of silence.

"Well, this is a little bit out of the blue. I know you've been taking on more solo missions these past few years, but you've always told me that you weren't looking to move up."

I didn't want to lie to him, but I also couldn't tell him the real truth so I countered, "I'm looking for new challenges, not really for promotions. You know I'm always looking for exciting things and I think this is what I need to keep me engaged mentally."

He seemed to buy it. He was nodding his head gently.

"Well you are one of my best men, if not my best, but

I don't want to stand in the way of someone who has earned their shot. I will give my supervisor and the intelligence supervisor my vote of confidence for you."

I tried not to jump up and down in my seat. "I appreciate that, sir. You don't know how much it means to me to have your approval."

He waved a hand at me, dismissively. "Don't mention it. Now get out of here and get ready to do your job. It's getting too mushy in here for me."

We shook hands and he patted me on the back and we went our separate ways. I was on my way to check out where I would be posted. They had me at one of the rear entrances. I always like to get a good observation of my surroundings before I do my post. I was about a block away from the building when a kid in ragged clothes ran up to me. He appeared to be about ten years old.

He put his hand out to shake mine and said, "Hello, sir." I shook his hand and looked down. There was a small note left in my hand. He quickly uttered, "Have a good day!" and ran away. I unraveled the note.

Dearest Simon,

Intel suggests that there is a group of ex-Maat members who will try and crash the party in an attempt to break relations and assassinate top diplomats in the process.

P.S. Don't get yourself killed. I'd hate to have to find another lover.

Lina is so charming. As of late, I've been doing this on my own, but I think this time, I'm going to pass this around to all the guards. I will, however, make sure they all know I've gathered the intel. After I had relayed the information, Claude put everyone on high alert. We knew an attack was coming, but the when and where was what was putting everyone on edge. I put out some feelers to the local messengers. I let it be known that whoever got me info on the group would get a pound of gold. I was sure that would make all the little birdies very motivated. I was not disappointed. Mid-way through the following day, I received a handful of messages, two of which were worth the time of investigating. With four days to go, I couldn't waste any time. I felt better about these things than I normally do because I knew there were dozens of eyes looking throughout the city. So I knew it wasn't solely on my shoulders.

The first tip was a local brewery on the south side of the city. The message said that four men were seen two days ago walking into the brewery, and no one has been seen coming out since. It wouldn't surprise me for a group of rogue vampires to take over a small business. All they need is less than a week. I mean, it's not the smartest plan if the business had orders. If they didn't fulfill the orders, you would have people coming in and knocking on the door, but we're not dealing with scientists here. It was a two-story building next to a lot of other two-story buildings in a business district. My initial plan was to use the gutter system to climb the side of the building and enter through the second-story window. It was easy enough, but I was worried the gutters would collapse and alert the men inside to my presence.

Once I got to the top, I found that the window was jammed. I weighed my options, then pulled out the dagger that I kept with me. I jammed it in the window frame and popped it open. It made a nice creaking sound as it opened but not nearly as bad as I had thought it was going to be. I was still on alert as I went inside the top story and I saw nothing out of the ordinary. No disturbances, no people. I made my way down to the first story and that's where I saw some flipped over tables and some blood. There was definitely a struggle here, but there didn't seem to be enough blood to say that there was a murder. I continued searching the first floor but didn't find anything of significance. I know they keep the brewery in the basement. If someone's still here, that is where they're going to be. I had to be aware of my surroundings as I entered.

As I opened the basement door, the scent of wheat and barley hit me like a ton of bricks. I had my dagger in my left hand, ready to strike at any moment. In the far corner of the room, there was a man sitting in a chair. His arms had been tied behind the back of the chair. I ran over to him quickly. He was still alive and breathing, but had been beaten severely. I could sense we were not alone in the room. I spun around to see four men standing about twenty feet from me. I instantly knew I was in trouble. These men were not vampires, not even close. All four men were wearing long jackets that went down to their ankles with basic white shirts and pants. I drew my sword with my right hand and put my left hand out.

I shook my head in confusion and asked, “Hold on, what the hell are you guys doing here?”

The three biggest guys dropped their jackets to the ground and started to remove their clothes. The fourth guy was clearly the leader; he stood in front of them. They started to breathe heavily, then the transformation began. Their arms and legs elongated, and they started to overload with muscle. Then came the hair covering their body and, lastly, their faces stretched out into that of a canine. I was staring down four Lycans in a basement with them blocking the only exit. I'm sure I've been in tougher spots, but I couldn't really tell you when. My heart was racing, I was waiting for a response. The leader looked at me, then leaned over and looked at the tied-up man.

With a thick German accent, he said, “You ask us what we're doing here, but I could ask you the same.”

I tried to stay stone-faced when replying, “I'm here investigating possible rogue vampires, what are you doing?”

“We have cause to be here. This man is selling our products without giving us our cut of revenues.”

Though we make up only about one percent of the population, most of the long-life entities or supernatural creatures have taken over vast industries. The Lycans have taken over half of Europe's beer market.

One of the Lycans leaned towards me. Breathing heavily, he asked, “Can we rip this parasite in half?”

I had to give them a reason to not attack me. So, I bragged, “You may be able to take me, but I'm going to take two heads with me. You can choose who.”

Their leader held his hand out to steady his men. “If I order my men, they would gladly lay down their lives.”

I had to get diplomatic. “We can all walk away from this. I don't give a rat’s ass about you or this situation.”

“What's to keep you from running, to gather the rest of your leeches?”

“I am the authority on matters of this kind. This human doesn't concern me. If he's wronged you, that's for you to deal with. My people have bigger issues.” I had a death grip on my sword. In an open field, I might have been able to take them. In this enclosed space, I might get a couple of shots in but then they would fall on me. I seriously don't think I’ll make it out of here if they decide to attack. The leader turned sideways and the others followed suit, to make room for me to walk through.

"I'm giving you one opportunity to prove my men wrong. If we hear that your men came looking around, we have your scent and you will be hunted," he warned, calmly.

I nodded my head, sheathed my sword, and with confidence, walked straight through them. When I walked out of the building, I had to shake my whole body to release the tension. I honestly wasn't worried about them coming after me. The majority of Lycan are straight forward, they'll tell you exactly what they're going to do. So if they said that they'll leave me if I don't come back after them, then that's exactly what they'll do. Not that I am overly concerned that I could not handle them on equal ground. I'm not going to interfere with them if they do not interfere with me. Now I have to go investigate the other lead. Let's just hope it doesn't end up putting me in a dragon's den.

This lead came in because there were three men who checked into a hotel which was mostly patronized by the same individuals that passed through. So it throws up flags whenever new people decide to stay there. When I went in the front door, I went directly to the woman behind the counter.

"Have you had some unusual patrons in the last few days?"

She had a look of concern on her face and she spoke very fast, "I don't want any trouble, sir."

I was trying not to lose my temper. "I didn't say you were in trouble, but I need to know if you have some guests who are not normally here."

"There were three men who came a few days ago. They said that they were only going to stay a week but they paid me for a month. They're in room four now. I don't want any trouble, sir."

My mood was already deteriorating. When I got to room four, I investigated the door and saw that it was a solid oak door. If I struck it just right, the door would stay mostly intact as it came off the hinges. I wasn't going to wait around if I was wrong. I'll pay the innkeeper for the amount of damage. I wasn't going to give them a chance as soon as I entered. I lined up and kicked the door close to the hinges. Though the door was solid, it still splintered into a dozen pieces. I sprinted in as soon as I kicked the door, not wanting to give them any time to react. I moved in fast enough that pieces of the door were still hitting the person that was directly in front of it, ten feet away. I sprinted and hit the first man to my left with my shoulder, sending them flying against the wall. The third was sitting at a desk with a type of fuse in his hand. I leapt across the room and tried to kick him in the side of his head, but he was fast enough to get both forearms up to block the shot. He yelled to the other two men, "Kill him!" I immediately knew these were the men I was after. I saw the man who had been standing in front of the door when I kicked it down. He had a piece of shrapnel from the door lodged in his left shoulder. His left arm was hanging at his side limply, while he was brandishing a metal rod, possibly a fire poker, in his right. Blood was trickling into his eyes from where he had been hit in the forehead by the door. His attack was lazy and had no chance of success. I ran forward, and with a horizontal strike, I cut halfway through his waist and his wrist that was hanging to his side. I spun and finished him with a strike to the back of his neck. His head tumbled to the floor.

The one that I had initially knocked into the wall dove at me. I fell underneath him, putting both of my feet into his stomach as we fell. I kept rolling backwards, then I pushed with everything I had, launching him into the opposite wall. This guy is really starting to piss me off. The loud mouth of the three tried to swing a punch at me. I ducked and hit him with a left hook and a right straight punch that dropped him. Looking back, I was glad that I trained in the art of fisticuffs. Most Nigrum Gladio thought it was a waste of time. I was trained from a young age to never lose grip on your sword, but you should be prepared for everything, even a fist being thrown at you. I could hear the one that I had flung into the wall getting back up. I turned to see him running at me like a berserker. I put my left hand towards the top of a blade and slammed it into his chest almost at running speed. I knocked him into the wall and forced the blade to his neck. I could feel it biting in and I started pushing with my left hand harder and harder. I felt the blade starting to cut through my gloved hand. I didn't care. I kept slamming and slamming and slamming until I felt the crunch of the blade cutting through his spine. I turned and pointed the sword at the last one.

With a desperate look on his face, he yelled, "Don't come any closer or I'll blow this whole place to sunder." I had my sword pointing at him, but in an act of compliance, I brought my sword across my body, down toward my hip. I now saw exactly what they were working on. There were wine barrels that I assumed were full of gunpowder. Now, what he took as an act of obedience from me, moving my sword downwards, was actually me covering the visibility he had of my left hand. As he stood over the barrel with a piece of parchment that was lit, I knew I had to end this quickly. My left hand blurred as I moved it in an upward motion, snatching my dagger and peeling it from its sheath, letting it fly. Before he even realized what happened, it penetrated his right temple, all the way down to the guard. I rushed over to him before he could fall on the barrel, grabbed the paper, and crushed it in my hand. His eyes were still wide open, but completely devoid of life. I quickly removed my dagger and decapitated him with my sword. I had practice throwing many times. My master, when I was first learning the art of swordsmanship, said to never throw your weapon. He also told me that you should always have a trick up your sleeve. I'm not quite sure why, but these vampires got under my skin. I'm normally unemotional about operations like this, but something about this situation had me vexed. I assumed it was the anxiety of not knowing whether or not I would be able to stay here. I found all of the men's coin pouches, then I bagged up their heads. I walked downstairs and threw the coin pouches on the front desk. I looked the woman directly in her eyes and I focused on my own, putting her into a state of hypnotism.

"I apologize for the mess I made in your room. You will not go up there until tomorrow morning. You can use the coin to repair any damages. Have a great evening," I coaxed her in a gentle voice. I would be sending over cleaners to retrieve the bodies and clean up most of the blood, as well as the gunpowder barrels, leaving only a smashed-up room. I sent a message to Lina that I had stopped them. She would be able to relay the message quickly to Maat or one of the head elders, seeing as how she had gotten a few promotions over the last ten years. I went back to the headquarters and debriefed Claude on the events that occured. Then, I wrapped my hand and got into new clothes before leaving for my duty.

The next two days went by uneventfully. While a few more dignitaries trickled in, word of me foiling the plot to blow up the event had circulated through most chambers in the city. I had received a lot of hand shakes and pats on the back. I was hoping this would strengthen my case to Ecne and the elders so I could stay. It was so hard to tell what was going to happen with everything being so crazy as of late. The night before it was set to begin, I started putting out my ambitions to the influential leaders. I went to my post to begin the shift for the night. Claude came by to speak with me for a moment, and he seemed to be in a better mood than normal.

“How's it going out here tonight, Simon?”

“Not too bad, nothing of concern to report. You seem awfully chipper this evening, sir.”

“I'm ready to get all this over with, and I'm ready to stop dealing with Maat’s people,” he laughed as he finished.

I took a deep breath and said, “I can imagine.”

He put his hand on my shoulder and, with a fatherly voice, said, “I can't promise you anything Simon, but I put in a good word for you, and from what I hear it sounds good.” That lifted my spirit, but I steadied myself. I didn't want to get too enthusiastic about the possibility.

The leaders and politicians started to file in. It was pretty boring stuff, basically nodding and bowing to the royalty, and checking the seals and passes of the less well-known or connected. When the last of the people on the lists entered, we closed off all of the entrances. Half of the guards stayed outside to walk the perimeter, and the other went inside to watch the halls. I could vaguely hear what was going on inside the main hall. It mostly sounded like normal political bullshit. People talked about how great the other people were, but when in reality everyone knew they hated each other.

The ceremonies were coming to an end when a man poked his head out of my door and said, “Simon, you're wanted in the hall.”

At first I thought that there was an altercation or someone I needed to escort out, but as I entered the chamber, the majority of the attendees were looking at me. Ecne was standing on the stage smiling. I'm not a fan of being the center of attention, so it really unnerved me when they cleared the walkway. Everyone was looking at me and a couple people were waving me on to go up. I did my best impression of somebody who wasn't a bumbling idiot as I walked up to the stage. Ecne put his hand out to shake, the whole world seemed to slow down as I put my hand out. I could see faces in the crowd staring up at me with fake smiles. Some of the faces I knew, most I did not. As I stared around the room, I could see people pointing up at me. I could see others whispering to each other with hands covering their mouths. Then, I saw her standing at the bottom left of the room.

Lina was in Maat's entourage of maybe ten people. She was wearing an amazing, silk, sapphire blue dress that fit her immaculately. It had gold threaded designs across her chest and back. The only woman who had a dress that stood out more was Maat herself. That was because she was wearing a solid gold dress that I swear it didn't only reflect light, but produced its own. Our eyes met, and for a moment, the corner of her lip turned ever so slightly, giving me the faintest glimpse of a smile, then it vanished into a generic neutral face. That was enough for me to perk up and straighten my shoulders even more.

The world came back into real motion and I shook his hand firmly, but I didn't try to out-grip him. Ecne spoke with a tone that carried throughout the hall. He was supremely confident talking in front of the crowd.

“Ladies and gentlemen, I do not want to take up much more of your time with my incessant chatter this evening, but I felt it wouldn't be proper not to introduce one of the men for whom this evening would not be possible.” At that, the rest of the room who may have not been wholly paying attention, turned their gazes up toward me. “This man single-handedly thwarted a group of conspirators who wanted to blow this room to kingdom come.” He let gasps and the murmuring go throughout the room for a moment. “This man's name is Simon, and he's one of my best Nigrum Gladio. For the past ten years, he has been preserving this transition in the background, unbeknownst to most of you. Normally, I would do this in private but I think this occasion deserves a more grandiose presentation.” I shifted my eyes around. All of this sounded great but I had no idea where he was going with this. Ecne was handed two items. One appeared to be a medal or pin, and the other was a small box that could fit in the palm of your hand. As he went to pin the medal on my chest, I tried to get a good look at it. It was the image of a sword crossing over a fist. Both fist and sword were black. The only pin I've ever seen that was similar to this one was the one Claude wore from time to time. Ecne held the tiny box in his hand. Then, while half facing me, and half facing the crowd, he announced, “For your immaculate service to me, and your fellow brothers in arms, I am promoting you to colonel of the Nigrum Gladio. You will be only outranked by Claude. You will be an intricate part in keeping my new world in order.” He opened the box to reveal my very own seal. I stood as still as I had the whole time, but inside I was losing my mind. *This isn't what I wanted, I made it clear what I was aiming for. Where did it go wrong?* Then I looked down and saw the face of an angel. This time when our eyes met, all I saw was anguish. She quickly looked away. I took the seal and shook his hand again. This whole thing was a whirlwind. People came up to me, slapped me on the shoulders, and shook my hand.

After the festivities were over, I made my way into the back corridors where I found Ecne talking with a few of the nobles. I waited until they were done shaking hands. As they walked away, I stepped up to Ecne.

"Sir, may I speak with you?"

He casually put his hand on the small of my back, and put his other hand toward an open door, then said, "Of course, Simon." We walked into an office and he closed the door behind us.

When I looked up at him, his whole demeanor had changed. It felt like the temperature in the room had dropped by ten degrees. Gone were the eyes of a happy politician. All that remained were the eyes of a predator. Like those of a shark: emotionless. You knew they were designed to seek out and destroy.

I treaded lightly with my words and tone, "Sir, I wanted to talk to you about the promotion." He stood completely still, but I could feel energy building up in the room that he was trying so hard to suppress.

His face looked like a statue when he blatantly said, "Yes?"

"Well, sir, I greatly appreciate the position that you have bestowed upon me, but I was hoping to work my way into the intelligence department. I have gained a great amount of contacts—" He cut me off before I could finish.

With authority behind his voice, he barked, "Do you

think I'm a fool?"

"No sir, of course not."

"How long has this land been my domain?"

"Thousands of years, sir."

"For millennia I have controlled these lands. Did you not think that I knew what you were doing, running around with one of Maat's pets?"

Shit. I had never felt fear like this since I was a young child.

"The only reason that you are not dead by Maat's hand already is because she does not have the eyes that I have here, nor will she ever, and the only reason that I have not disposed of you myself is because you have been effective." I could not quantify the fear I was feeling at that moment. I was standing in front of a damn near demigod while his anger was pointed directly at me. "I need effective men in my new world. Bid your farewell to these lands of your ancestors, for you will never see them again, and no matter how effective you are, I will not tolerate disobedience again." He walked out of the room and left me alone with my fear, sorrow, and my thoughts. One thing I will say, me being alone with my thoughts is not where you want me to be.

Chapter 14

When I woke up in the morning, I got out of bed to find a letter had been slid under my door sometime during the night. I picked it up and walked over to my balcony. I felt the cool morning breeze blowing against my face, it was refreshing. I opened the letter and carefully, I began to read:

Dearest Simon,

I know you. Last night you were probably scared out of your mind, but I know you. So after you got done crying like a baby, you probably got pissed and tried to figure out who you could wack over the head with your sword to fix the problem, but don't worry. I'm not going anywhere. We are not going anywhere, we'll figure this out together. It'll be just another secret mission to complete. After all there's only an ocean between us.

I looked out at the vastness of the ocean—no land in sight. I walked back inside my cabin to get ready for the day.

We arrived in New Amsterdam six weeks later. I am not a fan of long sea voyages, let me tell you. I was happy to be back on land, just not happy to be on land I was unfamiliar with. We were told that there were magnificent cities in South America, even some rivaling European cities in magnificence and population. Well, this place was pretty much a shithole. The population here, at least among the colonists, was less than the population of the city of Liverpool, and that's for the entire colony. Ecne had told us that he was going to facilitate more population transfer, to bring more humans. He expected by the beginning of the next century to have ten times the population. He said the goal within one hundred years was to be close to two and a half million people.

The Nigrum Gladio's job will be to keep vampires from thinning the population until a time where the population is sufficient enough to sustain normal feeding. We were also to keep vampires from turning the natives until we knew enough about them. That could run rapidly through a native population that was not used to defending itself. This is what Claude was most worried about. He was going to post our numbers greater in Boston, New Amsterdam, Dover, and Saint Augustine, though our numbers would be greater in the towns our best men would be: the ones who went after the rogues, and who ventured into the native lands. Claude had put me in charge of that group. He said his experience would net him a better effect with the nobles in the towns, while I was used to traveling the countrysides. His points were not invalid, but I felt as though somehow I was going to take a lot more risk than him. So I wasn't looking forward to our first meeting.

The building that we had set up was actually quite nice, maybe the nicest building in the area. It was brick and mortar on the outside, and on the inside we used the same carpenters that Wyckoff did to build his house. I knocked on Claude's door, which was already wide open. He saw me and his face automatically lit up.

"Simon my boy, I know this isn't where you wanted to be, but I am awfully glad you are here." We traded grips and I sat down.

"Well I'm glad because I'm stuck in this shit hole, and

you have to share it with me." We both laughed.

He put his arms out as if to show me the place and then said, "It's not that bad."' I raised an eyebrow, not believing him. "Okay, okay. It sucks here, but it won't forever. I've never seen so many resources being sent in such a short amount of time. We're going to be having hundreds of people being ferried over here every month." That got my attention. It is not cheap to cross an ocean. To ship hundreds of people every month, it's going to cost him a fortune. No wonder he drained all of the accounts, and called in all the debts that were owed to him before we left. Claude could see the realization on my face. "It will have an avalanche effect. The more people are here, more people will come here. He's investing heavily at the beginning. It's already worked in South America and we are financially reaping the rewards."

I couldn't help but ask, "So, what is going on with South America?"

He put on a fake smile. "Most of the leaders are stationed in South America, as well as the army. It's much more developed than up here, so it's easier for them to set up command, as well as homes for the nobles, and with that amount of power in the area, fear will keep most in line."

"Ain't that the truth."

"At least we don't have the problems they have down there." He handed me a paper with a list of directives.

I left the office and went over my directives as I went down High Street. Of course the signs say "Hoogh Straet", but I'm English and if I know the English, these signs will be getting translated in the not-so-distant future. At the heading, it acknowledges that, with my rank, I can accomplish these in any way I see fit. I do not have to ask for permission or any resources. If I needed something or someone, I got them. That was always my biggest issue, having to go through all the red tape to get what was needed for success. At the top of my directives, it stated I was to not stay in one town more than three days, unless on assignment. I had to make contact with the local tribes around major settlements, and trade with them to get intel on possible dangers. So this was going to be fun. I've basically become a nomad and an ambassador to people I know nothing about. Lina won't be able to call me an uncultured swine anymore, but I'm still not eating those snails. I shutter just thinking about them.

I headed back to the cabin to collect my equipment. I was going to carry three bows, some jewelry, and a musket. I'm sure natives would find these items desirable. The treasurer waved me over.

"What the hell do they have you doing?" he wondered.

"I'm the new traveling salesman, haven't you heard?"

"Well, remember, we're in every town along the way if you need supplies," he declared, throwing me several sacks of coins.

Looks like Windsor will be my first stop. It's half a day's ride to the north along the coast. The ride was amazing. With such small cities and so few people, the air was fresher than I've ever smelled. I came upon a cliff that was overlooking a small cove. I couldn't believe what I was looking at. His head started coming out of the water about forty feet from shore. As it got closer to shore, it became apparent that it was a massive being. When he reached the beach, he must have stood twenty feet tall. He had the features of the natives: long black hair, caramel color skin. I think you could say he was handsome in a way. He had an anchor sized rope over his shoulder.

Then I saw what the rope was attached to. There was a huge splash in the water. When I looked closer I saw that it was a whale. The giant was hand fishing a damn whale. As I looked further up the shore, I saw native people with knives, bowls and plates. He was bringing the whale as food for them. I told my horse to giddy up and spurred it on. I made it to the beach to see the giant in a struggle with the mammoth whale. He had about ten feet of rope ahead of him. He didn't see me approach, but I decided to grab the rope and help him pull. As soon as I started pulling, he looked up. I motioned my head toward the edge of the beach. He nodded to me and we pulled as hard as we could. The whale was so strong. It was unbelievable. My legs felt as though they were on fire. My hands were getting shredded by the rope. After a couple of minutes, I could feel the beast giving out. Just then, the pulling came easier and we started rushing up the beach. Once we had it all the way on land. The people started to cheer and clap their hands. The giant and I were covered in sand and water. I could hear the people talking amongst themselves.

Another adaptation for us vampires is that all we need to hear is a handful of words, and we naturally pick up languages. Scientists have said it has something to do with us luring in humans. Most of our gifts fall into that hunting category. I had heard enough to start picking up what they were saying. I heard them talking about me with reverence. The giant walked over to me, although it felt more like I was being approached by a tree. He loomed over me. I didn't have my hand on my sword, but my thoughts weren't far from it. His face was completely stoic, his hair matted to the sides of his head. Then he stuck his hand out. I thought I could see the crest of a smile form. It surprised me when he opened his mouth, and spoke in English. I was not hearing it as a translation like the natives. His accent was very similar to that of the Native I had met in New Amsterdam.

With a voice like a church organ, he spoke a deep bass, “Hey, not sure who you are, but I appreciate it. I’ve never had someone help with the fishing before.” We shook hands; this must be what it feels like for a baby to shake a grown man's hand.

“It looked like you could use some help. It was an awfully big catch.”

“Help is always good. Most people think that if you're big, you don't need help.”

“Don't I know it. My mentor always taught me that no matter how good you are, never turn down help.”

“Good saying to live by. I hope you have good travels through this land. I must go and feed my people. Oh, by the way, they call me Maushop.”

As I started riding away, the natives waved to me. One of them ran up and handed me a chuck of wrapped whale blubber. I bowed my head in gratitude and rode away to my next destination. I guess America is going to have some surprises for me after all.

When I arrived in Windsor, I found what seemed to be a quaint little town. I made my way to the office and found a friendly face. Philip had set up shop here. As soon as he saw me, he couldn't help but give me a hard time.

“Alright big boss, which ass cheek do I need to kiss?”

“It's good to see you too, Philip. How's America treating you?”

“One of the most boring-ass places I've ever been, until recently.”

“Really? I just got here and you've already got problems?"

"Hey, hey. You haven't even heard it yet. It might be something super amazing that you will love and there will be no issues."

"Really?"

"Probably not. Not with our luck. It'll probably be something nightmare-inducing."

"So, what's going on?"

"It looks like somebody is doing my work for me. I've had a couple rogue vampire incidents, but then everything stopped. After a couple of days, I sent word to James in Providence and Henry in Boston, and they reported similar incidents."

"So, we have a vampire hunter."

"I'm not so sure I would call it that. These vampires that they are attacking have been breaking our laws. I would have had to deal with them. No vampires that have stayed within the bounds have been harmed."

"I still don't like it. We are the law. When was the last incident?"

"Three days ago, just outside of town. It was the first time anybody had gotten a glimpse. A woman and her child we're being attacked by a newborn. They said it was a figure in a cloak that ran by and chopped the vampire's head off, and then disappeared without a word."

"Great. I love the strong, silent type."

Chapter 15

So, in America, I have giants, vampire hunters, and god knows what else I have to deal with. Doing a little investigating, I found the person and/or creature has a one hundred mile radius they've been traveling through. It's only been vampires who are committing vicious crimes that have been the victims. That tells me whoever this is fancies themselves a good vigilante. I don't see them stopping unless they are confronted.

I got word that there had been two vampire attacks outside of Boston. I moved quickly to get there before whatever had been attacking did. I actually found the vampire in question outside of the local brothel. He wasn't a vampire of significance. He was somewhere in the neighborhood of fifty years old from what my intelligence had gathered.

I've seen this a hundred times. He will wait until the end of the evening, and follow one of the girls home to snatch her along the way. He actually surprised me with how early he decided to strike. My pocket watch said it was only six o' clock. The sun was still high in the sky, illuminating everything. He followed her for about three blocks. She was actually pretty smart about taking the main streets, but it didn't matter. He took the risk and snatched her into a side alley behind a fishery and a warehouse. He may have thought that the smell of processed fish would cover up anything that came out of his attack.

Rarely do things work out perfectly for me, but it had gone exactly as I was hoping. I dashed in shortly after he pulled her in, but I hadn't been the only one stalking him.

As I turned the corner into the alley, I saw the figure strike the vampire in the side of the head. As he fell to the ground, I saw the figure getting ready to pull a blade from underneath his cloak. I rushed in and slammed into him with my shoulder, knocking him into the back wall of the building with a thud. The woman ran, screaming out of the alley. The vampire stirred and was getting ready to run after her, but I pointed my blade into his throat. The vigilante removed his cloak and rolled it up neatly and set it on top of a box. I'm a student of the history of war, and I don't believe I had ever encountered someone dressed in the type of armor he had on. This armor looked to be about five hundred years out of date. If I had to guess, I'd say he was wearing scaled horned armor. It also looked like he was wearing bronze gauntlets and shin guards. The two most fascinating things about him were his helmet and where he carried his blades. His helmet was also bronze, but what made it peculiar was that it was completely enclosed. Where his eye slits should be, were black glass of some form. His blades were attached to his wrist by some kind of mechanism. They were about two and a half feet long and very wide at the wrist, tapering off to a point still wider than most swords. He swung his arms down to his sides and the blades swung out like a hinge and snapped, holding in place.

He pointed down at the vampire and said, “This kill is mine.” His voice was muffled inside of the helmet. I heard a faint English accent.

“Well, now you’re talking bollocks. He's under my jurisdiction,” I responded.

"He's killed innocent humans and your people have done nothing."

"Hey man, I just got here. Give me a chance."

"I'll give you a chance to step aside."

"Seriously? I'm the one that makes the witty comments."

The vampire tried to crawl away. I proceeded to impale him through the leg with an iron rod that was laying on the ground. The warrior slashed down to decapitate him. I deflected his blow.

I tried to reason with him, "Please, don't make me kill you." He began to circle me. I could tell he was skilled by the way his feet moved. I didn't want to kill this man, but maybe I could incapacitate him. I threw a strike at his left shoulder, and he parried it with ease. He held his arms up in a position like he was going to block punches. This time I got creative and threw a double strike: one to the left side of his head, and the other to the right side of his body. They failed to hit home, like the first strike. This guy was really starting to piss me off. I decided to turn the heat up to see how long he could last. I began to throw blow after blow at him from all different types of angles. He wasn't faster than me, not by a long shot. It was almost as if he knew where the next strike was coming from and where it would land. We were in a dance and he always knew the next step. It was bordering on precognition, but I didn't sense anything in him but a human. The sound of swords clashing reminded me of a choir of people ringing bells. It was actually quite beautiful.

I stopped the attack and he said, "Your swordsmanship is commendable, maybe the best I've ever seen from a vampire."

"You're not too shabby yourself." I gathered in some

energy and I faked a movement to my right, then rushed forward for a horizontal strike on the left side. He slid under my sword and slashed slightly on my side. I tried to turn around to re-engage him but he had slid straight to the other vampire, decapitating him in the same motion. This guy right here, I've never liked and hated someone so much at the same time. "Why'd you have to go and do that?"

"I told you this was my kill."

"Now I can't let you off the hook. I've just started here. I am cleaning up this place, and believe me, I will put the fear of God into all vampires on this continent, but you can not be here again, or I will kill you." He made a quick movement with both arms and both blades swung back around and latched to his forearms.

"Let me give you a piece of advice: pick your battles wisely and be willing to live with the consequences." He picked up his cloak, unraveled it, and threw it back on in one smooth motion. He gave me a nod and then put his hood up, and walked away. I haven't been beaten skill-wise in a sword fight since I was fourteen years old. Sure, Claude and Michael have handed me my ass in the past, but that was more because of their power than their skill. There are moments in your life that you will never forget, this is one of those moments for me. I'm sure I won't forget it for years to come.

I went on to Boston and called a meeting with all available Nigrum Gladio. I beat it into their head that this is a new world and that we will set a new standard here. There will be no lag time with disciplinary actions against offenders. If we have a rogue, they are to be dealt with immediately. I even put a monetary compensation incentive for swift retribution. If we have an issue with the natives, we will use all diplomacy at our disposal before we use the sword. I wanted to gain allies before other groups started to set up shop here in North America. That was received with mostly positive feedback, especially from the younger members. They were all ready to jump feet-first into their new roles. There were still a few, especially the older members, who didn't think I deserved the position that I had. Being the diplomatic person that I am, I told them they can hitch to this wagon or they could be run over by it.

The treasurer wasn't too happy with me at first because I kept asking for more coin. He even raised the issue with Claude. After my results started flowing in, all doubts were erased. It's amazing how when you offer incentives to people instead of leaving them to their own devices, they tend to get things done. Of course, as I predicted, the number of incidents started falling rapidly. Again, when you know if you step out of line that the sword is coming for you immediately, you tend to stay inside the bounds of the law.

But with my new office came paperwork and all the new rumors. I'm not sure which I hated worse. No, scratch that. Paperwork is the worst, definitely paperwork. I had mounds of the stuff piling up on my desks and in my bags I carried around. I was able to use Claude's rule against him, because if I couldn't finish all the paperwork in my allotted three days, I would send it his way. Hey, if he's going to turn me into a nomad, I'm going to turn him into a paper pusher. One of the other banes of my existence is having to deal with everyone's issues. “Simon I need an advance...Simon I want reassigned” Blah blah blah. Such is the life of a manager, I guess.

I was riding into Providence when a small, well-dressed boy ran up to me.

"Sir, do you think you could spare a few bits?" The main currency over here is the Spanish dollar. People tend to cut the thing into eight pieces and they call them bits. I can sense a game being played here, so I threw him a full silver dollar. His eyes lit up with excitement "Sir, you've been so generous. Let me see if I have something I can give to you." He rummaged through his bag and pulled out an envelope. "Please, sir, why don't you take this as my gratitude?" I took the envelope and waved him on. Sometimes, I even get tired of these games. I opened the letter once I got back to my place.

Dearest Simon,

If you are receiving this letter, it means that you have learned to be charitable. Now I know that you have probably been thinking yourself to death, trying to come up with a solution to our problem. Well you don't have to worry about that, leave it to me. And before you ask 1. Because I'm smarter than you and 2. Because I don't want you to hurt your brain by doing any thinking. I can see that look on your face, don't get huffy with me. I'm only joking, mostly. I love you dearly, and my next letter will have my brilliant plan.

I could even smell her perfume, lavender with a touch of honey. I held the letter to my nose so that I could visualize myself with her. I didn't care that I looked like a giddy school boy. She's my lady and she is awesome. I took my nose off the letter long enough for me to ride to the office.

No sooner had I sat in my chair, I heard pounding on my door. I groaned as I got back to my feet and walked over to open the door. Whoever it was, they were being extra annoying today. They kept pounding on the door until I opened it.

"Ah, Christ. It's you Fitzroy."

"Thank you for the compliment. I am not Christ though, but we may have to pray to him if this ends up being true."

I scratched the back of my head. I do that when I'm nervous or annoyed. This should be fun.

Chapter 16

Fitzroy is the local sorcerer. He is currently on our payroll at the moment. All of the cabals used sorcerers. Ecne and Tū use them more like contractors, while Maat and Wendi have them like employees. They even have them in their personal guard. Mostly, they annoy me. Especially Fitzroy. He's the kind of sorcerer that will always tell you the sky is falling. Then he'll tell you that if you just get him this gem or more coin, he can stop it. He sat down across from me at my desk. His look was disheveled to say the least. With how much he got paid, you would think he could afford a haircut to go along with the fancy robe. He began speaking before I could find a sharp object to shove into my ears. Had I been able to do that, then only my ears would be hurting, not my soul.

"Do you remember that rumor that was going around not too long ago?"

"No, no I do not, but I'm sure you're going to tell me all about it."

"Is that sarcasm I hear?"

"Of course not. Dazzle me with your tail," I replied, unamused. He gave me an irritated look.

"There have been groups of humans and vampires alike venturing out west, several of these groups had vanished without a trace. Others have come back with a fantastical story." I interrupted him with a gesture of my hand.

"Could that be what these are? Fantastical stories of

people whose imaginations have got the better of them?" Fitzroy had been guilty of this in the past. His face filled with excitement and he wagged his finger in the air.

"That's what I thought too, until I went on one of these trips, about four days west of here. The natives call the land Dionde gâ."

"I appreciate that you have taken the time to get to know the locals, but I do not need the name of the flowers that bloom in the area or what type of berries are good to eat in the land. I need facts."

He got a little attitude. "Well, here's the facts: I went out there and my group was attacked by something with immense dark energy."

"What was it?"

"Hell if I know. I got the hell out of there."

"You didn't help them?" I asked.

"As much as I felt it necessary, I wasn't getting paid by them. I showed them the way out and I yelled 'run'. That's enough."

"Really? Are you that big of a coward?"

"It's not about being a coward. If I had to fight to stay alive, I would have done so. I had no obligation to protect any of them."

"What about a moral obligation?"

"Let's not start talking about morals. Your people feed on humans to live," he jabbed.

"Alright, alright. We can talk about your failings as a human being later. How long would it take me to get out there?"

"For you, five days to a week, depending on how hard you want to ride."

"Didn't you say it took you about four days?"

"Yes, but that was only because I made the trip easier

by giving us mostly flat ground to ride over. You will not have my magic to help you along the way. I wouldn't go out there without a small army."

I had Fitzroy make me a map, marking the landmarks along the way to find my way there. I also had him make me a backup map, which I had a messenger send to Claude, just in case I didn't come back so he could send an army. I tried to get more information out of Fitzroy, like what the animal or creature looked like, but he kept telling me that everything happened so fast and it was so dark, he couldn't get a good look. This trip was going to be four hundred miles one way, so I was going to need the best horse I could get my hands on. I was also going to make this an eight day trip out there. I didn't want to push the horse too far and then have to walk back. Along with my sword and dagger, I also took a bow with me. I'm not the best archer, but I'm competent enough to hunt or to hit any decent-sized creature. One of the younger guys out of the Nigrum Gladio in Boston caught wind of what I was doing. He showed up in full armor and had his horse fully packed for the journey. I tried to dissuade him, but I remember when I was new, I would have just snuck my way hundred miles down the road.

As we rode west and left civilization behind, nature took over. It was beautiful. The smell of waste had fallen away. The smell of farms was the next to disappear. As we rode on, the land was filled with red maple trees. They gave off a sweet scent that reminded me of cherries and almonds. We stopped at a creek to grab something to drink. It was the clearest freshwater I had ever seen. This must have been what all of Europe was like before the human population started to expand. Don't get me wrong, there are still places like this in Europe, but as the cities expanded, these places became fewer and fewer.

That evening, I decided to get to know my traveling companion a little better. We hadn't really talked the entire way, as we were trying to start at a good pace. We stopped for the night.

As the fire crackled, I started by apologizing, "I'm sorry, I didn't get your name." A look came over his face like when you start a trip and you realize you forgot something, but you're too far to turn back now.

"No, I'm sorry sir, I should have properly introduced myself. I'm Winston." I leaned over and knocked my wine cup against his. His mannerisms alone told me that he was new to the Nigrum Gladio.

"How are you liking life on this side of the pond?"

"It has its challenges but I'm excited to be here. It's like a whole new journey and I can't wait to see what the years will bring us."

I took a sip of wine. "Do you have any issues or concerns?" I paused for half a second, and reassured him, "You can be honest with me."

Winston shifted his eyes a little bit and then turned his head sideways slightly. "Well, I've been listening to Fitzroy—"

I quickly cut him off. "That's your first problem. Don't believe a damn thing that comes out of Fitzroy's mouth."

"You're probably right, sir, but he's been talking about the dark spirits that are all over these lands. He said if we don't do something about this, we too will end up like Roanoke."

"Roanoke was nearly a hundred years ago. People are still living here. Those people probably just ran afoul of the natives."

"Yeah, I think that's the consensus for most people,"

Winston said, unconvinced. I tried to take any tension out of the air.

“Let's make a toast to Fitzroy and his crazy-ass delusions.”

We smashed our cups together and finished off our drinks. Lying under the stars reminded me of when I was a boy. My mentor used to take me out camping in the woods whenever we had down time. Does that mean I'm a mentor now? Yeah, I don't know if I'm ready for that.

We rode on for a few more days before running into a group of ten natives. They also appeared to be traveling. They had bags, and the one that I presumed to be the leader, had an English satchel. That made me feel a little bit at ease because I knew they've been trading with Europeans. I wasn't sure about their dialect, or if it was a completely different language. So I had to get them to talk to me first. When they saw me, the women filed in behind the men. All of them had some form of a weapon. Some had knives, most had tomahawks. Two even had bows. A thought came into my mind: I had two spare bows from the previous trip. Their bows looked to be in rough shape. Even if they didn't want to use mine, they could surely trade them for something useful later on. I removed the two bows from my pack and slid off my horse. I held them out, not making it a sudden movement. I walked about halfway to one of the men with a bow. I stopped ten feet away and motioned with my hand for him to take them. He looked at me with a little suspicion and then snatched them out of my hand quickly. I slowly reached into one of the pouches on my belt. I retrieved three necklaces that were laced with pearls and gold, one for each of the women. As I threw the necklaces to them, their eyes lit up and they cut the biggest smiles I've ever seen. The rest of them started to talk amongst themselves which is exactly what I needed. I was able to pick up enough of their language and dialect to speak directly to them. I held up my left hand to grab their attention.

"I am Simon, and this is my friend, Winston. We are on a journey to Dionde gâ. We were wondering if we were on the right path?" I could see the shock on their faces that I could actually speak their language. They leaned over to each other and were mumbling something, but I could not hear clearly.

Their leader stepped a couple feet in front of the rest and spoke in a deep, rich voice, heavy with the native accent. "Are these gifts or are these payments to be your pathfinder?"

"They are simply gifts. You can keep them and be along your way, but we would appreciate it if you at least pointed us in the right direction." They went back to discussing amongst themselves. It only took them a few seconds.

"We will help you find your way. It is along our journey back to our home, not far."

I nodded my head and said, "As an act of good faith." I knew we were being watched. I could sense the creature's eyes upon us. I drew my bow back, pointed into the woods just to the right, and let the arrow loose. I heard the impact of my arrow. Then a short cry. The life was gone from the creature. I went into the woods and dragged out a buck deer. I handed it to the leader of the natives.

He looked at the deer, then held his fist in the air and let out a cry of "woo woop". The rest of the men followed suit, letting out their cry. They went to work on the deer. I've never seen someone field dress an animal as quickly as they did. We ate the most delicious venison over the fire that evening. It was amazing to get to talk to the natives and enjoy their company. They were so much different from the picture that is most often painted of them. In a lot of ways, they are similar to us. Most of our differences exist because they choose to live a mostly nomadic lifestyle. I told them stories of European gods and their deeds. They told Winston and I the story of creation. It was a fantastic story. A story of a floating island and sky people. In their story, no one was ever born, and they never died. Then, one day, a woman became pregnant and her husband kicked her off the floating island down to the waters of Earth and she was saved by two birds. These birds drug mud up from the ocean floor and put it on the back of a giant turtle which became the size of the entire continent. I found the story quite interesting. Winston, on the other hand, was enthralled. He looked like a little boy listening to an old man tell his favorite tale.

We continued the next few days the same way. They caught some fish to add to the venison. This was one of the best experiences of my life. To be among people who weren't plotting and scheming, but just trying to live their lives. The next day we closed in on our destination. I had learned the leader's name was Okwaho. He told me his name means 'the wolf'. I thought that was a great name for a leader. We walked to the top of a large wooded hill. As we crested the hill, I saw the point where two rivers create a great river. He was also pointing out little camps of natives all along the banks of each river. I wanted to try and get a little more information and see what he knew.

"Have you heard of any disappearances in the area?"

"People disappear in the forest all the time, especially those who do not respect it."

"Do you know anything about the recent disappearance of a group? They came through here about ten days ago."

"I can't say I have, but there can be spirits around this place. Angry spirits who use the power of the rivers to crawl from the ground." *Like a Native American demon crawling up from the underworld.* Okwaho pointed to the edge of the forest, passed the settlement. "We will camp there tonight. No need to walk through the village. If we arrive, they will expect to trade. We have no need for trade right now."

"How much further is it to your home?" I asked.

"Not far. One day's journey from there."

When we made our way back to the bottom of the hill, I found Winston playing a stick-ball like game with the rest of the group. I think they had adopted him into their family. If I happen to have been an observant person, one might think he was even flirting with the native women. It was no shock that everyone liked him. Winston's a likable guy. Winston is definitely good with a sword, but he doesn't strike me as someone that should be in the Nigrum Gladio. He seems more like someone's personal guard. He's very personable and easy for someone to like which would make him better for that type of role. I think when we get back, I will write him a letter of recommendation to a few of the nobles, and see if I can get him a better job which would suit his skills.

Once we reached the river, one of my concerns went away. I had wondered how we were planning on crossing this river. I mean, Winston and I could cross it without our horses. That is not something I wanted to do, nor did I know how the natives were going to cross. It appears they had rigged up a ferry system. It was the largest canoe I had ever seen, especially wider than anything I saw from the natives. Half of our group was able to make the journey at a time. These people were a lot more ingenuitive than anyone gives them credit for.

We followed a well-worn path through the woods. The air was heavy with the scent of peppermint. Okwaho told me it was from a wiigwaas tree. They had a beautiful white color to them. I hadn't ever seen a tree quite like that. The sun was setting behind the trees as we reached our resting point. That's when I heard it. The high-pitched scream of a native woman. As I turned around, Winston was already on the offensive. He slashed at the creature that was dragging her into the woods by her leg. Even with my eyesight and reflexes, I couldn't quite grasp what it was, maybe a big cat. Winston drew his bow and let loose three arrows faster than I've ever seen anyone do before. The arrow dove into the forest but I heard no response. Winston put the woman on his shoulder and began to carry her back to the group. She had a three foot long gash down her leg that was bleeding profusely. Before we had a chance to tend to her wounds, Winston was hit at the knees by a dog-sized creature. He spun and put his sword at a low guard. I drew my bow and tried to hit the creature while it was distracted. It rushed Winston just as I released my arrow. Right before they clashed, its form blurred and became a black bear twice the size of Winston. It hit him with so much force, it knocked him back to the edge of the forest. He was buried under fur, fangs, and claws. I let loose two more arrows which I was sure hit their mark. I looked at the woods, then at the group. I knew that if I left the group and they were attacked, they had no shot at survival against whatever this was. At least Winston had a fighting chance. These people did not ask to be brought into this fight.

I yelled at the group, "Circle up and get behind me!"

They all drew their weapons, and they began to chant, rhythmically, "Hi A Way Hi A OH." I could feel my night vision starting to pick up. I dropped my bow and unsheathed my sword. I was too tense. I forced myself to relax. I released my death grip on my sword, then got into a proper stance. I had seen that the creature liked to launch itself at its prey. I held my sword closer to my body so it couldn't target my weapon on its next pounce. I'm not sure what this thing was, but I knew it was a shapeshifter of some form. Thus, I knew it had to be sentient. I tried to play with its pride.

"Are you so weak that you hide in the dark, and that you attack from the shadows? I am here in the open. Face me!" I kept the fear out of my voice. Inside I wanted to be anywhere, except for standing alone against this creature I knew nothing about. I didn't know its strengths or weaknesses. All I knew is that it could shapeshift, and it was physically strong. As I used my eyes to scan the area of the woods where it jumped into, in my peripheral vision where there once was nothing, there now stood a giant creature. I've never seen one of these creatures. I had only heard about them. It reminded me of a bull, only hairier. Its head was bigger, and its horns were shorter and pointed upward. Its snow white fur and eyes black as the night stood out the most. We were both standing as still as any good predator does, waiting for its prey to make its first mistake. I took another jab at his pride since it seemed to work before. "The only reason you've been able to attack these people on this trail over and over again is because you haven't faced me yet. I'm going to spill your blood all over that nice, shiny white coat."

I think that pissed it off a little bit. It stomped the ground before charging at me. I knew it was going to be fast, but I didn't expect it to move with that kind of swiftness. I ducked to the right side and my blade sang out as it sliced through the air. I held it horizontal as the creature sprinted by it to bite into the side of its flesh. At the last second, it made a slight adjustment that moved it out of the way, but I still felt the blade cut. I looked down at the tip of my blade and there was blood there. The blood was way too dark to be human, but there was blood. I spun and pointed my sword at the creature as it turned around. I screamed at it, "You bleed, you die!" It charged again, but when it was about ten feet from me, it blurred and disappeared up into the night sky. It was fast but I could tell it was still up there. All of a sudden I heard the scream of a hawk. Then it came for me. As it dove on me, I swiped my sword left to right, trying to get a piece of it. I did get a piece of it, but not the piece I wanted. It hit the pommel of my sword. The hawk latched on and we began struggling for the blade. The first rule I was ever taught in sword fighting is to never let go of your weapon. The grip of this creature's talons felt like I was trying to pull a tree from its roots. I had to think outside of the box. I let go with my left hand and began smashing it with my fist. I didn't say it was a clever plan. It wasn't enough. A second or two later, the sword flew from my right hand. I unsheathed my dagger as the hawk turned and began barreling down on me. As I prepared to slash at the hawk, it began to shimmer. Next thing I know, there was a twenty feet long snake flying through the air at me. It hit me like a ton of bricks.

The mass was unbelievable; it began throwing its coils around me immediately. A sense of primal dread ran through me. It was all muscle and a sort of tackiness. It was glued to me, only moving enough to squeeze an inch more of the life out of me at a time. One moment, my body was filled with nothing but fear. The next, I was gone, and all that was left was animalistic instinct. I had no control over my being. I ripped into the snake with my fangs. Then, I began to do what I was designed to do. I began to drain the life-force from this creature. I wasn't really there. I was simply a passenger on this ride. It felt like sewage entering my soul. The whole sequence felt like it was going on forever, but in actuality, it was only a few seconds. The snake uncoiled faster than you could imagine. The world rushed back into my lungs. I was still running on instinct and adrenaline. I turned and made a dive for my sword. I turned around and the world was cold. I could still hear the chanting of the natives, “Hi A Way Hi A OH.” My eyes were covered in a fog as I shifted them back and forth. I tried to clear them. I coughed and blood leaped from my mouth. Reality came back to me. I was standing there with my sword clenched in my right hand. The white bull-like creature had returned and was standing before me. It took me yet another moment to look down. It's horn had gored me through my stomach. I had told the creature I was going to spill blood all over it. I just didn’t expect it to be my own.

Chapter 17

The head of the creature had changed from snow white to crimson red as my blood covered it. It pulled its horn from my body. I fell to my knees and lost my sword. The creature took two steps back, shook its head and snorted, spewing blood all over my face. The world was completely silent except for the low tones of the natives chanting. I felt a weariness like I never had in my life. I wanted to rest. I looked into the eyes of the beast. Its eyes were black beyond comprehension, sucking in all light and refracting nothingness. The chants began to rise in volume. There were no thoughts in my mind, just the echoing of the natives chanting. I found myself mumbling the chant as I choked on my own blood, "Hi A Way Hi A OH." A green light began to ooze from the earth. It slowly rose higher and higher until it was about two or three feet off the ground. I realized it was moving; it looked like the northern lights. As I focused as much as I could, I saw figures in the light. Little people dancing in time to the beat of the chant. They encircled the creature and began chanting, dancing, and stomping on the ground. The beast reared up on its hind legs and shook the ground with a stomp of its hooves. The earth began to open beneath it. What appeared to be the hands and arms of the little people grabbed it from below and dragged it into the abyss. The earth closed back over itself like nothing had happened. Except for a circle where they had been dancing, there was no more grass. All these beings seem to be translucent. Then one shape walked out of the mass. It was an older looking native woman, about three feet tall. She had the face and the demeanor of your favorite grandmother. She walked over to me and knelt down by my head.

With a sweet voice, she said, “How are you, young man?”

My mind couldn't comprehend her question; I was laying there, bleeding out. All I could muster was, “Who are you?”

The smile never left her face as she calmly spoke, “Are you asking who I am, or who we are?” She ran her hand across my forehead. She could tell I wasn't able to speak. “We are the Oh-Do-Was, and I am Squannit. You are a good man.”

I spit out some blood and muttered, “No, I'm not. I'm not even a man anymore.” I could feel my life energy fading away.

“Don't think me ignorant, I know what you are. You are kind, brave, and strong here.” She touched my heart.

“But I—”

“Am a vampire. That is the least of what you are.” She held my hand, and all I felt was love. I could feel the tears run down my face as I began to drift away. She started to chant. I couldn't hear the words, only the rhythm. Through my half-closed eyes, I saw the little people appear again. They encircled Squannit, and then I began moving. Squannit stood over me, holding her hands above my stomach. I felt my body leaving the ground. I tried to hold my head up. The only thing I could see before my head fell back was Squannit placing a glowing orb in my wound. The rhythmic chanting grew higher and higher. Then, just as I thought the sound couldn’t get any louder, a beam of green light shot through me into the sky. Everything went silent. Squannit raised her hands to the sky. Things began to peel off from the beam. I started to realize the beam had turned into a green translucent tree. It had sprouted from the orb she planted inside of me. She put her right hand on my forehead and reached up with her left. She plucked a piece of fruit from the tree. She took a bite, then lifted my head and put the fruit to my mouth. I bit into it. I couldn't describe it as a taste. It was more like standing in front of a tornado with your mouth open and the wind filling you up. My eyes shot open as all the weariness vanished. She let me down on my feet. "You are now part of me and I am part of you," she announced.

"Why did you help me?" I asked again.

"You've helped my people twice. It's only right that I repay the favor."

"Twice?"

"Tonight, and you helped my husband feed our people not that long ago."

I tugged at my memories, but only one thing jumped to mind. "Moshup is your husband? But he's…"

"A lot bigger than I. Good observation, but love knows no boundaries. Our bodies can't contain the size of our spirits, you should know that."

"What about Winston?"

"Your friend hasn't been forgotten by us." She slowly walked back into the green mass of spirits. The circle spun rapidly then sunk into the earth, leaving only a bare circle on the ground. I returned to the group of natives, where they all met me with embraces. We walked to the local tribe and told them what happened. They set us up in two large tents. We stayed the night and I walked the group the rest of the way to their home the following day.

Before I left, they had a small ceremony in honor of Winston and I. They presented me with a stone tomahawk. The handle had pictures carved into it. The stone head seemed to have some type of primitive ruins or writing on it. I accepted it graciously and made a slit for it on my weapons belt.

The trip back to New Amsterdam was uneventful, but gave me time to contemplate what matters in this life. All I could think about was how to get back to Lina. The whole trip I kept thinking about what Squannit said to me. *She is part of me and I am part of her*. I don't know what she meant by that, but I definitely felt different. Like there was something new inside of me, something greater. I also kept thinking about the beast that I took a part of, how dark and disgusting its energy felt. This will be something I can dwell on later though. For now, I have to put it to the back of my mind.

When I got back, I let Claude know what happened to Winston. I told him everything except for the part where I met the spirits. Claude told me that a high-ranking official will be gracing us with their presence in the next few days. So everybody was on their toes, crossing their T's and dotting their I's. Of course, two days later, my favorite elder stepped off the ship from South America. An entourage of twenty vampires escorted Áed from the ship. I was standing beside Claude.

I leaned over and whispered, "This should be fun."

Out of the corner of his mouth, he implored, "Why?"

"I had a run in with him when I was in Bulgaria."

He gave me a side glance and sighed. "Simon, why do you do these things?"

"Because I'm lovable and irresistible?"

"Yes, Simon, you are lovable and irresistible. Shit just loves to stick to you, and I have to be the one to smell it." We both chuckled before immediately getting serious again. As Áed walked by, we both bowed our heads and I tried to be personable.

"Sir, it is extremely wonderful to have you amongst us."

Áed kept walking, but I heard him say to one of his men, "Why is this fly talking to me."

I leaned back over to Claude and said, "I was playing around and he's hurting feelings."

"For the love of all that is holy, Simon, please shut up."

I guess after being eviscerated by a demon, things don't quite strike fear into me like they used to. After Áed had made his appearance, we headed back to the office. Claude had me sit down across from him at his desk. He had a slight nervous look to him, which was not his style.

"Listen, Áed will be here after he makes his first round with the nobles, and since he already loves you, let me do the talking."

I put my right hand to my heart, giving him a pitiful face. "Ouch, that hurts, Claude. But I'll let you do all the talking." He shook his head.

A couple of hours later, Áed and five of his men walked into the office. I don't think I've ever seen someone look down on a place so much as he did. He sat across from Claude, his legs crossed and hands in his lap very proper. I stood off to the side at Claude's right as he sat down.

Áed started the conversation off with his smug tone, "So, Claude, tell me about this place."

"Well, here we have vast resources of water, timber, coal, and metals such as iron and copper."

"That is good for trade. Have you found any precious

metals?"

"Not a lot here on the East Coast, but the small groups that we have sent to the West Coast have started to find deposits of gold and silver."

"Excellent. Start sending more people to the West Coast immediately. How have things been going here?"

"We've had a few bumps in the road but everything is mostly under control at this point. Simon has been doing a wonderful job of keeping the smaller areas in check."

Áed looked over at me. I was standing there with my hands on my tomahawk's head, doing my best impression of someone who is listening to the conversation, but not in the conversation. As Áed swept his gaze over to me, I swear someone turned the heat up by fifty degrees in the room.

He looked down at my tomahawk and said, "You're not turning into one of those savages, are you?"

I kept a straight face, even as my body began to tense. I tried not to pop my knuckles while squeezing my tomahawk. I had to think of a diplomatic response instead of the one I wanted to give him. "We need all of the allies we can get in this new land, wouldn't you think?"

"Oh, of course, but make sure they are the right ones."

I never broke eye contact with him. I responded flatly, "Absolutely."

"Well, gentlemen, it was a pleasure speaking with you. This place does not suit me. So, I will only be staying for a couple days, and then I'm headed back south."

"If you need anything while you're here, just stop by," Claude told him.

Then he stood up like the smug asshole he is and walked out.

Claude slammed his fist into the desk. "Christ, Simon!"

"What?"

"Don't give me that shit. You keep poking the bear. It doesn't just poke back, you know? It rips your head off."

"What, would you have me bow down and kiss his ass?"

"Yes, exactly because at his level he doesn't need a cause. He doesn't need reasoning. All he needs is to have a bad day and we are both dead, and there will be no repercussions. Ecne may be a little perturbed and may ask him not to kill the next people off-hand, but that's it. That is what this world is. You wanted to be in it, now you have to play by its rules."

I remembered my father's words in the back of my mind. *If you have nothing nice to say, don't say anything at all. Especially if you're talking to a friend or family.* So I nodded my head and walked out of the office.

When I got back to my room, I found an envelope that had been slid under my door. I picked up the envelope with eager speed. The scent of her perfume floated up to me. I felt a rush of excitement as my heart began to beat faster. I felt a little silly as my stomach did cartwheels while I was opening the envelope.

Dearest Simon,

As promised, I have come up with an ingenious plan so that you may once again find yourself in my arms. I have procured a ship that will be landing at Kittery in one week's time. This ship will take you to an island that is nearly uninhabited. It's an old viking island and only about a hundred or so people live there now. It will take about six weeks for you to get there. The rest is up to you. Do not delay. I will be waiting.

The rest is up to me. Like that's going to be the easy part. I could have gotten a ship. I looked at the bottom of the letter to see that she had written "P. S." and kissed it with lipstick. This woman drives me crazy, but I would move heaven and earth for her. My plan was to find a person I could trust to do a job and not ask questions. I knew just the man. All I had to do was leave out a few details, and he would do exactly as I told him with no trail back to me.

Chapter 18

Of all the places you might think to find an individual to do this sort of task, the library is not the first place that probably comes to mind. This man is a seeker of knowledge. If you offered him a job and he got to learn something in the process, he's all over it. I have employed him a time or two before. I knew that he could survive in tough environments. This was going to be somewhat of an epic journey for him.

Andrei was sitting with his legs crossed and a cup of coffee in his hand. He looks out of place in a library being a very large man. He is a few inches taller than I with a big brown beard that he kept rather well-maintained. He looks more of the tavern type of guy.

I snuck up behind him and said, "That's a pretty good book. Not big on the ending, though."

He turned his head and looked over at me, then said with his thick Russian accent, "Simon, you son of a bitch, we both know you can't read."

"Then I definitely couldn't read what this was on the shelf." I sat a bottle down on the table. His eyes lit up.

"Żubrówka! Simon, you are a gentleman and a scholar. Your intelligence is only surpassed by your generosity."

"You are a vodka man, right?"

"There's only two types of men in this world: men that drink vodka, and men who aren't really men."

"I think I might have heard that a time or two."

He held the bottle like it was a baby, and I couldn't help but laugh. "Where did you get this? I haven't seen a bottle of vodka since I've been to America." I grabbed a chair and spun it around so I could prop my arms up in front of me and talk to him.

"I have my ways. I might even be able to get my hands on another."

"Simon, don't beat around the bush. What's the price? There's always a price to be paid."

"I need you to write me a book." We spent the better part of the next hour going over the terms of the deal. I asked him to travel to all of the outposts in the northern territory. I needed him to make detailed notes about the economy, the population, and any predators or supernatural presence in the area. I also needed him to end his trip in Saint John's, and drop off the book to me in Kittery fourteen weeks from now.

After I left, my coin pouch was a lot lighter than when I walked into the library. Now all I had to do was convince Claude to let me take the trip up north. When I walked into his office, it had a heavy scent of tobacco smoke. He had recently taken it up. I think he thought it was fashionable since all the nobles were doing it. He looked like he was in a terrific mood.

"Simon, what brings you in?"

"Well, it's time for me to do something I don't really want to do, but has to be done."

"I swear to God, Simon, I am not in the mood for one of your dirty jokes."

"I'm genuinely hurt. First off, I wasn't going to make a dirty joke, and if I was, it would have been hilarious."

He waved his hand for me to proceed. "Out with it."

"A man walks into a brothel—"

"Simon!"

"I'm kidding, I'm kidding. All joking aside, I have to make a trip to the northern territories."

"Any particular reason to do it now? Have you heard something?"

"Nothing specific, but I do want to get familiar with the area, and I don't want to be up there during the winter."

"That's good logic, but I would kind of hate to lose you at this moment."

"What's going on, something serious?"

"No, nothing crazy. Just annoying. A local noble's wife has gone missing. He believes that she was taken by a rogue vampire, but anybody who knows anything about the situation is pretty sure that she left him."

"Well, this really isn't my thing, but I'll go take a look at it and see what I can dig up."

He shook my hand. "I appreciate that, and all of your hard work, Simon."

"No problem, sir."

What did I get myself into?

I made my way to the noble's home. It was one of the nicer houses in the area. It was a two-story home with an attic and a nice garden around the property. When I knocked on the door, I was greeted by one of the maids. She let me in and told me to have a seat on the couch and that she would go and get him. He came into the room at a brisk walk. The man was unremarkable in every way. He was below average height with palish skin, and a slightly receding hairline. He didn't even have the aura of a noble. A noble was normally an older vampire that had worked their way through politics or business. Those individuals almost always have the type of presence that seems like they own the place. If they are really old, you can even feel it physically. He had none of these qualities.

He vigorously shook my hand. "Thank you for coming. I'm dreadfully sorry I didn't introduce myself properly. My name is Tucker."

"My name is Simon. I hear you have an issue I might be able to help with."

"I certainly hope so. My Angel has been taken from me. Three days ago she vanished into thin air."

"And she wouldn't have left on her own?"

A look came across his face like I had just insulted his mother. "Absolutely not. She wanted for nothing. She loves me dearly, as I do her."

"Alright. Well let me take a look around and I'll see what I can dig up. You can sit tight and keep doing whatever you're doing."

He wasn't joking about her having whatever she wanted. I went upstairs to her bedroom and she had jewelry all over the place. She had the finest dresses. I walked down the stairs, checking for any signs of a struggle. One of the maids gave me a slight glance and I gave her half-smile in return. Continuing through the house, and into the kitchen, I saw no signs of struggle. If it was a rogue vampire, I'm sure she would have at least fought back a little.

I walked through the garden to see if I could find any tracks or disturbances. The maid's stare kept popping into my mind. I saw her on the side of the house, watering flowers.

"Ma'am, I didn't get your name earlier."

"Sorry, sir. My name is Rose. How may I help you."

"Well, Rose, I was wondering if you could tell me what kind of home life the two here had."

"Oh, very loving. Very loving. Sir Tucker just adores his

Angel."

"I noticed you didn't say that she adores him."

"I'm sure she does."

"Alright Rose, why don't you tell me what you know. You're not going to get in trouble, but I need to know what you know."

"Please don't tell the master. Angel has run off with one of the locals."

"Do you know where they might be?"

"He stays in the loft on the east side, above the brick-makers."

"Thank you, Rose. I found out this information all on my own and never heard it from anyone." She nodded her head eagerly several times, and I gave her a quick nod back. I was going to the east side apparently, to find a man's lost love.

When I arrived, the scent of drying clay was in the air. I could feel the heat from the furnaces rolling out of the building. The loft was accessed by an outside staircase on the side of the building. I saw a man coming down the stairs. He was a burly looking fellow. Definitely a worker from the factory. As soon as he went into the building, I made my way up the stairs. I checked the door and it was locked, but it was a crappy door handle. I popped it with ease. As I stepped inside, I was hit by a comet. Well, what felt like a comet turned out to be a frying pan wielded by Angel.

"You're not taking me back to him!"

"Christ, lady!" She took another swing at me but this time I grabbed it and ripped it from her hands.

"Sit the hell down now, before you make me angry."

"I'm never going back," she stated as she sat down on the edge of the bed.

The side of my head was throbbing but I'm sure rubbing it wasn't helping anything.

"What are you doing hiding out here?"

"Isn't it obvious? I don't want to be a trophy for a dreadful man."

"He seems quite alright to me. Was he violent?"

"No, he's just so bland, and a dreadful lover at that."

"So, you prefer your men to be poor?"

"No, I prefer my men to be strong."

"What's the plan then?"

"Well, I'm going to do whatever I want."

"Are you planning on telling Tucker?"

She crossed her arms and asserted, "I was going to get around to it eventually."

"Let's get all of this drama out of the way. I will go with you to make sure things don't get out of hand."

"Things getting out of hand is the least of what I'm worried about," she spoke as she gave me an irritated look.

A few minutes later, we were back at the house. As soon as we walked through the door, I caught sight of Tucker pacing back and forth. He looked up, saw Angel, and ran to her, putting his arms around her. You could tell by her body language that she was not interested in it at all. She took a few steps back, and I made sure that I was partially between them. She began to let him down in the not nicest way possible.

"Tucker, we are through."

"No, Angel, you can't. I'll buy you whatever you want."

"It's not about stuff. It's about me wanting a real man, and not some backwards paper pusher."

Then he did something I don't think I've ever seen a vampire of his age do. He began to cry, and his crying turned into a sob. My body started to contract in on itself. I don't do well with awkward situations like this. It was almost involuntarily the way my body was pushing me towards the door from the inside.

"Well, I'm going to show Angel to the door now. Try to have a good evening sir," I insisted, desperately wanting to remove myself from the situation.

As we walked out of the house, she looked over at me and explained, "That's what I was worried about."

I made my way back to the office to tell Claude that everything was taken care of. He seemed relieved to not have to hear from Tucker anymore. I could understand his pain now, having to deal with all these entitled pricks. I packed up my bags and grabbed as much coin as I could. The trip to Kittery was going to be a long ride. I met with Andrei one more time to make sure he had everything he needed. We both set out on our journeys. I just hope he was able to hold up his end of the bargain.

Chapter 19

It was a cool, wet morning in Kittery. The little droplets of rain that made their way underneath my hood felt like cold needles, barely touching my skin. I normally don't mind the rain, but I do when I'm going to be on a ship, especially in the middle of the ocean. Kittery was a small village, or it's what passes as a small town here. The stench of fish penetrated everything, overwhelming the senses. Then again, this entire place is a fishery. That's its lifeblood; people in New Amsterdam and Boston swear by it. My instructions were to find the ship that was sailing back to Iceland. If they happen to get blown off course, and I get dropped off at another location, that can't be my fault. As far as I knew, there was only one member of the Nigrum Gladio stationed here. I had sent word to him that he should do a sweep of all the countryside up to two miles away. The day that I told him to do it just so happens to coincide with this very day. I was hoping that he was a good employee and followed my directions. If I were to be seen here, that would blow my original cover story. I'm not saying I still wouldn't go, but I'd have to figure something else out.

The ship was unmistakable. It was a freighter. They were dropping off goods and it looked as though they were loading lumber. The markings on the ship, and the armor the men were wearing, were distinctly Norwegian. I walked up to the sailor who was directing the inventory and gave the code word, “Iceland.”

He looked at me with a knowing, stoic face and returned, “Iceland indeed.”

As I began walking up the gangway, I heard the man let out an impressively loud whistle. Then all the other crewmen hustled the last several pieces of lumber onto the ship. It gave me the impression that they were going slow intentionally, waiting for me. As they pulled up the anchor, the boat began to move out to sea. I could taste the salt in the air as the waves hit the side of the ship, creating a mist over the deck. I ran my hand down a case of smooth wood that had been freshly cut. I've always liked the smell of fresh lumber. I assume by the end of this trip, my views on that may change. I mostly kept to myself on the trip there. It wasn't a very exciting trip, which is good on a long ocean voyage. I never did get used to the swaying back and forth of the ship.

When we arrived, they booted me out so fast, I'm not even sure that the ship stopped completely. I hopped onto the dock and took a look around. The place was absolutely gorgeous. I could see snow caps in the far distance, and there were still some pieces of ice floating on the other side of the bay. In my general area, it was lush with vegetation. The hillside was covered in purple flowers and it reminded me of summer, high up in the Alps. The breeze started to blow against my face and wafted the smell of the local flowers, which was nice in itself. I picked up the scent of lavender and honey.

I turned my head and saw a cloaked figure walking in my direction. When they pulled their hood back, my heart leapt from my chest. Lina had her hair braided on both sides. I had never seen her do that before. Maybe it was part of her disguise. Either way, she looked more beautiful than she had in my dreams. I could hardly contain myself as I got closer to her. She turned from me and walked towards a small stone cottage. I followed her into the house and closed the door behind us.

The fireplace was well-fed and it was nice and toasty. There were fur rugs laid out all over the floor in front of it. As soon as the door latched closed, she slammed me against it and we kissed with the passion of a thousand suns. Her lips were soft and that perfect kind of wet. I could feel the warmth of her body, even through her clothes, as she leaned into me. Her skin was smooth and her hair felt like silk as I held it in my hand.

She whispered into my ear, “Welcome to Greenland.”

Soon the room looked like an explosion had happened. Our clothes were strewn all over the floor. We made such love, it would make the Greek gods themselves cry. Even after, we laid there intertwined in front of the fire for a while.

“I missed you,” I whispered to her before kissing her on the forehead. She was scratching at my chest.

“I missed this,” she rebutted.

I looked down and gave her a fake hurt look. “This is all you missed?”

She giggled, “Of course not, but a girl's got her needs too.”

“That's true. I am hard to live without,” I teased.

She playfully pushed me away and sat up, covering herself in a blanket of fur. She put a pot of coffee on the fire. I couldn't stop smiling, looking at her standing there with the fire Illuminating around her. She walked back over to me with a cup of coffee in each hand.

As she sat down, she warned, “You keep making that face, it'll get stuck in that position.”

"Then I would die with the happiest smile on my face."

"Simon, you flatter me too much. I like it."

"What have you been up to?"

"Well, it's been interesting. Let me tell you about it."

I sat back and listened to Lina tell me everything…

Lina

The pounding at the door sounded like they wanted to break it down in a panic. I whipped the door open.

"Yes, can I help you?"

"Sorry, madam, but Ahit is coming. She wants to speak with you."

All three of the first elders have been acting like they care about the structure of the cabal ever since we moved our headquarters to Paris. It has been rather annoying.

"Move along, Eric," I commanded.

He scurried away and a moment later, Ahit comes. She always wore extravagant clothes, even when doing the most mundane tasks. Today's gown was sky blue with red shoulder pads. I think she always wanted to present a strong, regal image because she's under five feet tall. If everyone is going to be looking down on you when you are talking to them, you should at least be better dressed than them.

"Lina!" she hollered at me from halfway down the hall.

"Your grace, to what honor do I owe the privilege?"

"I need you to deal with something. They keep pestering me with silly rumors that I do not have time for."

"Which rumors might that be?"

"The same rumor that has been going around here for the last fifty years: we have an infiltrator spy, if you will, inside the embassy."

"That's a very serious issue, should it turn out to be true."

"I have my hands full with setting everything else up. You know this area better than most. Use your little birdies to dig up some information."

"Absolutely, your grace. I will see to it at once. There shall be no spies on my watch." She gave me a once over, spun her head quickly the other direction, and her body followed her. She began speed walking down the hallway. I looked to my left and called, "Eric." I knew he was eavesdropping, and he came from around the corner.

"Yes, my lady."

"Did you hear all of that?"

He looked away slightly, mumbling, "Yes."

"Find me all of the information about this rumor and where its origins lie."

"Yes, my lady. Of course."

It didn't take him long to return. This time it was a light rapping on the door.

"Come in!"

Eric shuffled into the room. "My lady, I have news."

"Out with it."

"Well, it appears there is an informant among us. There is information that has been leaking out to Ecne's cabal that only an insider would know."

"What class of information are we looking at?"

He started twiddling his thumbs, and he spoke nervously, "It looks like financial information mostly."

"Bank statements?"

"Some of those, but I suspect the location of cash drops

and holdings are of the most importance."

"That is worrisome, but it also makes my job easier."

"How is that, my lady?"

"Any fool can get their hands on bank statements, but only a few know the location of our cash holdings." I saw the realization dawn on him. "You've done a good job. Now, run along, I'll handle it from here."

The last thing I need is people making Maat suspicious when I'm trying to do my own thing. I went around the city, dropping notes to my little birds. If this person was as sloppy as I thought, they would have the information on them by the day's end. When I returned to my office I found a note that stated I was to attend a meeting. It was to be department heads, as well as a few elders. The note also stated to be prepared for any questions about my office or current affairs. Because Ahit and Maat will be attending the meeting, everyone was on high-stress alert when they attended. Even Ahit, Oduda, or Anyanwu get nervous if they are in Maat's presence for too long.

I walked into the room and was hit with a proverbial wall of energy. I was by far the youngest in the room. Most elders try to keep their power tucked away, but even so, the auras we're filling the room. Maat sat at the head of the ornate table. It had the typical traditional Egyptian hieroglyphs carved all over the table top and legs. More than likely, it was stuff that flattered Maat. She was dressed in a gold, slender dress which was typical for her. Ahit sat to her right. Both of them nearly had the same scowl on their faces. The rest were department leaders in finance, weapons, military, and such. We went around the room, giving reports as to how our departments were running and transitioning. Of course it was all theater, for we all knew why we were really there. Maat stood up with her palms firmly against the table.

"Now that we got the pretending out of the way, you know why I have brought you here. Someone has betrayed us. I will not stand for this. Whoever it is, you will find them, because if I have to, this room will be less crowded next time. Do you understand me?" She made a slow sweep of the room with her eyes.

"Yes, your highness," we all spoke in unison.

I had set up an apartment for myself outside of the embassy. I know I'm not the only one who has a second residence. It's really the only way to be sure that you have privacy. The embassy has ears all over it, no matter how well you think you have your space vetted. A few minutes after I arrived, Eric showed up.

"My lady, these came for you."

"Thank you. Now run along and grab yourself a drink." I handed him a few coins. He gave me a little bow, spun on his heels, and left with a pleased look on his face.

I received a half a dozen notes from my little birdies. Five of the notes pointed to one particular woman. I don't get surprised often, but this one actually did surprise me. The list that I had compiled in my head was up to about ten people. She was on that list, but she was towards the bottom. Her name was Claire, and she had been working in the trade department for at least thirty years. I'm not sure where she was before then.

I tried to come up with a plan on how to deal with the situation. I could call the authorities, but where's the fun in that? I sent word to my birdies to follow Claire. I told them to report back to me if she meets with anyone, or plans to meet with anyone. It took them a few hours, but they got back to me with the information I desired. She was meeting with an Ecne operative at a small inn, on the south side of the city. I laid my light armor out. I knew I was going to have to move quickly if it got out of hand, which of course it would. I sharpened my karambit blades because a girl's got to accessorize. I also took a handful of nasty potions that could bring anyone down.

That evening, I followed Claire to the inn. As soon as I knew she had gone in the room, I leapt to the second story window ledge and listened carefully. It was Claire and another woman. I couldn't make out exactly what they were saying, but I could tell that it was getting heated. That was my cue to step in. I lifted myself up to the window, opened it, and made a spectacular entrance.

"What's going on, bitches?"

The other informant looked over at Claire and interfered, "Who the hell is this?"

"That's Lina. She is one of Maat's dolls. We have to kill her."

I looked over at Claire and tilted my head. With raised eyebrows, I piped, "Well, aren't you just precious." The informant grabbed a chair, and tried to swing at me. I ducked under and clipped Claire in the side of the knee, breaking her leg inward. The woman threw the chair at me. There was nowhere for me to go, so I put my forearms up to brace the impact. It hurt like hell, but it didn't take me down. I pulled my blades out and ran straight for her. I slashed at her face multiple times, but to no avail. She was too quick dodging both strikes. I decided I needed to play dirty. I stomped on her foot. I'm pretty sure I heard a few bones snap as she screamed. She tried to grab my throat. I knocked her hands away and sliced down inside of her ribs. She stumbled forward, grabbed the leg of the broken chair, and swung it backhanded at me. I tried to get my arm up to block, but she still clipped me partially in the back of the head. That one staggered me a little bit, throwing off my equilibrium. I needed to finish her off quickly before she got lucky and really hurt me with something. I threw one of my blades to the right of her face, which was enough to make her look away. I moved as fast as I could to get behind her. She caught a glimpse of me just before I got past her shoulder, which is precisely what I wanted her to do. As she spun, I slammed a small vial right into her mouth. Then, I hit her under the jaw and it shattered. She started to convulse. She was holding her throat, as it melted through her. I looked up to see Claire making her way to the door. I hurled a round glass bottle that struck right beside the door. The gas that burst forth enveloped her completely. She struggled for a second or two before succumbing to its effects. I knew Maat would want her alive so I concocted a nice potion to put her to sleep. I tied her to a board, not only to make her easier for me to carry, but I wanted information from her as well. I splashed water on her face to wake her up.

As soon as she came to, she started to stir and tug at the ropes that bind the board to her.

"Bitch, what have you done?" she screamed at me.

"Now, that's no way for somebody in your position to be talking."

"I might as well."

"It's that kind of attitude that got you in this position, all tied up, metaphorically and physically."

"You think you're so clever, don't you," she sneered.

"Well I would never underestimate my enemy, but one of us here is lying on the board, and the other is standing above them. But enough about me. We're here to talk about you. Why on Earth would you turn your back on Maat? Especially by handing over information to Ecne's people?"

"See, that's just it. You think you're so clever, but you have no idea what she is up to."

"Since you seem not to care about what Maat thinks, why don't you enlighten me?"

"Your beloved queen has lost her mind. She is preparing to lay siege to the Norse gods and the Greek gods' lands."

"You're talking madness. Is she a narcissist? For sure. Does she sometimes border on the egomaniacal? Absolutely, but she's not suicidal."

"Do you think I would turn on her for no reason? I have a good life here. I want for nothing. This is about more than me. I have heard the conversations that she's had with the elders. She wants to prove that she is better than Ecne. He always played conservative when it came to the gods, never encroaching upon their land, and scolding any rogues that did," Claire explained.

"Maybe that's true, but for good reason. She doesn't have the power to take them down."

"Oh, I don't think she does, but that's not the way she sees it. She sees them on an island now that she owns all the lands around them. There's no one to tell her no, and she can flood their area in theory."

"Lord Dracula would never sanction it."

"I don't think he knows. Honestly, I think she believed he would have to back her once she starts the wars."

Just then, there was a knock at the door. Before I could even start walking towards the door to open it, in walked Maat's private guards. The four men were in their Spartan-like armor. They had their cloaks on so other people couldn't tell, but I knew. They were walking with their spears, which was kind of a dead giveaway.

The leader, who was the tallest of the bunch, looked down at me and declared, "My lady, we will take it from here." I was more pissed at myself than at this prick. For I was the one that let them know where I was going to be. I didn't plan on the conversation being so tantalizing though. I gave the guard an account of what happened. I only left out a smidge of the conversation. That evening, Maat called a meeting of all her heads and nobles in the area.

As we stood around the throne chamber, I could hear the whispers and rumors swirling. Maat walked into the room and silence fell upon us all. She had the full attention of everyone in the room.

"Everyone in this room is among my most loyal and most trusted. Tonight we captured a traitor that was among us, and now I will show you the fate that awaits anyone who would do the same."

The wall beside the throne opened to reveal a secret room that seemed to be twenty feet by twenty feet. Claire was chained to the middle of the floor. Her mouth had been gagged. Maat pointed to her.

"This is what happens when you cross me. You enter the dragon's fire!"

The sorcerer beside her pointed his staff at the room and uttered a word I couldn't comprehend. The entire room was instantly engulfed in flames. Claire let out one scream and then it was over. She was no longer visible. There was not so much as an audible gasp throughout the room. It seemed like the energy tightened in the room. At that moment, I began to believe what Claire told me was true.

Chapter 20

I sat there with my coffee, silently trying to let what Lina told me sink in. All I could think about was how to keep her safe.

"You have to be careful. She's going to be looking for any suspicious activity. I know you wouldn't do anything against her, but that's not the way she would see it if she found out about us," I warned.

She reached out and grabbed my hand. "I love how much you worry about me. Even before us, I've always been cautious. You always have to be prepared for the knife in your back, at least on our side."

I squeezed her hand. "You're the smartest person I know. I can't help but worry about you. I will find a way for us to be together for good."

She ran her fingers up and down my arm. "How many people will you have to thump on the head to make that happen?" she asked.

"As many as it takes. I'll fight time itself if it dare not speed up until the next time I get to see you."

"Oh, time travel. I like it," Lina giggled.

"You know I'm a man of many talents."

"That's certainly true," she put in as she flashed a teasing little smile. "So, tell me what you've been up to."

I told her about all my adventures and mishaps I've had since I got to America. When I told her about my battle with the demon, she almost cried. After I had finished telling the rest of the story, we curled up in front of the fire and fell asleep.

When I opened my eyes, I saw that she was already awake and dressed. She usually was. She's more motivated in the morning than I am. I looked up at her and chaffed, "Did I die and go to heaven?"

She smiled and rolled her eyes. "Flattery will only get you so far. Time to get dressed."

"But I don't wanna," I groaned as I put the cover back over my head. I could feel her walking towards me. Then, all of a sudden, the covers were ripped away from me in one fell swoop. "Jerk!" I screamed. She threw clothes at me, and I put them on at a snail's pace to annoy her.

We walked through the meadows, enjoying nature and each other's company. The weather was perfect. The sun was out and shining. Every once in a while, a slight breeze came through and chilled us as it came down from the mountains.

I hadn't really thought about it until that moment, but I turned to her and asked, "Is it safe for us to be out in the open like this?"

"We're perfectly safe here; this is one of the few places on Earth that has no vampire presence whatsoever," Lina reassured me. I fell back into a sense of security again.

Suddenly, we stumbled upon a body and all of my sense of security faded again. It looked like a man, only more mushy. We were about a mile outside of town, and we hadn't seen another person for about an hour. By taking a quick glance over the body, it would be difficult to believe that a human did this. There was too much damage. If a human did indeed do this, a single human couldn't have done it. We cautiously made our way back to the village.

There were only about one hundred or so people within

hundreds of miles, maybe even thousands, but, in any town, you can always count on there being a tavern. I went straight to the bar and ordered two of the house specials and a bottle of wine. While I still had his attention, I asked, “You guys having any trouble recently?”

The bartender looked exactly like an old school viking from the books I read years ago. He had a long, white beard that was braided in two on either side of his chin, and though he was going bald on the top of his head, he had long braids that went halfway down his back.

He looked at me with an almost disinterested look and stated, “There's always trouble in one form or another. What type of trouble are you talking about?”

“I found a body about a mile from here in one of the fields. Looks like a man that had his whole body crushed,” I responded.

The bartender nodded. “That would be Jacob. He was out prospecting. I told him it was a bad idea. Nobody knows what's out there,” he stated matter of factly.

“Do you have any idea when that might have been?”

“I haven't the faintest clue, but I'll tell you the same thing I told Jacob and every other passerby that comes through here: stay close to the shore, and don't venture too far from town.” He handed me two plates of fish and potatoes along with a bottle of wine.

As soon as I sat down, Lina quickly inquired, “Were you able to get any useful information out of him?”

“Information? yes. Useful? Not so much. All he knew was that the man's name was Jacob, and apparently he was prospecting for gold.”

“You would really think in a community as small as this, they would keep track of their people a lot tighter.”

“Well, the bartender seems very nonchalant about it.

He advised me to stay near the shore."

"From his body language, I would say this isn't the first time something like this has happened."

I tried to tell her I agreed but I had a mouth full of fish. It came out all gurgly

"Honestly, Simon, can you not talk with your mouth full?"

I swallowed and said, "You really need to try the fish. It's amazing."

She shook her head and took a bite. Her eyes opened wide. "Wow, that is good."

"I told you."

She took a sip of wine, then remarked, "You're not going to let this dead body thing go, are you?"

"Of course not. This is too interesting." My response was almost automatic.

"So, are you thinking nighttime or daytime?"

I finished the last bite of my food and pondered, "Well, seeing as how I believe we're dealing with a creature rather than a human, we should probably do this in the daytime."

"I think you're right. If it's a type of predator, they will probably be adapted to nighttime."

I stirred that thought around in my head for a moment before speaking, "I really don't think it's a predator. I didn't see any bite marks or claw marks on the body at all. No signs of anything trying to eat it either." I could see the gears moving in her mind.

"Territorial?"

"I think you're on the right track with that."

After we finished our food and wine, we headed back to the cabin. We gathered up all of our weapons. I hooked on my sword and dagger, while she buckled on her blades and potions. We headed back out to inspect the area. If my hunch was right, and it was a territorial creature, it wouldn't be too far from the body.

As we took a closer look at the area, I started seeing imprints in the ground. I hadn't really seen them before, but that was probably because of their size. I initially was looking for signs of a human in the area. These indents were the size of the three large human feet. If I was correct this creature only had three toes. That narrows the suspects down a bit. Judging by the depth of the footprints, it has to be massive in weight as well. I didn't see any dermal ridges that would suggest a human-like creature. Lina came back over to me with a disappointed look on her face.

“No hair, no blood.”

“I would say by the size of the creature's footprint, and how deep it goes, there probably wasn't much of a struggle.”

“I don't think it was an ogre or a cyclops. They would leave a distinctive odor behind.”

“Well that certainly narrows down the possible culprits,” I concluded. We continued to follow the tracks until we hit a rocky area up the hill where the tracks stopped. Lina was looking off into the distance, drumming her fingers on her belt. “What are you thinking?” I asked her.

She turned her head when she came back to the current moment. “Everything needs some form of shelter. That's what we need to be looking for.”

“A cave is the most likely place for something to be in this area. There's not enough trees around for something to bed down, especially something that large.”

We moved further up the mountain. The chill in the

wind coming down from the glaciers was amplified as we got higher. Whatever type of creature this was, it had to be impervious to the cold, especially if it lived up here during the winter. I'm confident that no human could live up here during that season. As we made it to the top of a plateau, we could see the opening to a large cave. Lina gave me a side glance.

"What do you think?" she pressed. I tried to see past the darkness in the mouth of the cave.

"I think we found our creature's home."

"What makes you say that?" she asked as she pulled out her blades, warily.

I pointed to the right of the cave entrance. "See those piles of stones? That's not a natural formation."

"What kind of creatures—"

Suddenly, I saw a dark object out of the corner of my eye heading straight for Lina. I dove and tackled her out of the way just in time for a stone the size of a wagon wheel to lodge itself where she had been standing. I leapt back to my feet and looked at the creature standing some fifty feet away.

"God damn troll!"

Lina looked up at me. "That's a troll? I've never seen one in real life, only in books," she stated.

"Yeah, it's a troll alright. I've only encountered them one other time. It wasn't fun."

The troll stood about twelve feet tall and half that width at the shoulders. Like most trolls, its body had adapted to its environment. Rocks have been adhered to its skin like armor. Its legs were as thick as tree trunks, and its arms were as wide as a man at the waist, ending in gigantic three-fingered hands. I drew my dagger because I knew my sword was pretty much going to be useless against his rock armor-like skin. I was going to have to find small openings to stab it.

The troll bellowed out with a voice as gravely and deep as you would expect from a creature that large, "Have you come to steal my things like the last one?" The troll speaking reminded me of a ten-year-old child.

Lina lifted herself to her feet and spoke with authority, "We have not come to harm you. We only want to find out why you killed that man."

"He kept stealing my things, and you're with him!" He hurled another rock our way.

The thing about trolls is that they are immensely strong and extremely tough, but they are not very flexible, nor are they fast side to side. I ran straight at him, and at about ten feet away, I leapt over him and kicked him in the back of the head. It didn't hurt him at all, but that wasn't the purpose. I wanted to disorient and frustrate him. Lina followed my lead and we darted around and over him several times. He got lucky and swatted Lina. She flew about twenty feet before hitting a boulder. I lost it and latched onto his back and began stabbing him in any open spot I could find. He began to flail and tried to rip me off his back. I started punching him in the side of the head as hard as I could. I felt the pain shooting through my hand, but I didn't care. He got a hold of my shirt and threw me over his head. As soon as I hit the ground, I ran as quickly as I could and hit him in his left leg with my shoulder. It buckled him and he tumbled to his back. I pulled out my sword and was about to stab him in his throat when I heard two deep voices cry out, "No, don't hurt him!"

As I stood on his chest, I looked up and saw two trolls. It was obvious that it was his family. It's hard to tell trolls apart, but by the size of the two, I could tell it was his wife and child.

Lina shouted, “Stop!”

I looked over. She seemed fine aside from a couple tears in her clothes. I hopped down from the troll's chest and cautiously walked backwards toward Lina. I never took my eyes off of him. When he rose back to his feet, the sound of grinding rocks echoed off of the side of the mountain.

He bowed his head and said, “Thank you for the mercy.”

Lina pointed at him and interrogated, “Why did you kill that man?”

“He kept sneaking into our home and stealing our things. I tried to tell him to not come back, but he came back and tried to burn us.” Standing there, the adrenaline was still coursing through my veins, but I realized that anyone would have done the same to protect their family. It was hard to tell, but it looked as though he had a sad look on his face. “I'm sorry, I thought you were coming to hurt us.”

“That was never our intention. We only wanted to figure out what had happened,” I reassured him.

He waved at us to follow him into the cave. We were both still a little weary but we followed him in. The cave was actually nicer than I had anticipated it being. It was relatively dry and they had multiple fires going. The heat was bouncing off of the interior walls and began to warm us up immediately upon entry. I'm not even sure if trolls got married, but what I assumed to be his wife pulled out what looked to be two stone chairs far too large for us to look like anything other than children in. But we sat anyway, out of respect. I tried to build some sort of rapport with him.

"Do you have a name that I could call you?" I implored.

"Everything has a name. You can call me Ognar, and this is Islar, my love, and my son, Yungar."

Lina chimed in, "Are you the only ones here?"

Ognar looked confused. "Here in this cave, yes."

Lina chuckled, "No, I meant in the area."

"Oh. Well, no. Most of my people live closer to the center of the island. We live the closest to the shore. I am able to pick up things to trade from the ocean."

"Do the others interact with humans?"

"Not really. Most of my people are not as nice as I am."

He offered both of us a slab of walrus fat. We took it, not wanting to hurt his feelings. It was actually delicious. I'm not sure how Lina felt about it, but she put on a good face. We finished our meals, thanked Ognar, and made our way back down the mountain.

We made three different signs and posted them at the dock, at the tavern, and just up the hill. We hoped that they would deter most people. We spent the rest of the week walking up and down the beach, mostly staying inside, and simply being with each other. On our last night, she told me that we would have to figure out another way to meet. Greenland is only accessible for a couple months out of the year. By the time I returned to America, summer would already be over here. She promised to keep sending me letters and I told her I would do the same in return.

The morning came and there were two ships by the docks. We held hands, and even with the mist coming up over the dock and feeling the cold ocean water, I didn't want to let her go. I looked deep into her eyes.

"Wish we could stay here forever." She kissed me, and

her lips were like embers.

When she pulled away, she smiled and said, “There's only an ocean between us.” I stayed on the dock and watched her sail away. I've got to find a way to get back to her. I hopped on to my ship. I could still taste her on my lips.

Chapter 21

When I arrived back in Kittery, Andrei was there waiting for me. True to his word, he had indeed written me a book. We talked for a couple of hours about specific things that weren't touched on in the book. Then I chartered a boat that was sailing down the coast to New Amsterdam. I figured that would give me more than enough time to read through the book a couple times. When I met back up with Claude, I didn't want to have to rely too much on the book when he asked me questions. Claude is good at sniffing out bullshit, but I'm a world-class bullshitter.

When I arrived at the docks, there was a big commotion. I saw the person that the crowd was hovering around. He stood a full head taller than everyone else. As I came off the ship and began to move closer, I realized how much taller he was. I am a handful of inches taller than the average man, but he was that much taller than me. Not a giant of course, but compared to the average man, they might think so. When I got within a hundred feet of him, I felt it. An immense aura permeating off of him. I've only felt something like this a few times in my life. Different types of beings give off a certain auras, even when their power levels are similar. It feels different. This power felt like a vampire, but on a massive scale. There was only one vampire that I can think of that was that tall and had this much power surrounding them. I made a circle to get out in front of him to see if I could see his face. Most of the people surrounding him were vampires, but there were some humans that happened to be out. I stood there waiting for him to pass me by. When we were within a couple feet of each other, he lifted his head and looked over his shoulder at me. From under his hood, I could see the tattoos over his face. It could be no one other than Tūmatauenga. Inside I was rippling with tension, but I kept a straight face and nodded to him. I thought I saw a slight smirk from him, and then he turned his head away and continued walking. I made my way to the office to speak with Claude.

He was smoking like a chimney when I walked into his office. His office was spotless and his desk was clear of all but the two papers he was looking at.

He looked up and said, “Simon, thank God you’re back.”

“It's good to be back. I thought there was a fire in here.”

“Very funny, Simon, but Ecne arrived last week to inform us that Tū was coming to look at the new world.”

“Is this a good thing or a bad thing?”

“It's not necessarily a bad thing, but you never want too many powerful vampires in one spot. The egos can cause them to do disturbing things.”

“Are we running guard duty on this one?”

“I know, from what I hear, this will be a smaller occasion than the transition. Plus, Tū has his own warriors with him, and from what I hear, he welcomes challengers.”

“Yes. When I first saw him at the docks, his power radiated out maybe even more so than Ecne.”

Claude looked around, then said, “More than likely, in a straight fight, Tū would take him. Hell, he would probably take any vampire in a one-on-one battle outside of Lord

Dracula."

"If I'm not mistaken, isn't he his people's god of war?"

"Yes. While Ecne and Maat were building, and Wendi was influencing thought, Tū was conquering every island in the ocean, drinking the blood of his enemies and anyone who stood in his way. He has never stopped being a warrior. Anytime Lord Dracula has needed to go into battle, Tū is who he has called first."

"So, what's the plan?"

Claude pushed his papers to the side. "For now, let's go over your report of the northern territory." We spent the next hour or two going over the report. I tried to lean as little as possible upon the notes I was given.

I went back to my house to try and take a nap. You don't get the kind of rest you think you would on a ship. I was hoping that I wouldn't even be invited to the gathering. Alas, there was a knock on my door a few hours later. As soon as I opened it, I was given a letter with Ecne's seal on it. It was just as I had presumed. I was to attend the meeting in my traditional Nigrum Gladio dress armor. I knew Andrei was still in town. I wanted to pick his brain about Tū. If anyone outside of high ranking officials knew anything about him, it would be Andrei. We met at a local diner because I needed to get something in my stomach anyway. My belly was gurgling. I hadn't fed on blood or food for a while.

As soon as I sat down, he inquired, "You're not sending me to the other side of the continent, are you?"

"Rest easy, my friend. It is only a conversation this time."

"Thank God. I still have saddle ass from the last one."

"I bet you do."

"So, what information do you seek from the all-knowing?" he asked while stifling a grin with the piece of steak he was shoveling into his mouth.

I was trying not to talk with my mouth full, but I explained, "I need to know about Tū."

"What would you like to know about the most fearsome vampire warrior on earth?"

"I assume you know he's in town."

"Indeed."

"Well, we are throwing a small get together for him it seems, and I want to know what to expect from him and his people."

"In that case, you should know he hates weakness or perceived weakness, but even more than that, he hates cowardness. His people are all about dominance. If you bump into one of them by accident, they will take that as a challenge, and if you apologize for it, he will ridicule you in front of everyone for it."

"So, you are saying I need to stay out of the way?"

He took another bite and shook his hand unevenly. "Not quite. You don't want to be the person cowering in the back of the room either, they'll see that. You're better off standing somewhere towards the middle. Hell, even the front, and make sure you're projecting a look of strength."

"Why do I feel like this is a no-win proposition?"

"I wouldn't get so worked up about it if I were you. They may only be here to take a look around, maybe set up a port of their own as they're known to do."

"That's easy for you to say."

He raised his glass and said, "You are correct sir, and thank God for that."

"How I wish I could go back to your side of the fence," I claimed. We finished up our food and I made my way to the location of the meeting.

I always like to get in a little early to make sure everything is looking alright. Claude was already there as I expected. I learned my promptness from him. The rest of the crew rolled in shortly after. Michael, Olbrecht and Phillip came over and shook my hand. As the last of our people filed in, we took our places. Tū and his men came in a minute or two later. He had ten men with him, and they all looked to be warriors. We had prepared special seats for them, so they could sit across from the highest ranking officials. From the looks on their faces, none of them were happy to be here. Tū waved to one of our hosts, and they came over with several big bottles of what I presumed to be alcohol. Tū spoke with a powerful voice and accent. I had heard some elders imitate it before, and they told me it was an islander accent.

"This is a real man's drink. I brought it to you from the island of Okolehao."

After we all got our glasses filled, we raised them.

"To friends," we all saluted.

The drink wasn't half bad, most of the time when dignitaries bring their own drinks, it tastes like horse piss. This on the other hand had a sweet flavor to it. From the looks on everyone else's face, they agreed. Ecne looked over to Tū who was sitting beside him on the right. They both had thrones in the centre of the wall.

"It tastes just as delicious every time I drink it," Tū proclaimed. He took a big drink and said, "Ecne, this place looks like shit, but if I know one thing, it's you know how to build. In a few hundred years, this will be the capital of the world."

Ecne raised his glass and cheered, "Hear, hear!"

We all followed, "Hear, hear!"

Ecne lightly smacked the arm of the chair and insisted, “Enough about me and this place. How have you been doing?”

“Well with the mortals moving around more now, discovering places as they call it, I've had to deal with your European friends a lot more.”

“Oh, they're just dreadful, aren't they?” Ecne said through a laugh. Tū raised his eyebrows.

“I've had to keep one or two in line myself when they arrived on my beaches.”

“Oh my, I hope you didn't get cross with them.” Laughs bursted throughout the room with that one. Tū slapped Ecne on the shoulder, a gesture that no one else on Earth could probably get away with.

“Let's have a show,” Tū suggested.

“Say the word and I'll bring the women in. I know your taste. I don't lean that way, but if any of your men prefer boys, I don't judge.”

“We can do that anytime, brother. Save that for later. What do you say to some combat entertainment?”

“What do you have in mind?” Ecne probed.

“How about one of my men versus one of your black swords?”

“To the death?”

“Of course not, my brother, I wouldn't want to take one of your men from you,” Tū reassured.

One of his men stepped forward towards the middle of the room without being prompted. He was nearly as large as Tū. They were so similar that, if I didn't know for a fact he wasn't, it could have been his son. Michael stood up and took one step forward. He was a good choice; he was one of our oldest and most skilled. Tū looked at him and shook his head in disagreement. Claude stood up quickly.

Normally, you wouldn't have an official as high as him participating in something like this. Tū shook his head again and pointed his finger at me.

Why, why the fuck not. I really didn't want to do this.

I don't know if Ecne could sense it, but he chimed in, “Michael is one of my finest; he wants the challenge.”

“Come on, brother. You wouldn't refuse my choice. It doesn't matter who it is, the outcome will be the same. Why not let me pick?”

Ecne gave me a nod. “This is Simon, he is an up and comer. He has much promise.”

I stepped to the middle of the floor to face the islander. One of the other islanders threw him a metal version of their shark-toothed wooden club. It was an intimidating piece of weaponry. I pulled my sword from its scabbard, released my belt, and kicked it to the side. I wanted to be as fast as I could be against this man. We stood ten feet from each other. I held a two handed grip. While I went with a traditional middle guard, he used a low guard with his sword below his hip. We stood there and began taking measure of one another. He started projecting his aura, and now I could see why Tū was so confident. He was definitely a millennial. He was easily seven hundred to one thousand years older than me. That's when something began to creep into the front of my mind. I had been trying to tuck it away and not think about it.

The last ten years, I knew that my strength had grown exponentially. From the sorcerer, to my run in with the demon and the spirit, I could just tell. I didn't want to really find out myself, or especially let anyone else know. I didn't want to get in a measuring contest with him, but I needed to gain a bit of respect from him. So I completely stopped his aura two feet from me. That received some interesting looks. I think I even saw a grin on Tū's face. I decided to do something I would never do, and something he'd never expect. I dropped my sword and put my arms out to my sides. I saw the look of confusion come over him. As soon as he made the slightest move with his front foot, I struck. I even surprised myself with the speed. I hit him with my left elbow in the center of the face. I started pummeling him with punches before I finished with a kick to his leg. I jumped back as he finally got a swing off with his club. I picked up my sword and looked at him. He had blood coming from his nose, mouth, and from a cut under his left eye. It wasn't that it hurt him so much as it disoriented him and pissed him off which is what I was going for; an angry fighter is a fighter that makes mistakes. I knew one hit from his club could be the end of the fight for me.

He rushed me and swung wildly. I stepped under the club and sliced his right thigh. I leapt in and tried to stab him with a thrust, but he caught me off balance and hit me with a left knee to the stomach. I felt a couple ribs pop. I had to keep moving to stay out of range. I knew I had to finish this quickly, or he would. I took a half step forward. He came down with a vertical strike, which I parried. I took a step to the left, then brought the point of my sword to his throat.

Tū stood up and clapped. "Yes! Excellent! Good showing," he exclaimed.

Ecne tried to keep a straight face but even he was surprised. I had a hard time controlling my breathing. I hadn't ever pushed myself that hard before. Tū waved me over and reached out to shake my hand. When we shook he pulled me in and urged, "I can sense the strength inside of you. Next time, don't hide it."

The only good answer I could think of was to nod. I went over and shook Ecne's hand as well. He seemed a little off, but there was nothing I could do about it at this point. I went back to my seat next to Claude. I felt a few pats on the back. I assumed it was Phillip's and anothers' of our order. A few more nobles stood and talked about nothing of significance.

As we began to funnel out of the room, Ecne pulled me off to the side. I was definitely worried; there was no telling how he was going to react. I stood with my arms properly crossed at the hips. As Ecne stood a foot from me, he complimented, "You did well in there today."

"Thank you, sir."

"How did you beat him?"

"He was strong, but he was sloppy. Skill beats strength."

"Maybe if your powers are close, but he should have had a massive advantage over you."

"I'm pretty sure he was stronger than me," I told him.

Ecne squinted slightly in suspicion.

"It appeared to be that way, however, you did it. You represented us extremely well." He turned and walked away. I felt the tension release from my shoulders. I tried to sneak out, but I was discovered by Claude. He slapped me on the shoulder.

"Simon, that was impressive!"

"You know I do what I can."

"I wasn't sure that Michael was going to do well against him. You've always been terrific with the sword, but how were you able to move at those speeds? Have you been excessively feeding?"

"I'm not sure. I keep up on my practice."

"Alright, if you're keeping it close to the vest, that's

your business."

I finally got back to my room. I fell onto the bed. I stared up at the ceiling, running through everything that happened. I'm not sure what this means for me, or if this puts me further on the watch list of Ecne. I want to keep a low profile, but there always seems to be something pushing me to the forefront. I heard a slight sliding noise by the door. I got up cautiously, but when I looked, I didn't see anything at first. But then, from the corner on the floor, I saw it. An envelope. It was blank on the outside, but I could clearly smell the scent of lavender and honey.

Chapter 22

I was dead tired when I laid down, but the letter gave me a second wind. I tore into it like a kid on Christmas day.

My dearest Simon,

I hope your trip was well. I have some splendid news! I will be arriving in the New World in two months. We should arrive in the town of St. Augustine. I have been instructed to set up embassies there, and in a town far west called Santa Fe. If you happened to be conducting business in those areas at the same time, I wouldn't mind if you paid me a visit.

My heart tried to rip itself out of my chest. I couldn't believe she had found a way to make it over to me. We were still going to have to keep our guards up, but with her being on official business, things will be a lot less stressful. I hadn't been south yet, so it should be easy for me to convince Claude that I need to be down there in a few months. I'll do some work up here to ease some pressure off of him. Of course as soon as I put that out into the universe, I heard frantic knocking on my door. I whipped the door open quickly, hoping that I would startle the person who was trying to knock my door in. The man standing in front of me was sweating and was out of breath.

"Somebody better be dead. I was just about to fall asleep," I grunted.

"About a dozen, sir. You need to come with me."

I quickly grabbed my gear and ran behind him.

When we arrived at Claude's office, the place was bustling. We went inside and Michael, Philip, and Olbrecht were already there. I put my hand on Michael's shoulder.

"Do you know what's going on here?" I asked him. He shook his head.

Philip walked up to me and greeted me. "Christ, Simon. Have you heard what they're saying?"

"No, what is it?"

"They say we're being attacked by sorcerers."

Claude walked in and the room started buzzing. He gestured for everyone to be quiet. A woman came up to him and whispered something into his ear.

"Quiet, everyone. I know there are rumors flying around, and some of you were pulled from your beds. Our outpost right outside of Stamford was attacked a couple hours ago. Intel suggests it was one sorcerer. There was a group that came down from Boston to meet and exchange information, and the building they were in exploded." Murmuring growled throughout the room. "Quiet down, please. There were more than a dozen inside. After the explosion, he began systematically killing the survivors. Those who did survive the explosion without serious injuries have tried to set up a perimeter, keeping him from leaving the area while backup arrives."

"Are we bringing our own magic into this battle?" Michael chimed in.

"No, we do not have access to a sorcerer of our own at this point. I have put the word out to find Fitzroy. I know he won't fight, but maybe he can give us some intel."

Olbrecht jumped in, "How many of us are you sending?"

"I am sending the four of you, and up north, you should

be meeting up with four from New Haven. Hopefully there are still a few survivors left there when you all arrive. Simon will be coordinating."

I guess I had to ask the obvious question. "What do we know about the sorcerer?"

Claude sighed, "A lot less than I would like. All we really know is that as he was attacking the survivors, he kept saying that he was bringing light to the darkness. That could be a coincidence, or he could be with the Lightbringer Society."

I really didn't like hearing that. The Lightbringer's are a bunch of sorcerer fanatics who think that all vampires should be eradicated. They are not to be taken lightly. Sorcerers are already strong enough. When they have trained to fight vampires, they are beyond deadly.

I looked at the men and announced, "Make sure that you have everything with you. If you think you might need it, take it. I don't care if you think it's overkill. I want every tool at my disposal."

We each packed a bag, then we grabbed the four best horses in our stables. These horses are bred for speed and endurance beyond any horses that you may see on a racetrack. We also fed them a special endurance elixir that will allow them to nearly run at their maximum speed for half an hour. We try not to do that often as there's a high likelihood that they die of exhaustion after it wears off. The horses should get us nearly there; we may have to run a few miles on her own. Michael and Olbrecht were stonefaced in the saddle, while Philip did a good job of hiding it, but I could tell he was concerned. I trotted up beside him and smacked him on the back.

"Follow our lead and we'll all make it out of this."

He gave me a short nod and we continued on. I thought

about the challenge ahead. I had personally never battled a sorcerer, but I have seen them in action. I remember around a hundred years ago, Claude led a group into battle against a sorcerer who'd seemingly lost his mind. We lost a few men that day. Even Claude sustained some bad injuries that took him a while to recover from. That sorcerer was possibly the most powerful one that I had ever even met. His strength made Fitzroy look like a child. The way he was able to control fire was unbelievable. It was like the element was alive, and all that it wanted to do was devour.

Claude has made us train for many different scenarios. Battling against a sorcerer is one such area that we have trained for. The horses made it to within five miles of Stamford. We hopped off, loaded up our bags, then took off running. We vampires are fast, one of the fastest predators in fact. We could have made the trip even faster but we were trying to conserve energy. We did the last five miles in about ten minutes. As we closed in on the town, I could smell the burning wood from the building. The sun had started to set behind the horizon. That should give us a slight advantage the longer this fight goes on. Everyone dropped their bags and began to strap on their weapons and armor. Michael combined the two sticks to make his spear while Philip loaded up his pistols. Olbrecht pulled out his mace, and began sharpening the edges with his stone. I kept it simple. I had my sword, dagger, and tomahawk. We did our traditional huddle up like we did any other time we all went into battle together. I tried to make sure my voice came across with confidence and authority.

"Alright guys, we are going to create a half circle around him. No matter how close he gets to us, or we get to him, we should always be ten feet or more apart from each other. I don't want to give him an easy way to hit more than one of us at a time. We're going to keep our distance at the beginning of this. I want to see if he gives away his strategy. Then, once we figure that out, we can close in and take him out." We put our fists in the center of the group as our traditional send off into battle.

As we made our way out of the woods, the destruction was everywhere. There was charred wood, stone, and brick all over the ground for a few hundred feet. We spread out and ducked behind some crates. Philip got behind a turned over wagon. We heard a noise coming from behind one of the barns. I made a hand gesture to tell the others to watch that area. A moment later, out walks a thin man in plain brown pants that are tattered with holes all through them. In his right hand, he carried a wooden staff with a small crystal ball at the top, and in his left hand, he was dragging a woman by her hair across the ground. I recognized her from Germany. Her name was Hanna. Her hair was singed and her skin was blackened up and down her body. She was struggling, but barely. She had no fight left in her except for the vague primal notions to live as she slapped at his hand.

He stopped and made a clear gesture of smelling the air. Then, with a voice that sounded like his throat was filled with phlegm he said, "Come out and face me you leeches of darkness. I can sense you out there. I am the bringer of light. I have your last one here, will you not try and save her?" He pointed his staff to Hanna about two inches away from her skin. Tentacles of electricity leapt from the crystal ball. Hanna screamed as her body convulsed. I thought I even heard some bones break in her back.

I looked at Michael and he nodded his head. When you

work with someone for so long you can tell what they want to do. I moved out from behind the crate, and I did my best to bring his full attention to me.

"Hey, shit head." His head whipped around and his eyes met mine. His eyes were dark and bloodshot. Something in his eyes told me he wasn't right in the head. A smile came across his face that made him look even more like a madman. He dropped her to the ground.

"I knew they would send more. You are like moths to the flame."

"Yeah, exactly like that, if the moth had a three foot sword that he was about to hack you to pieces with," I taunted.

"So arrogant are your kind."

I made sure I didn't take my eyes off of him. From over his shoulder, I saw Michael lining up his spear. He threw it with everything he had. It couldn't have been moving faster if it was shot from a cannon. The sorcerer never moved his eyes from me, but at the last second, he brought his staff up in a blur. It deflected the spear enough that it missed his head by inches. We both ducked back into our hiding spots, anticipating some form of strike against us. Olbrecht leapt from behind his crate and began running at the sorcerer. The sorcerer pointed his staff at a boulder and launched it with invisible force at him. Olbrecht didn't lose a step; he hit the rock with his mace and shattered it into a thousand pieces. He immediately threw the mace overhand like an axe at the sorcerer. Then, he directly leaped into the air with his sword. The sorcerer wasn't fooled. He deflected the mace with a flick of his left hand, then pointed with the staff and an invisible wall of force hit Olbrecht in mid-air, sending him flying back a good thirty feet where he struck a tree.

Philip wasted no time jumping from behind the wagon. He fired off one shot of his pistol and rolled, then fired another shot from a low angle. It's like the sorcerer had seen it coming and put up an invisible dome around himself. The bullet ricocheted about three feet from him and went two different directions. He held the staff out towards Philip and lightning erupted from it, ripping up the ground in its wake. Philip tried to dive out of the way but was struck in his left leg. He continued to roll until he was behind the wagon again. I could see, and even worse, smell the burning flesh of his leg. The sorcerer let out a laugh that made my blood boil. He then pointed the staff back at the twitching body of Hanna, and hit her with an invisible force. A cloud of dust enveloped her. He looked over in my direction and said, "Is this the best you have to offer? The eradication of your species will be easier than I thought."

I'd had enough. I stepped out and met eyes with him again, and Michael walked out behind him. We began circling him. He kept his eyes on me and both of his hands on his staff. I began moving side to side as I advanced towards him. Michael came directly at his back. He fired off a shot of force that hit me in my left knee and knocked me off my feet. Michael swung down to try and cut him in half, but the sorcerer stepped to his left and as the sword and Michael came forward, he swung his staff and hit Michael in the side of the head with brute force. Michael stumbled to the side but regained his composure almost immediately. He began using beautiful technique, slashing away at the sorcerer, but he could never quite hit him. I don't know what kind of magic he was using. Either something to make him superhuman-levels of fast, or he just knew what Michael was going to do next. He swung the staff and a blur hit Michael under the chin, partially lifting him off the ground. Then he hit Michael with another wall of force that sent him back into the wagon. A piece of a wheel had gone through Michael's shoulder and impaled him to the wagon. I can see the sorcerer was aiming to finish him off. I lunged and swung at his head and I almost got it. He moved his neck a half an inch, so I only took some of his hair off. He whipped his staff around and I ducked. We continued for a couple seconds, throwing and dodging each other's blows. He leapt back to give himself some space. That was the first time he'd ever given ground during the whole battle. He smiled at me with crooked yellow teeth and said, "Finally, a worthy challenger. I shall keep your head as a trophy."

I couldn't help myself. "We'll see whose head is on whose mantle at the end of this." I moved forward and I started forcing reserve energy into myself to increase my speed. As I had him following me to the right, I moved my left hand down, and in one motion, removed my blade from my pouch. It moved end over end faster than any time I've ever thrown. He swiped his staff across his body to intercept, but I was just a little faster and it sliced his right shoulder.

As I saw the blood, I became excited. The adrenaline began to flow through my veins even faster. I even started to salivate. The predator inside of me wanted to go in for the kill. Before I could figure out my next move, he pointed his staff to my left and fired off a bolt of lightning. I dodged to my right and that's when he put out his left hand and hit me with a wave of force. I went flying through the air, and my sword went even further than me. I hit the ground like a child throwing a doll. I don't know if it was from the impact of his magic or the ground, but I could feel my ribs piercing my lungs. I let out a scream; it wasn't a scream of pain, but a primal scream of anger. *How could he do that? Come into my territory, kill my people, and hurt my friends. All the creatures that I had fought and killed, literal demons have not made me bow. Who was he to me? Nothing. I am the greatest warrior of the Ecne cabal. I bow to no man.* I stood up and every breath I took, the pain surged through me. I latched on to that pain and used it to fuel the raging fire within me. I showed my fangs and screamed, "Come on!"

He grabbed his staff in both hands and pointed it from his hips at me. "Let us end this." Then, a torrent of lightning poured from the staff and raced towards me. At that moment, I had no idea what I was going to do. I only knew that I wasn't going to back down. I pulled my tomahawk from my belt and held it in front of me as the lightning struck. The stone of the tomahawk began to glow as it intercepted the lightning. The ruins began to pulse. I can feel my whole body vibrating, trying desperately to hold on.

The sorcerer leaned forward and screamed, "Die!" He poured more energy into the lightning; he was about to kill me. Suddenly, Lina's face appeared in my mind, and then her smile. He was going to keep me from ever seeing her again. That's when I lost it.

My world began to turn red and I screamed, "No!" I drew back the tomahawk and threw it at him as hard as I could. It absorbed all the lightning as it went. It struck him directly in the chest. There was a burst of electricity and a wave of energy as it hit him. I lost myself to the predator inside me. I ran forward and leaped into the air, I vaguely remember a shocked look upon his face. I dug into his throat with my fangs. Everything was red after that. The next thing I remember is Olbrecht pulling me off him.

Chapter 23

The trip back was mostly a blur. We all travelled in the back of a wagon. I hardly remember waking and holding on to my tomahawk. We were all dealing with injuries, but I felt more mentally damaged than physically.

"Simon, you need to rest for a while," Claude told me after the others left. That might be the only positive thing to come of all this. It was the perfect excuse to head south and meet up with Lina.

"I need to go down south anyways. I have yet to see that part of the land. Plus, the warmth might do me some good."

"Yes, I agree. Make a report about what you learn along the way, but do not push yourself too hard."

"Well, depending on how I feel, I may try to go out west as well."

"Feel free, but do be careful. Not much is known about what lies out that way," he warned.

I packed my bags as well as my trading supplies for the natives along the way. My first major stop would be Jamestown. As I rode, my body felt perfect. I was healed physically. Mentally was a different story. There was something in my head that I couldn't quite shake. There was a feeling of fear, anger, and despair. I think what I feared most, was that I would let these feelings transform me into something I never wanted to be. As I rode in the cool late Autumn air, I fell into a trance of breathing in and watching my breath come out. It reminded me of home. We're at the time of the year where winter is barely kissing you. I enjoyed the different colors of leaves on the trees that had changed, and the damp smell of the leaves that had already fallen. I didn't push myself. I had plenty of time to make it to St. Augustine. I enjoyed being out on my own. No one to fight, no reports to write. Just me, the trail, and nature. It was a feeling of relaxation that I hadn't had in many years.

My parents passed when I was a small child, but one thing I do remember is riding through the countryside like this. We never needed a reason. My father would just throw us on the saddle and tell us we were going for a ride. There's something warm about that memory that I can always hold onto. I think that's one of the biggest problems with vampires. As we age, we lose that memory, and humans become another animal that looks similar to us.

The forest gave way to an open field of mostly dirt. If you've lived in the cities most of your life, it's hard to explain, but there's something about dirt that's been freshly blown around by the wind. It has a certain smell to it, maybe it has to do with the clay or something, I don't know. But you don't get it when you're walking in the cities where all the dirt has been packed down for hundreds of years.

If the weather permits, I will try and sleep underneath the stars as much as I can. I was about a day away from Jamestown when I decided to stop for the night. I got a sizable fire going, and as I lay there looking up at the stars, I thought about how far I had come. I came from nothing. I was a nobody, just a sideshow attraction. Now I'm on the other side of the ocean, in a land where a couple hundred years ago, ninety-nine percent of the people didn't even know existed. People look to me for leadership. I'm no leader, I'm only a guy trying to live my life, but things keep getting in my way. I have to deal with them like anyone else would. I threw another log on the fire then I laid my head on my pack. I thought of Lina.

"Not long," I whispered to myself as I fell asleep.

I woke to the sound of the fire popping. It was still pitch black outside. Normally I'm the kind of guy who can sleep through a thunderstorm. I sat up to take a look at the fire to make sure embers weren't going to start a grass fire. I saw a figure sitting on a stump in front of the fire. I jumped out of my bedroll, but I asked very calmly, "Who the hell are you?"

The figure turned towards me and I could see them clearly now. They looked unlike anything I had ever seen before, and I have seen a lot of strange things. They were humanoid in shape, but they appeared to be a mixture of bird and insect. Though they were sitting, they could have been six feet tall or more. They had three toes and four fingers. The two most prominent features were the creature's wings and their face. Their wings were similar to that of a butterfly, and their face looked somewhat like a praying mantis. Beyond all that were its eyes. They were as red as the embers in the fire.

The creature turned its gaze to me and said in an accentless feminine voice, "It's nice to finally meet you, Simon."

I would have had something snarky to say, but I was paralyzed. I realized the voice wasn't coming from the creature's mouth. It was speaking to me directly in my head.

"Can you hear me?"

"Indeed, I can," the creature continued to say to me in my head.

"Who are you and why are you here?"

The creature was as still as a statue, almost like it was sleeping, but that voice popped into my head without delay.

"My name would be of no consequence to you, and you will not need it for this conversation. I have felt you for some time, and with you being this close, I had to see you."

"Okay, Mrs. No-name. What do you mean you have felt me?" Normally I'm the one entrancing people, but I couldn't look away from those red eyes. Her voice became soothing to me.

"We all have our burdens: you have a thirst. It's not for blood but for strength, and I have the burden of being a harbinger."

I was confused. I didn't feel like I was trying to take power of any kind and I didn't think anyone would view me that way. I didn't want to get into an argument with a potential supernatural being but I couldn't help myself.

"I don't have a thirst for power; I'm not trying to take control of anything," I snarked in my mind.

"You failed to listen to my words. I did not say power, I said strength. You have a thirst for strength because you see danger for the ones you love, and you will need strength to protect them. You'll do anything to obtain that strength for them."

I had to think about that one for a moment. I have grown immensely in strength over the last dozen years. Those moments all seemed random to me. It's not like I sought out all of those battles. I decided to ask a question of my own.

"What are you the harbinger of?" I thought I saw her move slightly this time.

"Now, that is a good question. I can feel moments, people, and places that will create great sorrow or destruction."

"Hey! I may kill a rogue vampire or a crazy wizard from time to time, but I'm not causing destruction, let alone sorrow."

"Everywhere you walk you create tremors. Your intent matters little. Destruction is certain, the sorrow is less so."

"So if you came to warn me or something—"

"I am not here to warn you or stop you from doing anything. I'm simply here to meet you." She reached out to me and just before she touched my face, I woke up.

I sat up and looked around but there was nothing there. I had this overwhelming sense that it wasn't a dream. I don't know, maybe I need a drink. It was a little hard getting back to sleep but I managed.

When I woke up in the morning, I made it a priority to make it to Jamestown before nightfall. I made good timing, even getting there before the tavern closed. After last night, I needed to get a few pints of ale in me. As I got off of my horse, a few of the locals walked up to me. They began shaking my hand and smacking me on the shoulder.

"We heard what you did," one said.

Then another jumped in, "You're a fuckin' legend."

I smiled and waved as I walked into the tavern. As soon as I made it in, I made a beeline for the bar, but I was intercepted by two more people.

One of them said, "Open battle with a sorcerer and you came out victorious? Your skills must be immense."

There was a lovely woman standing beside him. She gave me a once-over with her eyes then gushed, "With that kind of confidence in battle, I wonder what else is immense..."

I just laughed. "Thanks, but I'm only here to relax and have a drink." Then, from somewhere behind me, I heard a voice.

"Well, aren't you Mr. Popular."

I knew that voice anywhere; it was unmistakable. I didn't even turn around. "I traveled across the ocean to get away from you, but yet here you are."

I heard a slight chuckle.

"Well I was going to buy your drink for you, but now I think you've hurt my feelings."

I spun around and teased, "You don't have feelings, and hunger is not a feeling." We both smiled and Rattenfänger gave me a big hug. "What the hell are you doing over here?" I asked.

He gave me a sideways glance and said, "You know me, I have to sample all of the world's fruits."

I shook my head and chuckled. "So how long have you been here?"

"A few weeks, but I've already heard the tall tales of the wizard killer, Simon."

"I still don't understand how word travels so fast in such a new colony."

"What's the old saying? You could never outrun a rumor."

"The worst part about this one is it's true. We haven't had any problems with sorcerers over here until the other day," I responded.

"They say he was very powerful. Did you make it out in one piece?"

"Physically, he beat me up a little, nothing I haven't ran into before, but it was mentally where he nearly broke me," I said after taking a drink.

He put his arm on my shoulder and concerningly

asked, “Is everything alright? What happened?”

“I'm not sure exactly what's been happening ever since I came over here. I keep running into mind-melting situations, and now I'm even having crazy dreams that I've never had before.”

“Well, Simon, why don't you tell old Rattenfänger about this dream? I'm pretty good at interpreting these sorts of things, don't you know.”

I proceeded to give him the rundown of how things have gone since I've been here. We ordered a few more drinks so this conversation wouldn't seem too much like therapy. Our waitress ran us over two more pints. She was a beautiful woman of African descent. Her accent would tell you Jamaican, but her English was perfect other than that. Of course Rattenfänger turned up the charm.

“I don't believe that I have seen a woman so beautiful and so good at her job in all of my days,” he blubbered.

She gave him a sly grin. She knew the game.

“And I don't believe that I have seen a gentleman dress quite as lovely as you in all of my days.”

Rattenfänger made an exaggerated motion of putting his hand on his heart. “Be still, my heart. I thought I was the flatterer.” That got a laugh out of her and I. He kept fishing, “So, what shall we call you?”

She was hesitant. “I'm not really supposed to talk to the patrons but—”

Just then, the owner, an older, bald man with a pot belly walked up to her and demanded, “Quit talking and get back to work.”

I could see in Rattenfänger’s eyes that he was not pleased with this. His flute was in his hand so fast it was like it appeared from thin air. He played a couple of notes and the owner turned right around and walked back to the bar. Rattenfänger put his elbow on the table and his chin on his fist and said, "Go on."

She looked around for a second then answered, "My name is Amancia."

"What a gorgeous name!" Rattenfänger exclaimed.

She looked over at me and claimed, "You're Simon, some famous warrior everyone is talking about." She turned her gaze to Rattenfänger then continued, "I'm not sure who you are though. You must be somebody special to be with all that coin you've been throwing around."

I had to jump in.

"Why, ma'am, this is the world famous Rattenfänger! He is a bard, a model, and an exterminator when the problem presents itself."

Rattenfänger cut in quickly, "I do not exterminate. I merely move them to a more appropriate location, but everything else he said was true."

"I like you. You're funny," she laughed.

Rattenfänger looked over at me, and I knew he was going to do something stupid.

"How would you like to see the world, Amancia?"

She looked at him with a puzzled face. "I'm not free to go."

"Let me worry about that," he replied.

I gave him a concerned look. "What are you doing?"

"Simon, don't worry your pretty little head. I got this, chap." He pulled out his flute and began playing a beautiful melody. One by one, the handful of patrons began falling asleep. The tavern owner laid down behind the bar and went to sleep himself. Amancia looked astonished. Rattenfänger smiled at me and said, "World famous."

"More like infamous," I replied.

He grabbed her hand like she was royalty and she stammered, "They will come for me."

Rattenfänger kissed her hand. "If I had left here without you, I wouldn't have been able to forget you, but they already have."

As we walked out of the door, Rattenfänger jumped and clicked his heels together. He couldn't have been more happy with himself. I now had two unexpected traveling companions, but I could use the company.

Chapter 24

The rest of the trip went perfect and smooth, although I had never heard someone ask so many questions as Amancia did. Rattenfänger was more than happy to indulge her every question, and anything else her heart desired. When we arrived at St. Augustine, Amancia began to cry. Rattenfänger put his arm around her.

“What's wrong?” he questioned.

She looked up at him with tears still in her eyes. “It reminds me of home.”

Indeed, this was a beautiful place. The sand was a color of white that I had never seen before. The water was see through; you could actually see some fish darting back and forth. It was unlike any other beach I had seen in my life. The temperature was amazing for this time of year. I could imagine New Amsterdam having snow covering the ground this time of year. While here, the sun was warming our skin like a summer day back home. A slight breeze brought the smell of the ocean to us. The sand even gave way when we walked across it in a more pleasant way than the sand on the beaches did back home.

Amancia took her shoes off and walked part of the way into the water. She flicked some of it back at us playfully. I've never been much of a beach guy, especially since I was reborn. Mostly because being completely exposed to the sun doesn't feel that great to us. But I joined in the fun a little. I took my shoes off and walked through the sand.

The only place I could compare it to would be Greece. I never got lucky enough to be there during the summer. Somehow I always ended up stationed there during the winter, so I never got to experience their beaches.

We moved on to the market to get something to eat. Amancia was filling her arms with fruit when a man stepped in front of her. She tried to step around him, but he mirrored her.

The man spoke with a proper Spanish accent, "Now, where do you think you are going with those?"

"I'm going to pay for them," she replied unabashedly.

"I see no coin pouch. We don't tolerate thieves around here, especially runaways."

I moved to step in, when out of nowhere, a figure steps in between them and hits him in the jaw. I felt the impact of the punch in my chest. His knees buckled and he hit the ground like a sack of potatoes. When I approached the figure, it turned around to slug me then stopped. Lina had a surprised and excited look on her face. She gave me a kiss that I felt in my soul.

"I missed you too," I whispered as I held her tight. Rattenfänger walked up beside us.

"Lina, love, how are you doing?" he asked. She gave him a scowl.

"What's he doing here?"

I laughed. Rattenfänger looked back and forth between Lina and I.

"Am I missing something here, Simon?"

Lina is not a big fan of his; she thinks he's nothing more than a womanizer. Rattenfänger, he's a good guy. He's just an acquired taste.

I held Lina close to me and said, "Rattenfänger and his friend have accompanied me from Jamestown."

"How long shall they be traveling with us?"

"Fret not, my lady. Amancia and I, we'll be heading our separate ways. I wanted to make sure that Simon didn't get lost trying to find his way to you," Rattenfänger comforted.

"I do thank you for that. That was always a real possibility."

I acted like I was stunned. "I'm right here, guys. I have a perfect sense of direction..." I said as I playfully looked around like I was confused.

It was a great night. Lina had us over to the new embassy for dinner. Before the festivities started, I pulled Lina aside.

"Do you think it's safe for us to be having dinner out in the open like this?" I asked her.

"Don't worry, I only brought four people with me, and they are my closest confidants. We will be leaving two of them here, and then the other two will travel with us to Santa Fe. Then, we will leave them there to run the embassy out west." She walked her fingers up my chest as she said, "We will have the entire trip back to ourselves."

"Forgive me for ever doubting you," I praised, smiling.

She waved her hand dismissively. "We all can't have the mind. One of us has to go stabby-stab-stab."

I put on an embarrassed look. "That's my part, isn't it?"

She nodded her head and put her arm through mine, and I walked her into the dining room.

The food was absolutely delicious. As I sat there, the smell of grilled chicken seasoned with black pepper filled my nostrils. I started salivating at the mashed potatoes and butter. *This might taste better than feeding.*

As we all started to dig in, Amancia asked, "How did all of you meet?"

Rattenfänger was the first to answer, of course. “I met Simon shortly after he was reborn. What was that, two hundred years ago now? But anyway, I had run into him when he was having some troubles with a fellow swordsman.” He made a gesture of moving a sword back and forth with both hands.

I cleared my throat. “Well, that's not exactly how I remember it,” I proclaimed.

“Oh, really?” he quipped.

“The way I remember it, you were being chased by an angry mob because you forced their mayor to hand over a large sum of coin.”

He smacked the table. “They agreed to pay me that coin, and they tried to renege. It's not my fault that they’re liars.”

Lina and Amancia were laughing so hard, I think some food fell out of their mouths. Amancia looked over at Lina.

Lina wiped her mouth and added, “Oh, you know, Simon followed me around like a lost puppy and I decided to take him home with me.”

I rolled my eyes and said, “Really?” while the other three laughed at my expense this time.

It was a great night; times like these have been few and far between. The eating ended quickly, but the drinking went long into the night.

Lina and I snuck out into the night to prowl and quench our thirst. In her favorite fashion, we made our way to the section where the upper crust of society stayed. One difference here than from over in the populated cities of Europe is that these people kept nighttime guards. Not that it made much difference. Lina walked up to the front door guard.

"Please, sir, can you help me find my way? I simply got turned around." He never had a chance. She hypnotized him right to sleep and laid him by the door. We walked in like we owned the place.

The master bedroom was at the back of the house. Just before we opened the door, their live-in maid walked out of the bedroom that was across the hallway. As she opened her mouth, I was on her. I covered her mouth with my hand and stared into her dark eyes. She melted into my arms and I carried her back into her room and laid her on the bed. We walked into the master bedroom holding hands. We each took a side and began feeding. I don't know if it was the woman, or if it was being with Lina, but something made the blood taste so good.

We fell asleep in each other's arms that evening. My mind was clear for the first time in a long time as I slept.

In the morning, we were at the docks with Rattenfänger and Amancia. I gave Rattenfänger a hug and asked, "Where are you going?"

"Not quite sure yet. I want to show Amancia around a bit, but then I want to take her somewhere she can be free and use her intelligence to her advantage."

"Try not to get into too much trouble without me."

He pointed to himself and said sarcastically, "Who, me? Never." We both laughed a little, then hugged again.

"It was good to see you brother," I told him.

They walked aboard the ship and both waved back at us as they moved toward the horizon. As we walked back to the embassy, I asked Lina, "These two that are going to follow us to Santa Fe, can they handle themselves?"

She shrugged. "They're not warriors, but they shouldn't be a liability."

"I hope not. I don't want to babysit two people in an

area I don't know."

"Everything will be fine," she comforted.

"Famous last words," I muttered.

When we got to the embassy, we packed our things and headed out. We traveled by boat across the Golfo de México. It cut our time nearly in half, especially because the next fastest route would've taken us through swamp land. We unloaded a ton of supplies into the covered wagon we would be taking with us. I guess these two will need a lot of supplies at the embassy. We followed the Rio Grande all the way to the town of Ciudad Juárez. It was an odd area where you had mountains, desert, and lush greenery around the river. It was a feast or famine type of place to live in.

Once we made it into town, our two travel companions, whose names I had finally learned were Colette and Renee (both of them were French women who I suspect came from upper Society themselves. Either that or they have been very well trained since being reborn), went ahead to gather more supplies while Lina and I went to go and grab some food at the local tavern.

The place had a mixture of Spanish and Native American patrons; we stood out like a sore thumb. They all seemed a little weary as we first walked in. I looked around and saw that there were only about five locals, so I made a circle with my finger to the bartender and announced loudly, "One for everyone!" Lina raised an eyebrow at me and I shrugged back at her. "Couldn't hurt to make some friends," I whispered to her. All of the men in the tavern raised their glasses and mumbled their thanks.

After a few minutes, one of the locals asked us from across the room, "Are you passing through or are you staying for a bit?"

"Maybe a day or two, then we're headed up to Santa Fe," I told him.

"Be careful. There's something draining the livestock's blood in these parts," he warned, taking a big swig of his ale. Lina and I immediately looked at each other.

"One of yours?" she pushed.

"Not that I know of. Our people really haven't come out this far, unless they came up from the south."

I looked over and I casually asked, "Anyone get a look at the thing?"

Another man at the table across from him chimed in with, "I've heard it was small, but fast as a demon. It latches on to the throat of the animals"

The owner jumped in, "Y'all need to go ahead and shut up. You're going to scare away my business."

Lina looked at him confidently, like only she could, and reassured him, "We don't scare so easily." She turned back to the men and asked them, "What do you call this creature?"

The men all looked at each other and said in unison, "El Chupacabra."

She turned back to me and commented, "Doesn't sound that bad."

One of the men warned, "I wouldn't walk around the fields at night, ma'am. It hasn't attacked a person yet that we know of, but it could be dangerous."

Lina smiled at him.

"Trust me, she's way scarier than any Chupacabra," I contributed.

We decided to stay the night and see if we couldn't find out what this "El Chupacabra" was. We went out to the field where it had been happening. We bought three goats off of the farmer, and he left them in the middle of the property. Hopefully that would entice the creature to come in and feed. Renee and Colette wanted nothing to do with our little foray into this unknown territory. We had them both stay back with the wagon at the entrance. We figured if they were together, they would be able to at least fend off whatever kind of creature it was if it came for them. Lina and I separated and we made a circle in the opposite direction of each other, hoping that if the creature was in the middle, it would then be between us.

Damn it if it didn't work just the way I had hoped it would. I adjusted my eyes and I could see a creature not even three feet tall. It looked like the most emaciated person you could think of. Its head was a cross between a human and a bat. It had two long skinny canines. I assume that's how it punctures its prey and then sucks the blood from the holes. Right as I saw it, it noticed me and made a run for it. The thing truly was a fast little bugger, but the problem was that it ran right in the direction of Lina who promptly snatched it up and had ropes around its arms and legs before it had a chance to do anything. I walked over to take a closer look at this El Chupacabra. It was struggling against the ropes but they seemed to be holding. Something was off. I know I'm a long way from my traditional territory, but I'm normally familiar with most types of creatures. I can usually place a creature that I've never seen before and place it into a certain type of family. This creature had me completely dumbfounded.

We stared at him for a few minutes and then Lina said, "Can you feel that?"

I focused a little harder, and then I sensed it. He was a type of fairy. Not one that I had ever heard of, but it was definitely a fairy aura. I decided to do an experiment. I brought one of the goats over, and I let him feed on it.

Instantly, his body started to fill out and expand and before long, he looked almost human. He had pointy ears, an elongated forehead, and a smile that would make anyone jealous. His long dagger-like canines were just above average size now. Then, I heard something I definitely wasn't expecting when I first saw the creature. He spoke with a type of light British accent.

“Thank you, sir. I much appreciate it.”

Lina and I looked back and forth at each other stunned.

“You're a fairy?” I asked him.

“Give the kid a coin, he got it on the first try,” he said with great sarcasm.

“What happened to you?” Lina inquired.

“If you would kindly untie me, I shall tell you all about it,” he replied.

Lina removed his bondages. He sat on a stump and crossed his legs like a proper gentleman. He began his story.

“Well, I presume you would like me to answer the question of what happened to me. The easiest way to answer that is to simply tell you that we fairies use portals to come through to your world. Normally, there is no issue because as long as you know the combination or have the key, you can go back and forth all you like. The problem is somebody changed the lock when I came over.”

We were both still in a semi-state of shock; I'm sure we had stupid looks on our faces.

Lina tried to push for more information, “That doesn't tell me why you turned into that creature, and why you drank the blood of a goat and got back to your normal form.”

He shook his head as though he was agreeing with her question. “That creature is what happens when a fairy is away from our realm too long. Depending on how powerful you are determines how long you can be away before that happens. I am but a low fairy, so I turn within a couple days, and blood is the only thing that has enough energy to pull me back to my form."

I raised my hand like I was a child in school before asking, "Who changed the locks?"

The little guy smacked his hands together in glee.

"Another good question! I don't know, but whoever it is, they are very powerful."

"How powerful?" I asked.

"They would definitely have to be in the realm of a god."

Lina popped in, "Nobody below a god could shut down a portal."

He twiddled his thumbs for a second.

"They certainly could if they knew what they were doing. A sufficiently strong wizard or someone of that like, but this has been happening for a while, and with how widespread it is, it couldn't be just anyone, but someone on a god-level to do it at this scale."

I rubbed my chin with my index finger as I was thinking.

"Is there any way we can help you?" Lina offered. Now it was his turn to rub his chin. I couldn't tell if he was mocking me or not.

"I don't think so, but I will head to the coast and see if I can find me another door where the lock hasn't been changed." We all stood up and he shook our hands. As he was walking away, he said, "If you ever happen upon any of my people, tell them you helped out old Billy and they'll give you a helping hand." Then he was gone.

Lina looked over at me and shook her head.

"The stuff you drag me into..."

Chapter 25

As we continued on towards Santa Fe, I noticed the trails were not very worn. Luckily for us, it was a desert with hard compacted dirt and clay. So it was actually pretty easy on the wagon. There's nothing worse than trying to take a covered wagon somewhere that not many people have been before. You'll tear up the wheels, and having to repair those out in the wilderness is never fun.

The air out here is so dry. I could definitely see our water consumption increasing. I could see how this was an extremely dangerous trip for humans. At least the views were amazing. Off in the distance, there were beautiful mesas. I couldn't really remember ever seeing anything like that in Europe.

We happened upon some natives while we were refilling our water jugs. We traded some jewelry with them, and they told us that we weren't too much further from the town. That spurred us on to speed up a little bit and get there before the end of the day. We were all excited as we saw the town come into view. I think Colette and Renee were by far the happiest. They were not used to these kinds of trips. They simply wanted to get into a regular bed, with a roof over their head. Most of the buildings were of adobe construction, but you could tell the architects were very proficient. Colette and Renee didn't seem to be impressed, but I thought the buildings were terrific. They weren't the monstrous constructions that we were used to back in Europe. Every building, no matter how big, seemed very much like a home.

Apparently, Maat had sent two individual riders ahead some months ago and had them start construction of the embassy. When we arrived they were still working on it, but it was mostly complete. The girls quickly put me to work, taking things out of the wagon and putting them in their proper location within the embassy.

I was carrying a desk in when I looked over to Lina and muttered, "This is why I hate moving."

"You'll be alright," she said, smiling at me.

"You don't know that. I could die at any moment; this could be the end. Vampires, demons, werewolves, I handled them all, and I help you move once and that's what takes me out," I went on sarcastically.

"You're such a baby, Simon."

I retorted with a classy, "Waaah!" She shielded her eyes from me and tried to walk away. "Don't act like you can't see me!" She disappeared into the far room and I laughed.

After about an hour, everything was inside. Lina was setting up her office, while I was pacing back and forth down the hallway.

"Why don't you go outside and play," Lina called out to me.

"I'm a grown ass man, I'm not going to go outside and play," I countered.

"I hear there's a tipi set up north of town," she replied with her sweet, condescending voice.

I poked my head in her office. "Which direction did you say?"

She smiled and shooed me away, "Get out of here."

And with that, I made my way out of the embassy and decided to explore the town a little.

One thing that became apparent about Santa Fe that I hadn't seen anywhere else: there were some Spanish people who had natives for slaves. Now I don't know if it was more of an indentured servitude, or if they had been sold by the locals, but it was definitely a difference I noticed. Back east, I don't think I had seen one native slave. The one thing that made me think that the Spanish hadn't come in and enslaved everybody is that I had seen free natives walking around as well. There were three natives outside of a massive tipi. They were cutting and moving wood into the tipi. I walked up to them and asked, "You fellows need any help over here?"

They looked at me, then at each other. I think they were surprised that I could speak their language. With a deep native accent, which I grew to love, the older gentleman said, "If you want to help, you can drag the firewood inside."

I piled the wood onto a rug and I was able to move most of it in one go which of course I got looks for from the gentleman because I think that was beyond a normal human's ability. Once you have been around for a few centuries, you start forgetting what the limits of normal humans are. I'm not so sure the younger gentleman liked me very much. I mean, he looked older than I looked, he was probably in his thirties. He kept giving me weird looks. I don't know if he didn't like outsiders or what. I watched them prepare the wood, making a large fire pit in the center of the tipi. The tipi looked much larger from the inside, but it still felt cozy. The older gentleman turned and looked at me, "You seem interested in our culture. Would you like to join us in our ceremony?"

I mean I really had nothing going on. I assumed Lina would be busy for a few hours. I gave him a little nod and replied, “I would be honored. What do you need me to do?”

“Take a seat on one of those rugs by the fire.”

I sat down while he went around and set a few more things up. The other one sat beside me on the rug to my right. He was still giving me a little side eye, but I just smiled back at him. The older gentleman threw something on the fire and it began to smoke. Then he walked over to me with a bowl that was filled with a murky looking liquid. He motioned for me to take it.

“Drink deep of it, and your mind will be free.”

I guess I couldn't back out now. I figured it would be easier to go ahead and take a big gulp and not try to taste it that much. Whatever plant this came from, I could tell it was not meant to be consumed. It had a very tangy taste to it. The natives began chanting, dancing, and banging drums. They started to use hand fans to blow the smoke around. Oddly enough, the smoke didn't burn my eyes like I thought it would.

After about thirty minutes, I started to feel like the world was wobbling. All of the colors inside the tipi felt like they were coming alive, and I felt myself swaying to the beat of the drums. I looked over at the younger native and noticed there was something different about him. He had fangs, like he was a vampire. Whatever this stuff was that they gave me, it was potent.

He looked at me and said, “It took you long enough to get out here.” At this point, I felt like I was in a different dimension. Whatever this hallucinogen was, it had turned my world upside down. I tried to pull my faculties together. I didn't know whether this was reality or not so I went with it.

“You've been waiting for me?”

He laughed, and it went through my head like an echo of distortion. “Not specifically you, but I have been waiting on someone from one of the vampire cabals to arrive.”

“Who do you belong to?” I asked. That drew a little bit more serious look from him.

“I belong to no one, and I claim no one.”

“Who were you turned by?”

He smiled and replied, “Some things are so far back that even the immortal mind cannot remember.”

“How long have you been out here?”

“Since the time of the ice.”

I was fairly certain I was having a conversation with my subconscious and it was playing games with me. While I was on this ride, I figured I might as well be entertained.

“If you're so old, you must be powerful. Why don't you have your own empire?”

He took a puff off of his pipe before speaking. “My people have chosen to live in harmony with the natives and the beings that inhabit these lands.”

“Most of the ancient vampires that I have met think of humans as nothing but cattle.”

“Vampires that are close to Dracula would have those views. We on the other hand are the reason that humans have been able to propagate all the way through the lands.”

That statement confused me.

“What do you mean?”

He smiled and said, “When we arrived here, there were giant cats, and there were bears and sloths the size of twenty men, but you do not see them now. We came to the realization that we could do the same for humans. Then, of course, the spirits began to manifest and the gods arrived. My people decided we would no longer kill humans. It did not take long for the ones of us who did not follow to fall victim to the protectors of humanity."

I felt a little bit of my faculties coming back to me. "How do you know Lord Dracula?"

"We go on walkabout from time to time to see how the world is progressing. We've had our eye on him for some time. So why are you here?"

"To help Lina."

"What is she to you?"

My mind started to clear. "Everything."

A smile that illuminated the entire room came over his face. "Ah, love. Nothing is worth more than love. Never let it go."

It felt like I was being dragged through a mineshaft towards the surface. I came to and the tipi was filled with smoke. When it cleared, the younger native who I had just been talking to had the same distrustful look on his face as before I drank. I couldn't tell if it was a dream or reality.

"Were we just talking?" I asked him. He looked at me like I was an idiot, which in all honesty, I probably was.

After leaving the vortex of weirdness, I made my way back to the embassy. When I walked through the door, I could smell the aroma of heaven, and by that I mean steak.

I heard Lina yell from the kitchen, "Did you have fun?"

I threw a snitch of sarcasm at her, "Absolutely not." She sat the food down and I dug in. It was so good. I took a drink of wine and said, "This is amazing. I knew there was a reason I kept you around."

She gave me a scowl and said, "Really?"

I blew her a kiss. "You know you love me."

She took a bite then wittily replied, "I tolerate your existence." We both laughed.

Before I fell asleep that night, I thought, *A full stomach and I get to lay beside the woman I love. Nothing can be better than this.*

Next morning, I decided to go for a supply run. After I had loaded everything up from the shop, I noticed two men arguing. It sounded like the Spanish man was accusing the native of pickpocketing him. Because I can't keep my nose out of other people's business, I had to try and calm things down, but like the way things normally do, it went south quickly. I made my way across the dirt street and tried to keep the sun out of my eyes. As I got a few feet from them, the native pulled back his hand. As he did, it turned into a giant cat's paw and he hit the man on the side of the face, gashing him open. I tried to back hand him, but he was quick. He ducked under my strike and ran for the door. I followed on his heels, then I tackled him to the ground. Before I could do anything, his lower body turned into that of a coyote. He slipped from my grip and kicked dirt in my face. I raced after him but he was so fast. I wasn't about to let him get away from me. I let my knife loose with my left hand and it hit him in the lower back. A scream came out that couldn't have come from a human. I closed in on him and he spun around and grabbed me by the throat. The crazy thing about it was that his hand was now a pincer from a scorpion. I grabbed either side of it to keep him from decapitating me. I put both of my heels in his chest and pushed with all the strength I had in my legs. FInally, I popped free of his grip. I hit the dirt road, came back to my feet, and removed my sword from its scabbard. He stood still like a statue but I could see his eyes shifting, anticipating my next move. I hopped to my left and then immediately pushed off to my right. He fell for it, and I stabbed him through the right shoulder. He came down on me with the arm of a bear. He smashed me into the ground then ripped the sword from his body and threw it. I started to get up, and I saw him run off into the distance. As I was about to give chase, his legs melted into that of one of those fast desert birds. Then he was gone. There was no way I would catch him now.

I drug my ass back to the store to check on the man who had been slashed. Surprisingly, he was still alive. The local doctor was tending to him. I walked up to the store owner.

"Do you know anything about that guy?" I asked him.

"I don't know who he is, but I know what he is."

"What's that?"

"He's a skinwalker."

"What the hell is a skinwalker?"

"It's a witch that has the ability to take the form of any person or animal." *Dammit, that's all I need. Another shapeshifter, and on top of that he's a witch.*

I went back to the embassy. Lina could tell that something was off as soon as I walked in the door. She quickly made her way to me.

"What happened? Is everything okay?"

"Oh, you know, just got in a fight with a shapeshifting prick."

She had a shocked look on her face. "Are you serious?"

"No, I'm lying. Of course I'm serious," I retorted like a sarcastic ass.

Lina looked at me with a straight face and said, "Nobody hurts my babe." I couldn't not laugh. She strapped on her potion belt. "Let's kill this fucker."

I let my jaw hang down. "You're so hot right now."

She laughed at me and looked over her shoulder. "I

know I am."

We went back to the store owner to get some more information. He had told us that you could tell a skinwalker by their smell. They smell like that of a dead animal. We don't quite have the scent capabilities of a werewolf, but ours are better than normal humans. We should be able to sniff him out of a group. The weirdest stuff follows me around, I swear.

We made our way to the tavern because everyone seems to come through there once a day. We sat close to the door and anytime someone would walk in, we would sniff the air like a couple of weirdos. Sometimes being weird pays off. Finally, we smelled a woman who came through and she definitely reeked of dead animals. I went in for a closer look because I didn't want to stab some lady who had just butchered a deer in the back. On my way to her, the smell became apparent. My nostrils began to burn the way they only do when you're around something putrid. The smell had a weight to it, and I could feel it permeating in the back of my throat. By the time I got in striking distance, I was fairly certain this was the skinwalker. I still had to make certain though, so I made a loud noise seemingly from out of nowhere beside them. It had the effect I was looking for. She was startled. She whipped her head around, and had inhuman eyes, something along the lines of an owl maybe. She turned towards the door, and right as I thought she was going to run, her right leg turned into that of a horse and kicked me in the chest. The blow knocked me back a few feet and I dropped to my knees and grabbed my chest. She took off for the door, but Lina ran full speed, jumped in the air and kicked her into the side of the bar. The impact was violent. I'm sure she had broken some bones. Lina ran toward her, but as she got within a few feet, the skinwalker opened her mouth and shot out a six foot long tongue that knocked Lina off of her feet.

I was back on my feet and running. I leapt across the room to impale the creature to the ground, but right before I landed, she rolled and my sword stabbed into the floor. The skinwalker raced out the doors. Lina and I were both outside in half a second's time.

As we gave chase down the center of town, I pointed for Lina to go left so we could flank the skinwalker. My adrenaline was pumping. I could feel the sweat coming out of my pores as the sun beat down on me. I started pulling up some reserve energy, and I could feel myself getting stronger. I closed in on the skinwalker. Before I got my hands on the creature, she turned to the left, directly into the blades of Lina. The cut went clear across the creature's chest, and she let out another one of those inhuman screams. Lina attacked from the front and I took the back, but we were having no success. Every slash that we threw at the creature, it dodged as it continued to change from one animal form to another. I decided to throw a different technique in, and try to impale the creature with an upward stab of my sword. Before I could get the motion started, it grew a damn alligator tail and smashed it into me. Again, I found myself on the ground which allowed the skinwalker to focus on Lina.

She was holding her own, keeping the creature on its toes and defensive. She stabbed both blades down at the same time, but the creature grabbed her wrists in mid-motion. Then, from behind the creature, came a scorpion stinger that slammed its way into Lina's side. I could feel the monster, the predator inside of me, taking over. I couldn't stop it even if I wanted to. I didn't want to. I wanted to kill, to take, to feed. I leapt while the stinger was still inside Lina, and stabbed it through the stomach. Immediately it turned to run away, ripping my sword and the stinger away from us. Lina threw two bottles of her potions out ahead of the skinwalker. They exploded, creating a wall of gas. The creature slid to a stop before hitting the gas which would surely do nothing good to it. By the time it turned around, I was already on it. I was hacking and slashing at speeds even this creature couldn't keep up with. I'm sure the creature was screaming but the only thing I heard were my battle cries. I stabbed my sword down the skinwalker's shoulder blades. The blood splattered all over my face and into my mouth. The beast inside me ripped its way free and I bit the creature on the other side of its neck, ripping away flesh, and swallowing as much blood as I could. The skinwalker pulled free of me and headed in the opposite direction back towards Lina. She met it with an explosion from one of her viles. The creature was engulfed in fire. As it turned around, I finished it with a blow to the neck from my sword. It's head fell to the ground, and its body continued to change forms as it fell to its knees. I began to hack at its body uncontrollably until I heard Lina's voice.

"Simon, I'm okay." I turned and rushed to her. I dropped to the ground to check her. "See, it's already healing," she reassured me as she showed me her side. The predator that had come up from inside of me started to release its grip on me. I could feel my eyes getting hot. She pulled me in and held my head to her chest. I heard her heartbeat, and the rhythm soothed me. I sank deeper into her embrace.

All I could hear in my head was, "*It's okay, we're okay.*"

I don't know how long it took us to get off of the

ground, but we eventually made our way back to the embassy. Colette and Renee immediately went to work, taking care of our clothes and getting a hot bath ready for us. My mental state was mostly back to normal by the time we got in the bath. She sat on one side of a copper tub and I sat on the other. I had to say it felt pretty amazing to lay in the hot water. I had to get my feelings from earlier off my chest.

"I'm sorry I lost myself back there."

"You don't have to apologize to me, Simon. I know it's because you care about me."

"More than anything. I love you, you know."

"And I love you," she responded. She then lifted her right foot out of the water. "Now rub my foot, you peasant."

"Yes, ma'am."

Chapter 26

The trip back was much more fun than the trip out. We were alone, and we didn't run into a single hideous monster the entire time, if you can believe that. I walked Lina back to her ship at the St. Augustine docks. When we got to the dock, I held her hand and told her, “Be safe over there.”

She gave me a slight grin. “Don't worry about me, I'm just dealing with a demigod that's losing her mind. You're the one dealing with things nobody's ever seen before.”

That drew a smile on my face. “I love you, Lina. I can't see you soon enough.”

“I love you. You do whatever you have to do to come back to me. You just come back to me,” she bidded me, looking me directly in the eyes.

I took those words to heart, and I did whatever I had to do to survive to see her the next time. This became our routine over the next forty-five years. I would go meet her in Greenland during the summer, and then she would come and we would travel the southwest.

Things have become progressively more volatile as the years went on. Maat had begun her push into parts of Greece, as well as Scandinavia. Anyone who second-guessed her vanished shortly thereafter. She had become paranoid, so Lina and I had to take as many precautions as possible not to be seen being too cozy with each other. We had both been trying to stay low key, but the issue was that she was already holding a position of significance, and doing very well at it which gave her notoriety while garnering her promotions.

As much as I tried to stay in the background, I had become somewhat famous, or infamous, depending on your point of view. I became the one everyone called to kill what went "bump" in the night. I tried to play down that picture of me, but Lina said that the rumors of me had made it to Europe and beyond. All that was going to do was bring unwanted attention to me.

The weather started to warm and spring gave way to summer. It was time for me to head up north and catch my boat to Greenland. As usual, I headed over to Claude's office to let him know that I was leaving. Also as usual, I had just got done solving one of his local problems to butter him up. I knew as soon as I walked in the door something was off. He was usually in a cheerful mood when I came back from cleaning up a mess for him. There was a different energy in the room. I figured I would break the ice.

"A horse walked into a tavern and the bartender asked, 'Why the long face?' Nothing? Not even a tiny chuckle, what's going on?"

He looked disheveled, and I'm pretty sure that he had been drinking. He looked up at me with sad eyes and replied, "I'm not feeling it right now, Simon."

"I'm sorry, is everything okay?"

"I'm not sure yet, but I'll find out soon enough."

"Do you want to talk about it?"

"It's not something I can really talk about," Claude said, the burden seemingly weighing on him.

"I'm getting ready to head up north; I wanted to let you know before I jumped on the trail."

He looked up and pleaded, "Do you think you could stay, at least for a few days?"

"I wish I could, but if I don't get there by a certain time, the local riffraff might think I'm not coming and I don't want to run into a shitshow up there," I explained to him.

He let out a deflated breath. "I thought so..." I felt bad leaving Claude like that, but I needed to leave now to make the boat. As I was walking out the door, Claude yelled to me, "Take care of yourself, Simon." I gave him a nod and went on my way.

The whole trip to Kittery, I kept thinking about Claude. It wasn't like him to be in a sad mood, and to be so stand-offish. I really did wish I had more time. I would hang out with him to try to make him feel better.

I love the smell of the woods up here when it turns over to summer. I've even come to appreciate the buzzing insects because when they start to appear, I know it won't be long before I'm off to see Lina.

I arrived at the town, and even though I tried to keep a low profile, I had become friends with the man who ran the general store. We shot the breeze for a little while and he had his stock boy load up my cart before I headed off to the boat. As I was loading the supplies onto the boat, I thought I heard someone yell my name. Off in the distance I heard, "Simon!"

Now this is not where I told Claude I would be. So it would be very odd if someone were to be here looking for me. I came out from underneath the boat, and as soon as I stepped back onto the dock, I saw them. Michael, Olbrecht, and Phillip were walking toward the dock. In my head, I figured I could play this off. They don't know the route I take to do my tour of the northern territories. I could feed them a line of bullshit of where I am sailing to.

It shouldn't be too hard to convince them.

Oddly enough, they stopped about twenty feet before they got to me. I had expected them to walk right up to me and shake my hand. Something was off, I could tell by their body language they weren't coming to greet me.

Michael took the lead and spoke up first, “Simon, my brother, we need you to come with us.”

“What's happened?” I asked. “I have all my things ready for my northern territory tour.”

Olbrecht looked over at Michael and Michael nodded to him. Olbrecht turned to me and shook his shoulders out a little bit. “You need to come with us, we'll take care of your things.”

I started to lose my patience. “I am your superior, now tell me what the hell is going on.”

Philip had the saddest look on his face of any in the group when he begged, “Don't make us say it.”

“How about this? You can tell me now, or I am going to get on this boat, and you can go to hell.”

Michael took the conversation over for them, “We're bringing you in.”

“On what grounds?”

“Conspiracy, and collusion with a spy.”

“Collusion with a spy? What are you guys talking about?”

“We know about Lina. Maat’s people are taking care of her as we speak.”

A fire erupted inside my soul. “She is not a spy, did Claude give this order?”

They could all feel the tension rising. Olbrecht decided to speak up, “No, this came straight from Ecne.”

Now it all made sense. That's why Claude was acting the way he was. He knew there was nothing he could do about it. That's probably why he asked me to stay, because had I not shown up here, they couldn't have called me guilty. All I could think about was Lina, and what was happening to her. My breathing became heavy, and I could feel the pulse in my neck. They reacted as I would if I was in their situation: they drew their weapons. I could feel their auras pushing forward. Fifty years ago, I would have been intimidated, but after the creatures I have faced, this seemed almost normal. I had no idea if I could defeat, or even survive, them. All I knew was that they weren't going to stop me. I was going to give them one last chance to call this off.

"You think that you are the apex, that you are the strongest and most deadly warriors in the world," I paused and began building my aura. I don't know how big my aura is but I had to try and gain some type of advantage to make them second-guess themselves. I pulled my sword from the scabbard and continued the build out of my aura which was already rivaling all three of theirs. "You think you can be the judge, jury, and executioner. Your strength has deceived you. If you stand against me, I will take that from you. You are not what you think you are, and I am everything you fear that I am!" My aura enveloped them and everything around us. Philip was shaking when he pulled the hammer back on his pistols. I looked over at him with a bone-chilling glare. "If your first step is not backwards, you will fall."

I could feel my pupils automatically dilating to envelop nearly my entire eye. I could see everything clearly, down to the little micro twitches of their fingers on their weapons. Michael made the first move as I knew he would. He threw his spear as hard as he could. Just a hair's breadth after that, Philip fired off a shot from his pistol. In one motion, I stroked my sword left to right, deflecting the spear and coming down on to the bullet with my blade. I even surprised myself with that; I wouldn't have thought it possible. Before I could get my hopes up, Olbrecht was coming down on me with his mace. I caught the blow on the cross guard. I felt the vibrations from it permeate through my body, but I held. I knew I couldn't stand in one place for very long. I leapt back and saw Philip raising his other pistol. Before he could fire it, I swung my sword in an upward motion and knocked it out of his hand. He hesitated for a moment and that's when I grabbed him by his chest plate and headbutted him in the face. I spun and launched him, with one arm, about thirty feet away. He rag-dolled against the ground; I was hoping that would give him his way out of this fight. He was always the closest to me and I even mentored him for a while.

Olbrecht was on me again, swinging wildly with his mace. Though his blows were powerful, they were slow and easy for me to dodge. As he came over the top to strike me in the head, I ducked under, stepped to the side, and kicked him in the side of his knee, collapsing it inward. Michael tried to stab me in the back, and not just metaphorically this time. I spun away, deflecting his sword. Then, there we were, standing face to face in an open field of battle, just like when I was a teenager in the tournaments. I was going against a far older opponent who didn't stand a chance. He came forward with speed that I remember mesmerised me when I first became a part of the Nigrum Gladio. Now I could track him the whole way and knew where he was going to be. I parried his blow and sliced him across the shoulder. I started to walk diagonally away from him with confidence. Looking at him over my shoulder I said, "I told you this was what was going to happen. Now I'm leaving."

Michael still had a defiant look on his face. "No, you're not. We can't let you leave." Then he raised his hand. They must have thought that I was an exceptional threat because I had never seen so many members of the Nigrum Gladio as what came out of the woods that day. There must have been fifteen members' swords at the ready. Some of their faces, I recognized. Others, I had no idea who they were. It didn't really matter because even if I was as strong as all of them put together, which I didn't think I was, the sheer number of attacks and angles I would have to deal with couldn't be overcome. I took a shot in the dark and pulled my tomahawk from my belt. It helped me against a sorcerer, maybe it could help me here. I was going to hit them first and put them on the defensive.

Right before I took off, a sound of cracking wood and tree limbs came from the forest off to our right. Everybody looked, and exploding from the tree line was Maushop. He was moving at a speed a horse couldn't match. He hit the group of vampires like a cannonball. Bodies and swords went flying everywhere. Michael tried to slash him, but I came in underneath his attack and blocked his sword. I immediately elbowed him in the side of the head as hard as I could manage. It dropped him to the ground and I'm sure I broke some bones with that blow.

Mashoup looked at me and yelled, "To the boat!" So we ran like hell.

The crew of the boat were all tough Scandinavian sailors, but even they looked afraid. I don't know what Lina paid them, but it must have been good because they didn't run. I leapt into the boat from about twenty feet away and started pulling up the anchor. Maushop started pushing the boat with all his might, propelling us into the ocean. He then turned around and proceeded to club a handful of vampires who tried to get to the boat. My tomahawk started to glow green, and out of nowhere, a giant whale appeared underneath us. It gripped the anchor in its mouth and dragged us at three times the speed we could have managed otherwise. I looked at the whale and said, "Thank you, Squannit," and I swear the whale winked at me.

Once we were about a mile away from shore, the whale disappeared into the depths. I looked back and hoped that Maushop was okay. I looked around at the crew; these guys are professionals. Not a single one of them had a question or complaint about what happened. The entire trip there I kept thinking about what Michael said. *Was Lina okay? Did they capture her, or was he lying?*

As we arrived on the choppy shores of Greenland, I already had a sinking feeling because I didn't see Lina waiting for me at the docks. As soon as I stepped onto shore, I saw Maat's warriors approaching. They couldn't tell right away who was who because I was wearing the same cloaks as all the crew. I tried to stay with a handful of them as they made their way up towards the general store. These were true professionals; they already knew what I was doing, they just didn't know which one was me.

As soon as we cut the corner of the first building, I took off. My cloak flew away from me but it didn't matter at this point. I could hear them questioning the crew for a moment until one of them came around the corner and saw me sprinting up the hill to the interior of the island. I hated to do this, but the only way I was making it out alive was with some help from an old friend. As soon as I made it to the mouth of the cave, I yelled "Ognar!" He came trotting out, and the ground shook while rocks and dirt fell from the ceiling. He waved with one hand.

"Simon, why must you yell?"

"I'm sorry, my friend, for bringing this to you but I had nowhere else to go. I'm being hunted and I think they have Lina."

"No need to apologize. You are family, and we protect our family." He let out a whistle, if a whistle sounded like a volcano erupting. The warriors crusted over the hill. They were distinctly Maat's. They had gold-plated shoulder and bracer armor that had her wings insignia on them. They also had a few vials similar to that of Lina on their belts. I knew from first-hand experience that you do not want to be hit with one of those.

I looked over at Ognar and warned, "Watch out for any bottles they throw."

He made a deep rumbling sound. He picked up two boulders which each had to weigh at least three hundred pounds. He hurled one to the left and then one to the right of the group. Then, he ran down the center of their line. I barely had any time to react, but I followed closely on his heels. I leapt off my right foot and then pushed off his shoulder with my left. I came down with a blow that severed the arm of the first warrior. Ognar slapped two at the same time and sent them flying. That left us two against nine, not bad odds.

The real fighting began as they pulled out straight-bladed short swords. Their weapon's main effectiveness is piercing. They were using a lot of lunges and stabbing motions. I was easily able to parry them off to the side and use my slashing technique to keep them at that distance. One of the warriors thought they were going to be clever. He tried to slide in close to me and cut my ankles out from underneath me. I blocked his sword with a left-handed motion and then kicked him in the face with my right foot.

The first of the potion bottles came next. Ognar put his giant hand beside my head right before it hit me. I could hear it sizzle against his skin. I think the rocky armor protected him from most of it. One of the warriors had managed to get behind us, and launched himself at Ognar's back. I deflected his blade away, but it left me open and one of the others stabbed me in my right side. Suddenly, I heard what sounded like a stampede of bison. Everyone looked up the hill, and there were only two of us smiling when we saw six more massive trolls coming down towards us.

Ognar smashed one of the warriors into the ground before saying, "Go, we can handle them."

Maat's warriors began to hurl vials at the oncoming trolls. Again, I couldn't believe I had someone defending me like this. I've never had anyone support me in all my time since being turned. I started running down towards the shore. One of the warriors broke off and came for me. I turned to try to take him out quickly, but I didn't catch the vile he threw. It hit me on my left side. It ate through most of my armor and my left arm felt like it was on fire. My thoughts went from pain to rage as I darted straight at him. I was far too fast for him; he had no time to react as my blade slipped through the bottom of his throat and out the top of his skull. I kicked him in the chest, ripping my blade free and continued my escape. I caught a fisherman who was headed out. I threw him one of my coin pouches that was filled with silver coins. He looked befuddled, then looked inside and saw the silver.

He looked back up at me and I insisted, "There's more where that came from if we go now!"

"Hop in," he said.

We were off. I can't believe I've been chased into the ocean twice in such a short amount of time. I gave him another pouch of silver and told him to get me to Ireland. The man had a Scottish accent so I knew he had been there and was familiar with how to get there. I could see it in his eyes that he didn't really want to do the journey, but I gave him enough silver to be more than worth it. He could easily resupply in Ireland and fish his way back and still have plenty of coin left over. As we closed in on our destination, it seemed that the sea decided to turn against us. The North Sea started to rise all around us. The waves were too much for the small fishing boat. We capsized and it tore the ship apart. I grabbed a large chunk of wood and threw the fisherman on top of it and hung on.

Chapter 27

We washed up on shore a few hours later and I drug him up on land. It was just as shitty on land, the rain was pouring down. As if destroying the boat I was on wasn't enough, fate had conspired against me once more. This must have been where they planned to drop me off at once they captured me because there were Maat soldiers walking up and down the shore. I tried to look inconspicuous, but one man dragging another man out of the ocean kind of draws your attention. I tried not to let them see my face and hoped they wouldn't recognize me, but I heard them murmuring to each other once they were about fifteen feet away. I attacked immediately, slamming fists, knees, and elbows into both men. They laid there bleeding and broken.

Just as I thought I was going to make it home free, I looked up. There stood a nightmare: it was Ahit. She looked even more irritated than normal, I don't know if it was me or if it was because the rain had matted her hair to her face. I let out my weariness and frustration, "God damn it!"

She didn't even have the courtesy to gloat. She looked at me stone-faced and exclaimed, "God will not save you from me!"

I was so weakened from the shipwreck and healing from the acid burn. I didn't know how much of a fight I could put up. I knew that I wasn't as strong as her before all of that, but I wasn't going out without a fight. I took one step to the right to draw her in. I knew she wouldn't make the first move. So as soon as my foot was in the air, she came at me. I was able to duck under her first strike. I turned and swung my sword down at her back. In almost a blur of motion, she turned around and grabbed the hilt of my sword with her left hand and slammed her right fist into the side of my head. It felt like somebody had dropped a house on me. My whole body went numb. I saw her hand coming down to grab me, but I was powerless to stop her. She picked me up with her left hand and lifted me into the air by my neck. The only thing I can really remember was the raindrops falling on my face. There was something soothing about it.

The next thing I remember was waking up in a cell. It felt like they beat me all the way here. It felt like my body was one big bruise. The cell was made out of thick masonry rock and the door was a thick steel door with one slit big enough so you can see your tormentor's face. I heard a voice coming from the door. They banged on the door.

"Simon."

"Yes, what do you want?" I groaned.

The man cleared his throat and said, "Her Majesty will be here shortly to address you." Then he walked away. I must be a big deal if Maat herself was going to come talk to me, but I don't get it. I'm not really anyone special in the grand scheme of things. Even with the position I have now, I'm no more than halfway up the ladder. There are a lot of people who wouldn't even know my name.

It couldn't have been more than an hour, when the door unlocked. True to the messenger's word, as the door opened, there stood Maat. She radiated power and beauty, the likes of which I had never seen. Ecne tended to keep his aura contained. In that way, she was more like Tū, though I was told that he wasn't showing but a fraction of his energy. I went to stand up and pay her respect. Her face turned from a look of disdain to anger.

"Sit down, you shall not stand in my presence. You are a dog, even less. A snake. I should make you lie on the floor."

So I sat back down but I still wanted to be cordial. "Your majesty, I'm not sure how I've wronged you. Maybe you have some bad information." *Great, now I've insulted her.*

Her lips began to snarl.

"You infiltrated my ranks and tried to turn one of my daughters against me. No, I think my information is good."

"That's not how it happened at all. I love her. I've never asked for any information and I've never relayed any to my people."

"Speak another word and I'll rip your heart out where you stand. You know nothing about love." She paused for half a second. Looking in her eyes, I could see she was gone. "I will cleanse the memories of you from her mind, and if that doesn't work, I will cleanse her body." I could feel the predator in me trying to claw its way out. I had to tell myself that I couldn't help Lina if I was dead. She shook her shoulders and smoothed out her dress. Her eyes went back to that of a person that had their faculties together. "You will be publicly executed in three days, like any other spy."

So it looks like they're going to decapitate me in a few days, and then they're going to try and break her mind and have a wizard extract memories of me from her. I had to try to get out of this cell tonight.

Oddly enough, even though we are night time creatures, the place was not as busy once the sun went down. I listened for the pacing of the guard, and when I knew he was his farthest away, I walked to the far side wall and hit it with a massive forearm strike. Red light permeated through it like it was protected by a magical field. I felt hopeless; there was no way I would break down this wall. Then I heard a sound which I couldn't make out at first. The sound kept going. The rocks that made up the wall were moving. I don't mean they were moving like they were falling. They were moving like they were being deconstructed. I stood in front of the wall as stone by stone, they floated away so there was an opening big enough for me to walk through. I took a step out cautiously and there he stood: a man from my past.

Agrippa didn't look like he had aged a day even though it had been over fifty years. He stood tall with his staff beside him.

"They weren't lying when they said you kicked up a hornet's nest," he said.

"Agrippa, what are you doing here?"

"How many times have they beat you over the head? I'm here to save you obviously."

"I get that, but why? Why risk it?"

"All those years ago, you wouldn't let them kill me. I shall not let them kill you."

"Do you know anything about the state of Lina?"

"What I do know is limited, but she is alive and she is in solitary."

I wanted to go back through the front doors and rescue her, but I knew I had no chance of that at this point. I have to get more help, more strength. The image of the being with the red eyes flashed in my head. I remembered her words, that I would seek strength and I would cause destruction.

I looked around and spoke frustratedly, "I wish I had my gear."

Agrippa scoffed, "Do you think I'm an amateur?" He pointed his staff at the ground beside us. I couldn't make this stuff up if I wanted to. A bag with my sword attached pushed itself free from the loose soil. Agrippa raised one eyebrow. I looked at him with a stunned face.

"Okay, that was pretty awesome."

"Thank you. Now, enough lollygagging, there is a boat waiting for you. Go!"

I sprinted down to the shoreline, and another old friend was waiting for me. As commanding a presence as ever, Joan waved me into the boat. I shook her hand, then I pulled her in for a hug.

"You didn't have to do this."

"This place has been hell since Maat took over. I've watched her destroy too many things and too many people. I wasn't going to let her take you down too." I was trying to keep my emotions in check, but I think she could see it in my eyes. She put one hand on my shoulder and then handed me something wrapped in cloth. I looked at her, confused. I started unwrapping it and she said to me, "Elizabeth sends her regards." It was the scepter of Erisvorsh. I looked befuddled.

"What am I going to do with this thing?"

"Elizabeth told me that all you have to do is push your will into it, and it will do what you need it to, whatever that means."

I had no idea what that meant either. I grabbed the scepter and jumped in the little sailboat. I drew the sail down and Joan gave me a push. I was lucky. There was a nice breeze this evening, propelling me away from shore.

I had to think of where I could go, where I would be safe, who might help me. I started sailing north, but I wasn't the only one. It didn't take long for them to realize I was gone. There were two small boats coming from behind me. I held the scepter, and banged it against my head softly, forcing myself to think of a plan. I pointed the scepter at the water in front of the two boats. I began to visualize what I wanted to happen, bringing it together inside my mind until it was a clear picture and it felt real.

"Now!" I screamed. The jewel glowed a beautiful blue color like a miniature star. The water around the two boats began to thrash and waves crashed into both sides, forcing the two ships in on each other. They smashed with enough force to break them in half. The soldiers began diving into the open ocean. I conjured up another vision in my head and pointed the scepter behind my boat. A current of immense strength forced me quickly out of sight of the men. I knew where I was headed, but it was the last place I ever thought I would step foot.

When I landed on shore, it reminded me of Greenland. I had never been to Finland before. In fact, most vampires have never ventured into these lands. The Norse gods rule these lands, and they strike down anyone who encroaches on their territory. I stopped in Kemi to gather supplies before heading up the Kemijoki River. The scepter worked as well in the river as it did in the open ocean. Only a handful of people saw me on my way up the river. It must have been a strange sight seeing a boat go against the current faster than it could go down.

I was in Rovaniemi within a matter of hours. I was always told that their home on this realm was east of the city. I could be chasing a fairytale or I could be walking, it was a suicide mission either way. I didn't feel good about this. I didn't see any other alternative though so I kept moving.

A few minutes later, I saw a rainbow that looked like it was pulled straight from a fairy tale. The colors were so bright it looked as if it was almost solid. Before I could crest the hill, two viking warriors started their way down. We locked eyes immediately and I put my hands in the air to show that I was no threat. Apparently they weren't buying it because they drew their swords and started running straight for me. With my hands still up, I yelled, "I don't want to fight." My words fell on deaf ears. I dove out of their way as they closed in on me. I rolled back to my feet and yelled once again, "I don't want to fight!"

They circled me and one of them said, "You have come to the wrong place if you did not wish to fight. You will not reach the gates." I removed my sword and they smiled like a couple sadistic bastards. Their skill was on par with the best humans I've crossed swords with. They were far too aggressive. They underestimated my speed and I was able to out-maneuver them. I dropped the first one with a cut across his thigh. The second took a slash across his hamstrings and he hit the ground instantly. I made a break for the top of the hill. As soon as I came over the top, I saw where the rainbow met the ground. It was mesmerizing, but all of those feelings soon went away once I saw the other handful of viking warriors. I'm sure I didn't look very cordial coming down the hill with my longsword in hand. They all let out a war cry, picked up their swords and came charging for me. I stayed on the outside of the group, never letting them surround me. It took all of my skill as I deflected and parried blow after blow. I lightly slashed, elbowed, and kicked until I had felled them all.

I heard two loud noises like two large boulders falling.

I looked up to see two men standing about twenty feet from me. One had his back to me with his hands behind his back, and the other was staring daggers through me. Both men were a foot and a half taller than me and they were both heavily laid with muscle. But the one who was staring at me was exceptional; he had more muscle on his frame than I thought a human could have. Then of course, I knew they weren't human. The power I felt coming from these individuals was unlike anything I'd ever experienced. The only thing comparable was the few times I've been in the presence of Lord Dracula. Their auras were completely different from his though. No wonder we've never pushed into their territory. These two could probably take down an entire vampire army themselves. The Asgardian that was staring at me was easy to identify. He had long blonde hair and where the color of his eyes should be, were streaks of lightning. I could also see electricity flowing down his right arm and ending in the hammer he was willing. Thor, the god of thunder, was not pleased that I was here. His chest was heaving. When he decided to march for me, the other Asgardian put his hand to the side, blocking his way and said, "Brother..." His voice was very mellow but had such authority in it.

Thor took another step into his hand and said with an echo in his voice, "This vermin dares intrude into our territory."

Though he was still facing away from me, I could see him sigh and he said once again, "Brother." Thor looked at him and the lightning in his eyes flashed even stronger. He moved his hand from Thor's stomach to his shoulder. "You of all should appreciate what he has done. Against all odds for his mission, he came here and he even took out what? Ten of your men." When he turned around, I saw he had as much muscle on his frame, but he was built more like a swimmer.

The thing that really stuck out about him were his eyes. They were like pure light and the more you looked at them, the more colors you could see, but they weren't like a rainbow. I can't quite explain it. Looking at him, he was definitely the better looking of the two, and understanding that he was Thor's brother, I had to guess he was Baldr. I think he saw the realization on my face and he smiled. He walked up to me and put his hand out to shake mine. I accepted the handshake and I was glad that he didn't decide to crush my hand, which he easily could have. "So, what brings you to us, friend? It is no small task getting here," he inquired.

"I need help. I must speak to the all-father."

He smiled and had an amused look on his face. "You must have found yourself in quite the predicament. You're a vampire and you have to reach for the kind of power that my father possesses to help you."

"I'm going up against Maat."

He put his arm around my shoulder and proposed, "Well in that case, I think we'll have a little stroll. This should be interesting."

Thor was still staring me down. Then, as if he was invisible, another Asgardian appeared from thin air. He was as tall but far less laden with muscle, but there was something about him that said he was just as dangerous.

He patted Thor on the back and chimed in, "Has it been so long that you forgot what it's like to be the underdog?" He looked over his shoulder and winked at me.

As Baldr walked me through the bifrost, it wasn't anything like I imagined it would be. One moment we were in the field, then there was a flash of light and I was standing in a throne room. Everything seemed to be made of metal. It almost looked like gold but not the right texture. There was a small section of stairs the length of the room. Standing up there, next to the balcony window, was a being that couldn't be mistaken. The all-father himself, Odin, stood like a mountain of power.

Thor walked up to him and sneered, "There is a parasite who wishes to speak with you."

Odin turned to look at me. He had a long, well-kept, white beard and a bright blue eye. One thing I wasn't expecting was that he didn't have an eye patch, only a scar down across a closed eyelid. Baldr pointed towards Odin and urged me to go to him. As I walked up the stairs, I felt as though I was walking towards a waterfall of power, and I tried not to get crushed down by it. Odin stood with his hands behind his back, staring out the window.

"You find yourself in rarefied air. You are one of the few outsiders in thousands of years to see my realm; Baldr must like you," he said with the voice of a general.

I tried to not get tongue-tied as I replied, "I'm honored to be here, sir."

"Oh, I'm sure you are. What brings you on such a journey?"

I took a deep breath before I spoke. "I've come to see if you could help me in any way."

He gave me an inquiring look. "But of course you have, that's not hard to deduce. I mean what do you need?"

"Maat has lost her mind. She is planning to attack you and the Olympians. She has taken the woman I love and I must retrieve her."

A massive smile came over his face. He gripped my shoulder slightly and shook me a bit. "Ah, love. No better reason to go into battle. Many empires have risen and fallen for love. The question I ask myself is why would I get involved in a quest to save your beloved?"

I straightened myself up and tried to look more professional. "She has become irrational. She plans to invade your lands. I think it is foolish, especially being in your presence, but she believes she can do it."

"What can you do for me?"

I mean, what could *I* really help *him* with? I decided to throw the first thing out that I could think of. "I could get you information, keep you informed."

He patted me on the back. "Simon, if I'm coming to you for information, then I am in far more trouble than you can help me with."

I had to go for my ace in the hole. I was desperate. I pulled the scepter from the bag I carried it in on my back. When I presented it to him, his eye sparkled and he grabbed it. He looked deep into the gem.

"Erisvorsh, how did you come about having this item in your possession?"

"I am very resourceful. It should be worth any help that you could give me."

"So it seems you are a bit resourceful." He handed it back to me. "I think it will help you more than you know."

I was running out of ideas. "I'll owe you a favor."

His eyebrows went up. "Owing a favor to Asgard is no small thing."

"Whatever price, I'll pay it," I vowed.

"Say it once more."

"I'll do it!"

His face turned from cordial to as serious as a judge handing down a sentence. He stood up tall, pushed his shoulders back and reiterated, "You have made a promise to Asgard, and you will keep that for no matter where you are, even if you are standing in the presence of Dracula himself. When Asgard calls, you will come to us, or Asgard will come for you." When he finished speaking, he immediately went back to his friendly disposition. He turned with me and we started walking down the stairs. "Can I see your sword?" he asked.

"Absolutely." I handed over my sword to him and he threw it to a dwarf.

"Sindri, take care of this and make it what you will," he commanded.

Sindri looked up at me and sought, "Nice blade for a human. What is it made of?"

"Wootz steel," I replied.

He looked at it like a drug addict looks at their drug of choice. Then he proceeded to talk to the sword. "When I'm done with you, you will be the sharpest sword any vampire has ever held."

He scurried off. Odin looked at me and said, "It won't be an Asgardian blade but it will be as good a sword as that sword itself can be. Since I will not be directly interfering in whatever assault you plan, this sword should make you more formidable, but take my words to heart, you still are not strong enough to take Maat down. You will need more strength. Where you are going to get that, I do not know."

I am starting to think that those two words are going to haunt me for the rest of my days. "More strength," I spoke under my breath.

He waved over a tall slender asgardian. I was pretty sure I knew who he was too.

Odin confirmed it when he called, "Loki, quit being antisocial. Come over and say hi."

Loki put his left hand out for me to shake which I

wasn't used to. When I reached out, he gave me a forearm gripping shake like we were in a guild together. He leaned over and whispered some gibberish in my ear. When he rose, he gave me another one of those winks from earlier. Sindri ran back into the room with my sword, if I could even call it that anymore. It was shining like a mirror and it had an Asgardian rune etched into it. The runes reminded me of the ones written into my tomahawk, but instead of green, they were glowing blue. He handed the sword over to me. It felt lighter; as I windmilled it, it whistled through the air.

Sindri yelled at me, “Try not to cut your own head off.”

“I shall do my best.”

“That's what I'm afraid of,” he mumbled as he walked away.

Odin shook my hand one last time. “Good luck, young warrior.”

I gave him a slight bow.

Baldr gave me a nod, then Thor and Loki walked me back to the bifrost. Neither said a word as I stepped through it.

Chapter 28

I was back in the field with the soldiers still bandaging their wounds. It made me wonder whether or not time was slower in Asgard than in our reality. I had to heed Odin's words. If I were to go up against Maat now, I would surely fall. But where do I go for more strength? I thought back to my time with the Native American shaman. I remember the vision that I had. There was only one place I could think of to go for that kind of power. I got back in my boat and began the long voyage down to Africa.

I did my best to avoid the European shoreline. Instead of going into the Mediterranean, I went around to West Africa and made landfall there. I could already feel myself slipping before I ever started what I knew I needed to do but never wanted to do. I wrestled with my conscience, but it didn't matter. I had to save Lina and I was going to do whatever it took. I began to slaughter on the Savanna. I turned into just another predator in the bush, killing and draining all the large animals that crossed my path. For a time, I tried to hold some semblance of humanity together, by dragging the carcasses to the edge of a village. Elephants, rhinos, and hippos, it didn't matter. As long as it was larger than a few humans. Inherently, animals do not have as much power in them per pound as a human does. But once you get an animal that weighs a few tons, it has as much power as a few humans.

It didn't take long for word to spread of the mass

slaughter happening. Different authorities started to hunt me: from mercenary werewolves to shamans. They all fell beneath the blade of my sword and underneath my fangs. Each one was easier than the last, adding to my strength. My blood lust had taken over me and I had become a rogue vampire.

My dreams haunted me. Dreams of a man I couldn't recognize. They called him Simon. He was feared in battle and loved as a friend. He seemed so familiar but I couldn't quite place where I knew him. Then, the vampires came for me. At first it was just a low-level crew of four soldiers. I stalked them like the lions I shared the Savanna with. They were standing in your basic one-two-one formation. It gives you an opportunity to watch all four sides. It also makes the front and rear vulnerable. I crouched in the high grass and waited for my opportunity. There was a split second where their eyes were out of my position. That's all I needed. I hit the one in the rear with bone-shattering force into the other side of the tall grass. As soon as we hit the ground, my fangs ripped his throat open to navigate the source of his power. The second I was gone, they found his body.

Just moments later, I was back on the prowl. I could smell their fear in the air; it was intoxicating. They had their swords drawn and ready. Who did they think they were, coming into my territory? These are my hunting grounds, and I allowed no intruders. They'll just have to pay and be an example to anyone else who would enter my hunting grounds.

Their eyes darted back and forth. It didn't matter; they were too slow, too sloppy. I took the first one in the throat with my talon-like nails. Pieces of him went flying into his fellow soldiers. I could feel their heart rates rising.

They began to panic. They slashed their swords at me but to no avail. They were destined to die by my hand, at this very spot. As the next one tried a double-handed blow, I ducked under him and smashed his wrists with my forearm. I heard the snapping of bone, then his screams of pain which I quickly silenced by snapping his neck. The last one tried to be smart and run for it. I picked up one of the soldier's swords and threw it at him. It tumbled end-over-end until it reached its destination, right between his shoulder blades. It went all the way down to the cross guard. It must have gone through his spine because he fell instantly. I proceeded to drain them all. They weren't particularly powerful vampires, but they were by far the most powerful thing I had since I've been in Africa.

I laid the body in the middle of the trail from which they came. I knew it would only be a matter of time before they were found. Once they were discovered, they would send more, and I would dispatch them the same.

My dreams haunted me again. They tried to tell me who I was, but I already knew who I was. I am the apex predator, the one that all creatures fear in the night. My dreams try to fill my thoughts with laughter and happiness. I know the truth. There is only hunger and pain. I thought I heard a voice say to me, "They're coming for you." I woke and leapt to my feet. What predators lurk in the shadows? What is there to challenge me? What am I to be afraid of?

My answer came in the form of a Maat hit squad. These were no normal soldiers. They were the equivalent to the Nigrum Gladio. So what? Their swords and daggers are no match for my fangs and claws. I had to make sure that my attacks were more precise and instantly brutal. There was one that seemed to be lagging behind the rest: easy prey. I waited for the right moment to strike. I saw the opening, and sprung to life like my big cat brethren. I didn't realize my mistake until it was too late. I was already in the air when I saw the staff he was holding. He hit a lever, and the end opened into a V shape. He braced it on the ground and hit me in the throat. He used my momentum to flip me over and slam me into the ground. I rushed to my feet, but the trap had already been sprung. I was surrounded on all sides with spears pointed directly at me. I could see it in their eyes: they were all professional, but none of them wanted to make the first move.

I heard from outside of the circle a powerful voice. "Nobody move," it boomed. Then a specimen of a man walked into the circle. He was a good half a foot taller than me and probably had a hundred pounds of muscle on top of that. He wore no armor, only a primitive loincloth. He was completely hairless from his head to his toes, which probably helped him show off his ridiculous physique. He had a traditional Zulu spear. I could tell that it wasn't normal. There was something about it, and I knew I had to stay away from it. He looked around at all of the men and said, "This is my trophy. No one interferes. I will take this animal down."

I heard one of the men respond, "Of course, Anyanwu."

That name jarred something loose in my head, something from the past. I've heard that name before. He must be a very powerful vampire. No matter. I would test that.

My first attack would be to see how he reacts. I circled him as soon as I thought I was a half a step ahead and launched my attack. I was moving so fast. I threw my left hand out to take his throat. He was even faster, barely moving out of the way and clubbing me in the back of the head when I passed him. I decided to go low on my next attack. I went in to take his ankle, but he stepped over to the side and slammed the side of the spear into my ribs, making me roll to the side. Sure he was fast, but I only needed to get a hold of him, and then I could rip him apart. I went straight for him which I think caught him off guard. I was able to get a few hits on him, including a cut across his cheek. When he grabbed a hold of me, I realized I was dealing with a different level of strength. He threw me fifty feet in the air and just as far, I smacked into the ground with a thud.

Anyanwu stood with his spear at his side and boasted, "It pleases me to see you like this, Simon. Feral and lost. They say he who makes a beast out of himself gets rid of the pain of being a man. I wonder if that is true?" Something in me began to stir. *I need that pain, I want that pain. Give me that pain back.* He looked down at me like I was a dog with mange. "Once I bring your head to Maat, she'll stop playing mind games with Lina. Seeing your lifeless face will finally break her."

A flood of emotion entered my mind Maat. Lina. It all came flooding back. It was like a fog had been lifted from my eyes.

When I could finally see clearly, there I was, standing in front of one of the most powerful vampires on earth. I was perfectly calm. He saw the change and gripped his spear tight. My hand touched the handle of my sword and it was like embracing an old friend. I pulled it from my scabbard and it hummed and shined brilliantly, reflecting the light on it's silver finish. As I gathered my focus and my will, the runes burst to life. Anyanwu took a defensive posture. I moved faster than I ever had. I faked a thrust to his leg and he barely moved to block it. Then I came over the top with a double handed slice. He was fast enough to raise his spear to block it. My Asgardian enhanced blade went through it like it was a piece of wood. My blade continued down and took his left arm at the shoulder. A look of utter shock came over Anyanwu's face, but he quickly recovered his wits. He tried to slash me with the handle of the spear. I was too fast and my technique was too good. I side-stepped him and brought my sword down on his right arm. He dropped what was left of the spear along with the section of his arm, right below the elbow. I stabbed my sword into the ground and bear-hugged him from behind. He flailed his half arm back at my head, but without a hand, he was powerless. I sunk my teeth into the side of his throat.

The amount of power was unbelievable. I felt myself instantly becoming stronger. As he slipped away, he fell to his knees. I put my fangs away and took a two-handed grip on his throat. With one swift motion I ripped his head from his body. His men's faces were riddled with fear as I showed them their leader's head. I circled and showed my trophy to them, yelling, "Go tell Maat that I'm coming for her next." The circle separated and I walked through, carrying the severed head of one of the most powerful vampires on the planet.

I knew this fear and shock from them would wear off and I would be hunted again soon. I remember when I first arrived here, I heard the local vampires saying that Tū would be arriving at Madagascar soon. I knew it was a long shot, but I thought that maybe he might help me. From here, it's probably a three day journey, but I could probably cut that in half. I gathered all of my things, as well as Anyanwu's head, and shoved off for the island. Once I landed, I was directed to head to the city of Antananarivo by the local informers. It reminded me a lot of

New York, and from what the locals have said, it was founded about the same time.

It wasn't that hard to find his embassy. It wasn't because it was the nicest building in the city, but because it was the only one with a large Polynesian man standing at the front door. As soon as the guard saw me approaching the front door, he put his hand to his weapon. Oddly enough he didn't draw it, he waited for me to walk up to him. I made sure to keep my hands away from my sword.

"I'm here to speak with Tū."

He looked at me with a blank face and said, "One moment." I couldn't help but look around, expecting a band of warriors to surround me at any moment, but the only thing that happened was the guard stepping back outside and saying, "You may enter; follow Loto."

I followed him down a hallway that split the building in half. We entered the main room through double doors. Tū sat on a throne that looked too small for his massive frame. If I had to guess, I would say it was to make him look even larger. Tū spoke before I could give him a traditional greeting.

"Simon, I thought you might make your way here."

I was taken back by that statement. "How did you figure that?"

"I have eyes and ears all over these lands. When I heard that you had fallen on the wrong side of Maat, and then I heard some feral vampire was killing her men in Africa, it wasn't hard to see who it might be. Knowing that I'm not far, it didn't take too much to think you might come see me." I guess you don't get to be millennials old without having a good feel about what's going on around you. He spread his hands. "So what is it you think I can do for you?"

“I don't expect you to go to war for me, but what I think you can do is plant a seed of fear in Maat.”

He leaned his head back. “Interesting choice of words. Would you care to elaborate?”

“Maat knows you fear nothing, so she would believe you if you told her she should worry.”

“What would I have her worried about?”

I pulled Anyanwu's head from the bag, and laid it at my feet. I saw some eyebrows go up around the room. Tū’s laugh boomed through the room.

“I knew it! Yes, I knew from the moment I felt your aura that you were something special. Every once in a while, a true warrior spirit comes along. You are one such spirit. I was hoping she wouldn't take you down so easily.”

“Will you help me then?”

He slapped the arm of his chair. “You need no help from me, but I will tell Maat that her enforcer has been laid to waste, and that you are far stronger than she gave you credit for.”

I bowed my head slightly. “Thank you.”

I began to walk out when Tū yelled to me, “I like you Simon, but I do not think you will weather this storm.”

I looked back over my shoulder and said softly yet confidently, “I am the storm.”

I could feel the smile of approval as I left.

Chapter 29

I still needed more strength, or at least more help. Hopefully the warning to Matt will get her to second-guess herself. She won't tighten her security because that would be a sign of weakness. That's why I did that display publicly. So she has to play it off as though I'm no threat at all, but inside, there is a seed of doubt. When I face her, I will need her to make a mistake, then I can capitalize.

I have heard of a place where one can access power, but I'll have to go back through the Gauntlet of Africa. I have no allies on this continent, no connections. I'll be going it alone until I can make it to Morocco. There, I have some contacts that can help me make my way back into Europe. I made a stop at Lake Ukerewe. The lake was massive, as large as any of the Great Lakes in the America's. I stayed the night at one of the locals' houses. I paid them six months worth of labor in silver. Had they known what was coming next, they probably would have asked for more.

The next morning, I heard screaming and yelling coming from all around the village. When I looked out the window of the shack, I saw a team of Maat's warriors escorting a wizard. They were throwing people out of their homes and demanding they tell them where I was. I couldn't let these people take the fall for me. I jumped down as they were dragging people around.

"Hey assholes!" I yelled. They all looked over and

dropped the people they were holding. The wizard walked in front of the group.

"Simon, this is where your path ends," he said.

"You sound a lot like another sorcerer who tried to take me down before I drained him."

He must've been paid very well, his staff had gold markings all over it. I knew this wouldn't be a one-on-one fight, because all of the other warriors drew their weapons as well. It didn't matter, I was going to have to take them all out anyway. Without any warning, a ball of fire shot from the tip of the sorcerer's staff. I was barely able to dive out of the way. Two of the warriors closed in on me. Which wasn't a very smart move on their part, because now their sorcerer didn't have a clear shot on me. The first warrior came at me with a downward swing. When our two swords met, mine sliced right through his. I quickly brought the sword back, decapitating him from behind. I kicked the other warrior in the chest, knocking him off his feet. Then came another ball of fire. This time it was close enough to singe the hair on the back of my head. I picked up the broken piece of sword and threw it at the sorcerer. It sliced the side of his shoulder, but didn't appear to faze him too much. As the warrior tried to get up off of the ground, I kicked him in his head as hard as possible. It dented in his helmet and I heard bone cracking. The next two warriors tried to come at me from both sides. I brought my sword behind my head to block the strike from behind, and then sidestepped and took both of his wrists off with my sword. I brought my sword back up, taking his head from his body. I did a one-eighty and met the other warrior's sword once again, this time breaking his. I hit him under the chin with my elbow, grabbed him by his chest, lifted him slightly, and started running towards the sorcerer.

The sorcerer unleashed a stream of fire, setting the vampire warrior aflame. Just before I slammed into the sorcerer, one of the two remaining warriors tackled me. I spun back to my knees, and in one motion, I pulled my dagger from its sheath and sliced deep into his throat. I caught the blade of the last warrior with my dagger and impaled him with my sword through his chest armor. Our momentum landed us on the beach. I spun and blocked an incoming fireball with my sword. Some of the flames splashed over and seared my right cheek. I took a half-step back and my heel touched the water; it gave me an idea. I pulled the scepter off of my back. I was really hoping this was going to work.

"Come on, the last sorcerer I went up against was twice as strong as you. Is that all you've got?" I taunted him.

He held his staff out like a spear and unleashed a stream of flame three feet wide at me. I lifted the scepter, and I already had the thought in my mind as a torrent of water twice the size of his flame came rushing forward. They met about twenty feet from me. The steam it produced was like a fog had covered the area. I felt him weakening as the stream of water overtook him. I jumped in the air and landed on his arm holding his staff. As I had him pinned down, I stabbed his other shoulder with my sword and knocked his staff away. I looked into his eyes and said, "I told you my path wasn't ending here." Then I took all the life force from him before heading off.

I straddled the line of the forests and the desert as I moved along northwest through Africa. As I sat by the fire, the sun disappearing behind the horizon, I thought about what was to come ahead. I kept thinking about what Maat was doing to Lina. I had to keep telling myself that we were both still alive. Whatever came our way, we were still here. I could still save her and we could still be together.

The next day, I closed in on my destination. I knew it was not going to be easy to get into this place if the legends were true. I was also not a fan of the desert which is precisely where I had to go. As I was a few days in, I had to keep reminding myself why I was putting myself through hell. No human would be able to make this trip by themselves. I had to pull a bit of reserves to keep the heat from frying my brain. When doubt started to creep into my head, that's when I saw it. The eye of the Sahara came into view; a wave of relief and excitement came over me.

If my intelligence was good, I needed to watch out as I entered the structure. As I looked around, I could understand how some legends say that this is the site of the lost city of Atlantis. As I made my way to the center, where the oasis lies, I started to feel a sense of unease come over me, like I was being watched. I stopped in front of the pond, knelt down, cupped my hand, and took a drink. I removed my sword from its scabbard and called out, "I fear you not. Come and face me if you will." I didn't have to wait long.

As my words were still echoing throughout the structure, an arrow came flying towards me. I deflected it with my sword quite easily, but I didn't think that was the best they could do. I began to see one arrow after another, after another, coming from the sky. I started deflecting and rolling and running as they kept coming. When the last one fell, I yelled, "Arrows? I come to you as a true warrior, and you use arrows?"

Suddenly, I heard what I both feared and hoped for at the same time. The sand began to move, and from it, a huge figure arose. It was humanoid in nature but it looked as though it had been put together with rocks.

The thing spoke with an echoey voice, "You trespass upon the city, you shall be removed."

I yelled back to him, "I don't know if you can look around, but there isn't a city here my friend."

It must be pre-programmed because it didn't acknowledge that I said anything and kept barreling forward. I sidestepped him and slashed at his knees. The vibration I felt through my sword was odd. When I looked at the guard, he had an aura that was pulsing where I hit it. He stomped on the ground and it felt like an earthquake, rendering me slightly off balance. He sped up at twice the speed he was running earlier and nearly crushed me with a blow from his hand. It finally clicked in my head what it was: a golem, a spiritual defender created by the people who lived here all those years ago. I put my sword away and pulled out my tomahawk. The ruins began to glow that beautiful green color. I stared the golem down, and we both began to run towards each other. If it was a sentient being, it may have found it strange that I was running right at it. I leapt with all of my strength. I put both hands on the handle of the tomahawk and came down right on the golem's forehead. His protective aura exploded and a whooshing sound along with gale-force winds emanated out from both of us. The creature fell to its back, and the light left its eyes.

A slow clap started to echo throughout the structure. I turned around and saw a man riding a camel slowly towards the oasis. My tomahawk continued to glow. He must be spiritual in nature. I knew nothing of the person, only a name and that they can grant favors. He stopped about ten feet from me. He sat up straight in the saddle and held the horn with both hands. "Simon, it is nice to meet you."

I guess I shouldn't be surprised that he knew my name. "I see your knowledge has not been exaggerated."

"But of course. I don't get many visitors to this location. I must know who would come all this way."

"I hear you can help people."

"Depends on what type of help you need. I can manage a great many things, but there are a few things out of my reach."

"So...are you a jinn?"

"Please, don't insult me. I walked this earth long before what you call a jinn, but I presume you would like a wish granted?"

"What I need is strength."

"How much strength? Who must you defeat, young Simon?"

I took a deep breath and explained, "I need to take Maat down."

He chuckled. "Is that all? Just enough to take down the likes of a demigod? You don't ask for much, do you?" He laughed a little more.

"So you don't possess enough power?" I jumped in.

His laugh continued for another half second. Then he leaned down and said, "I've been at this for a long time. I know all the tricks and games that you play. You know that I possess great power, no need to be rude"

"I think you were the one being condescending."

He reached over and scratched the camel's ear. "You know what, you're right. I wasn't being very nice about your request. It's just that the normal request is a kingdom or massive amounts of gold, but all you want is to kill an ancient being of your own kind. Why is that?"

"She has taken everything from me."

He squinted his eyes. "So she has your woman then? A story as old as time itself."

"Will you help me or not?"

He sat up straight again before asking, "What is my name?"

Luckily, that was one of the few things I knew. "You are Paimon."

"Remove all doubt. I will help you." He reached out into the air, and squeezed his hand like he was grabbing the back of a dog's scruff. He pulled downwards, and what happened next was hard for my eyes to comprehend. He tore what looked like a rip scar in the fabric of reality. After a few seconds, a figure began to step through. As they came through, they took two steps towards Paimon and grew from the size of a normal man, to being tall enough to look him directly in the eye as he sat atop his camel. I was in total shock. The only thing I felt, besides the shiver running down my spine, was the stinging of the desert sand on my face and the sweet smell of the water from the oasis.

If the ancient Egyptian dress, bronzed skin, and golden headdress wasn't enough for me to know, him having the face of a falcon instead of a human sealed it for me. He is one of the most feared entities on this plane of existence. He spoke with a baritone Egyptian accent, "Paimon, old friend, what do I owe the pleasure of your call?"

"I have a young man here who has a proposition I thought would be more suited for you."

Ra, the god of Egypt, turned to me. If looks could kill, and I'm not a hundred percent ruling out that they can't, he most definitely would have.

"What is the virus-infected leech doing here? Is this the

company you keep now?"

"You haven't even heard what he's here for; I think you will find it very interesting."

"What value could he possibly bring to me?"

"Well, this man would like to see Maat ended."

Ra looked at me. "What would you have me do? Walk into her stronghold and kill her myself?"

I was at a loss for words. "I mean if you could do that, it would save me a lot of time and effort."

That got a laugh out of Paimon, and even a small one from Ra who spoke, "It has nothing to do with whether or not I can, or even want her killed. She has pulled the wool over my people's eyes. They truly believe her to be one of my gods. If I were to kill her, and myself, it would look like I have lost control of my people."

"So, you won't help me?"

Paimon looked at Ra with a questioning face.

Ra thought for a couple of seconds before he spoke, "I think I shall help you."

Paimon jumped in, "Excellent! All I need is a finder's fee."

"Of course. Nothing in this world is free, I'm sure Anubis can accommodate you."

Paimon inclined his head slightly, then Ra turned back to me, "What I will do for you is make you all that you are. I will give you the Amulet of Awakening. It will allow you to access all your strength which is considerably more than you know. If you should fall, the amulet will vanish and you will take the fall completely, but if you somehow succeed, I will come for you in the form of what will look to be an avenger for a fallen god. I will take you with me and transform you into one of my vanguard."

Ra then handed me a necklace with a scarab pendant

on it. I looked at it for a moment, then put it around my neck. As soon as it touched my skin, it felt like it melted its way into it. I tried to remove it but it was a part of my body now. Ra walked up to me and looked down upon me, then said, "Good luck assassin." He stepped back through the rip scar and it closed behind him.

Paimon smiled at me. "It was good to meet you, young Simon. Would you shake my hand?"

I reached up and traded grips with him. As soon as he squeezed my hand, I was bombarded with visions: sitting in a boat with no oars or sail, standing upon a giant machine that was moving down rails, I saw myself standing around dozens of bodies, and then I was standing in front of a building made of metal and glass. A creature that looked like a cross between a werewolf and a gargoyle stared back at me with rage-filled eyes. Then I saw myself staring at Maat, while my world burned behind her. When I snapped back to reality, Paimon was smiling. He released his grip and said, "Good journeys, Simon."

He rode off into the distance and faded away.

Chapter 30

First things first, I needed to get out of this desert. I needed to make my way to Morocco; there were a few friends that I knew there. I could stop there, resupply, and get information that I needed to have. The trip took approximately a thousand years, or at least it felt that way. It was closer to about two weeks. I hid my armor in a bag I was carrying, and I even wrapped up my sword so that it was unrecognizable. I had to keep a low profile here. The city of Fez is too large and will have too many soldiers or mercenaries that would love to take me out. I knew a place that I could go where I wouldn't draw too much attention. It was my favorite tavern in the entire world. It had a little bit of a supernatural vibe and clientele.

I weaved my way through the streets and alleys. The aroma of the street food wafted underneath the hood of my cloak. I can't remember the last time I had a good meal, but I hope to rectify that soon. The entrance was in an alleyway on the side of an unassuming building. If you didn't know what you were looking for, you'd walk right by it. The door is painted to look the same clay color as the rest of the buildings, but if you look close, you can tell it is clearly made of some other type of heavy metal. There's a sign beside the door that reads in the Tamazight language, “Leave it at the door”.

Politics is strictly forbidden, or at least fighting over it is. This is a place for the supernaturals and predators to relax without the fear of being attacked. I still don't plan on revealing myself while I'm here. There would be nothing to stop them from having a hundred men standing outside waiting for me. You had to do a secret knock to get in. It really wasn't that big of a secret. It was two fast knocks, two slow knocks, and then three more fast knocks. It was really more just a tradition. Most exclusive clubs had some form of secret knock, plus it added one more layer of security. You really only had to be a certain prestige to be accepted. Even from a young age, as a vampire, I was well-respected for my skill and helping out the right people.

I knocked and the security window opened. The guard looked at me and I pulled back my hood slightly. He looked around and shut the window. After what felt like an eternity, but was probably only a few seconds, I heard the door unlock and it swung open. I recognized the guard as Rudolph. He is the most average-looking Moroccan man you can imagine. Just over five and a half feet tall, maybe slightly more muscular, dark hair, dark skin, and short beard. You wouldn't think much of him, but if you have the job of being the security at this place, you have to be a certified badass. I certainly would never be the one to cross him.

As I walked by he said, “Long time, Simon.”

“Way too long,” I replied. I made my way down the stairs. Once you reach the bottom of the staircase, there is a black velvet curtain. I could already smell the smoke and hear the music playing. As I stepped through the curtain, all my senses were engaged. From smells of delicious food to the playing of music, and the men and women dancing, covered in jewels. I forgot how amazing this place was. In the human world, creatures conceal their true appearance with magic or makeup. Down here, you are free to be who you really are. I passed by a table that had elves talking with a couple of wizards. Normally, elves will wear bonnets of some form to cover their pointy ears. They also typically have their bangs down to cover their larger-than-average foreheads. There were four ogres in the corner getting drunk. They used inherent magic to disguise themselves as human. There were all manner of races and even some legendary figures that you would know.

One person that did catch my eye was a man they called the Scion. They called him that because he could do things that other humans simply could not do. He was superhumanly strong, fast, and tough. The truth of the matter is, and most people here would know it, he is what we call an “involved”. They are humans whose parents are both one hundred percent human, and they use no magic to generate their base powers. In more ancient times, it would have been claimed that he was a scion of a god, hence his nickname. He is a very capable warrior and he is known to be a sword for hire. He is unmistakable; he looks like something Michelangelo would have sculpted: the perfect jawline, long black hair, and huge arms. I've heard it said that he reminds people of Beowulf or Achilles. People speak of how great a warrior Beowulf was, but I personally spoke with someone who saw Achilles in person. They told me that Achilles was a one man army, so I doubt he is quite on that level.

What has me worried is that I wouldn't be surprised if Maat had a price put on my head. So I turned out of his line of sight, and at the end of the bar, I saw the person I was hoping would be here. I walked up behind them and whispered, “I'm glad some things never change.” Rattenfänger turned, did a double take, then nearly tackled me with a hug. I patted him on the back. "It's good to see you too."

He squeezed me a little tighter. "I thought they had killed you."

"I'm like an ugly coin: you can't get rid of me."

"I heard what happened. I heard you broke out of prison. Then everything went silent. I thought they had done you in."

"I took a little detour through Africa to find myself."

"I caught word that something was hunting and killing vampires in central Africa. I was holding out hope that it might have been you."

Two mugs of ale were dropped in front of us. I downed half of it in one pull.

"God, that's good," I said.

He took a swig himself before asking, "So what brought you here?"

"I needed to resupply and get some information. That's where I was hoping you would come in."

"What do you need to know?"

"First, where are they holding Lina, and what type of shape she is in?"

He took another drink and sucked a deep breath in. "Well from what I hear they haven't been able to break her with their mental attacks, but I would not expect her to be in very good condition. They are holding her beneath the embassy in Paris."

I downed the rest of my ale which tasted like liquid gold after all this time. "I guess I know where I need to go."

Rattenfänger smacked the bar top and exclaimed, "I'm in!"

I gave him a skeptical look. "You're what?"

"I said I'm in. I'm with you all the way."

"I can't let you do that."

He laughed. "Nobody 'lets' me do anything. I do what I want" All I could do was laugh with him. He looked into his empty glass. "And what I want right now is for both of us to have another drink and get some rest before rushing into a certain doom."

"I'll drink to that."

So we did, but in the morning, I thought about sneaking off. Rattenfänger is truly my best friend, and I don't want to put his life in danger. Too many people have been putting themselves at risk for me, but if I knew Rattenfänger, he would be more pissed at me if I left him behind than he would if I took him to his death. Once we were both dressed and ready to go, which took him a lot longer than me, we headed off to Tangier to find another acquaintance. Rattenfänger thought it would be good to sing a ballad about our journey. I don't know how his spirits were so high because I was hot and sweaty and just wanted to get to the city, but there he went off singing.

"*The two best of friends*
will go off to defend
the woman the warrior loves.
Do not call us conceited
just because we know we cannot be defeated.
Noooooooo."

At this point, the cold embrace of death was becoming more appealing.

"Simon, what do you think?"

"I think if you do not stop singing, you will not have to worry about Maat, because I will beat you to death."

We entered the city in the evening. Even so, the docks

were still bustling which is not unusual for this being one of the busiest harbors in the world. I stayed back near one of the staircases that led up to the main walkway. I sent Rattenfänger to talk to him, seeing as how he's not wanted dead. I could see him conversing with the boat captain. It took him about two minutes and they both started walking towards me. I leaned out of the shadows and said, “Karim, good to see business is still going well.”

He laughed and smiled fully, which I know he didn't do very often since he lost one of his left teeth in a bar fight about twenty years ago. I met him about twenty-five years ago when he was in his early twenties. He is the best smuggler that I have ever met. If you need to get something, he can get it to you, and if you need to get something somewhere, he can get it there.

We shook hands and he said, “Simon, I always knew you lived dangerously, but you are one of the most wanted men alive.”

“I mean if you're only doing small jobs now, I understand. I'll find someone who's in it for the big money.”

He put his arm around my shoulder. “Simon, Simon… How much money are we talking about?” Rattenfänger pulled out a hefty pouch of silver. Karim's eye opened wide. “What kind of job are we looking at here?”

“The kind job where you take us to the edge of Maat’s domain.”

“Well you certainly don't do things half-assed, do you?”

I smacked him on the shoulder. “You know me, when I do something, I go whole assed! How long will it take us to get there?”

“Well, this trip normally takes me about a week.”

“We will be there in four days,” I said to him blatantly.

I was able to help push the boat to its limit. We actually made it in under four days, but I never told him how we did it. He just thought everything was perfectly favorable with the current, and I let him go on believing that. Rattenfänger and I were laying in special compartments that Karim had made for smuggling goods. The compartments were nearly pitch black. The only good thing was whatever he had treated the wood with in the compartments kept them completely dry. I could hear as we entered the river. It had a different rhythm than the ocean. If you've been around the water enough, you can tell the difference in smells when you go from the salty smell of the ocean to freshwater. I heard him acknowledge a couple of people but the boat kept going. I felt like we were getting close when I heard shouting coming from the shore. I heard a boat pull up beside us. The boat swayed as we were being boarded.

I heard Karim call out, "What can I do for you, gentlemen?"

A man with a nasally voice responded, "This is a restricted space, what are you bringing through?"

"I was not aware that there was a section of the river I could not pass through, but if you must know, I am carrying mostly spices."

This is where he earned his money, and boy did he ever earn it. The son of a bitch opened two barrels full of garlic, as well as some other pungent items. I could hear the two men backing away.

Karim upped the pressure, "Would you guys like to see some more? Here, a free sample of garlic, on the house." I heard the clove hit the floor.

"That is quite alright. Keep it moving."

"Will do," Karim said with a satisfied tone.

We only moved for about another minute before I felt

us bump against the bank of the river. Karim gave us the all clear, and we popped out of our concealment. We exchanged handshakes and hugs. Before he let go of my hand, he said, "Give them hell."

"I'll give them death. God decides where they go."

I handed the scepter to him and he nodded. Rattenfänger and I knelt behind a line of shrubs.

Rattenfänger looked me in the eyes and said, "I'm going to get you in that building, but I won't be able to help you once you're inside. I don't do well in close quarters."

"You get me inside, I'll do the rest. Maat might have magical defenses around the property."

He laughed, "She certainly does. I can feel it all around us, but their magic can't stop my music." He pulled his flute out and began playing the loudest melody I had ever heard from him.

On the other side of the shrubs was a brick walkway that was as wide as a road leading to the embassy. Rattenfänger walked down it, playing his flute, and guards began slowly walking towards him like they were possessed. He walked all the way to the front door, collecting all of the guards in the area, even the ones that we didn't initially see. He walked back down the path where I was hiding with a line of vampire guards following him. He gave me a nod to head for the door and I took off as fast as I could.

I stood there staring at the door handle, knowing full well that on the other side was probable death. I spoke words of strength out loud to myself, "My whole life I've been the matador, but today I become the bull."

I touched the amulet on my chest, and instantly my senses became more acute. I could hear guards on the other side of the door. I could smell them. My eyes were more focused than they had ever been before. I pulled out my sword. I was as ready as I would ever be. I put my left hand on the door and listened. I slammed my sword through the door, and when I pulled it out, it was covered in blood. I quickly opened the door and pulled the dead guard out of the hallway.

The embassy was covered in white marble. It was almost distracting. I made my way slowly down the hall, being sure not to make any noise. I stopped at the end of the hall when I heard a guard coming. I counted his steps: one, two. I swung my sword out and his head toppled from his body. I leapt down the hall and slashed through the next guard that rounded the corner. I peaked around the next wall. It was a set of stairs leading down to the next level. I stayed close to the wall as I crept down the stairs. The hall split at the bottom. I looked left to see a guard looking away from me, but I didn't see the one coming from behind me.

“Hey!” he yelled as he slashed down with his sword. I ducked under, kicked in the side of his leg, and as he fell, I took off his head. I immediately threw my dagger at the other guard and it slammed into his sternum. As he reached to pull it out, I speared him through the neck. He dropped and I knew others had to have heard me. Half a dozen men poured into the hall from the next room. I ran straight into the group, bunching them up which allowed me to slash and stab away. They tried to fight back but they had no room to move. It was a slaughter.

After the last had fallen, I moved down the hall. I turned into the first door which led to another corridor. I stopped and listened; I could hear a group of voices. I went through the third door on the right. It was a room similar to a balcony seating section at a theater. I crept to the doorway, and I could see a gathering of top ranking vampires. There, Maat was standing in the middle of the room. Then I saw Lina in tattered rags that passed as clothing. They forced her into a room that was through the back wall of the main room. I could see them shackling her to the floor. She fought but I could tell they had worn her out. Maat began to speak.

"This is the beginning of a new era. Those who would doubt me, or turn their back on our vision, will meet their end the same as this one." She pointed to Lina. "She stabbed me in the back after all the work I put into her, and the years of loyalty! Now she will meet the dragon's fire."

I had my opening. She was too busy boasting about her greatness to notice anything around her. I leapt from the balcony, and came down for the death blow. Half-way down, I was hit by a force of energy. It sent me tumbling across the ground. I came up with my sword in hand. I saw a handful of wizards, each pointing their staff at me.

Maat raised her hand to halt the group. "Stop! No one move." I looked around and all eyes were on me. She was wearing an ornate jacket that she slid off her shoulders. "Look here. This is the spy who has turned my daughter against me, but I am glad he is here." She turned her attention to me. "You have tried to undermine me from the shadows, and now you try to assassinate me. I can sense you have been associating with demons and gods, but now it's just you and me." She turned her head to speak to the group behind her. "Back up," she commanded. Everyone made a large circle. Maat had a wicked smile on her face. "This will be a learning lesson for everyone here. I will give you an opportunity to strike me down."

I could feel her expanding her aura. It was suffocating;

the air was thick with her power. I held my sword low on my right side. She didn't know how strong I had become. Though I couldn't compare to her, I had the skill advantage as well as the element of surprise. I couldn't beat her in a prolonged fight, but I could hit her first and that's all I needed. One strike and I could finish her.

I pulled my strength from deep within. With the amulet, it was so easy. I had it all at my fingertips. I could feel the sword vibrating. It wanted to bury itself in her flesh. The spectators faded into the background. I feigned a breath and twitched my left shoulder. Then, while I had her thinking left, I leapt with all my strength diagonally to my right. I immediately launched myself toward her. I focused all my strength into my sword as it was coming down over my head. I closed my eyes to concentrate all my energy into the strike. As I came down and finished the blow, it was like an explosion.

I opened my eyes. Maat was standing in front of me with my sword in between her palms above her head. My heart sank. I couldn't believe she could be that fast. She moved my sword down towards her chest, then snapped my blade in half. It sounded like a lightning strike landed in the middle of the room. She flipped the blade around palming the broken edge. She slammed the blade down into my right shoulder with such force, it sent me to my knees. It felt as though she had broken every bone in the right side of my body.

I could hear Lina scream, "No…!"

Our eyes connected for a moment. In that moment, I saw the best of my life: the last fifty-seven years flash before me. I couldn't hold it in. I vomited blood. The damage was so severe, even if she didn't decide to do anything else to me, I would probably die from my current injuries.

Maat turned from me to look at Lina.

"Her lust consumed her. Now so shall the fire consume her body." Maat conjured a ball of fire in her right hand, and threw it into the room with Lina. It felt like all the moisture in the world went into the room, as the fire erupted, engulfing her. I didn't hear a scream or a yell, nothing. Tears began to flow down my face. Maat turned around. Her smile transformed into a look of disdain. She spit her venom at me. "Where the fuck is your god now?"

My ability to talk had mostly faded by then. All I could muster was a few gibberish words. Suddenly, my left forearm began to burn. I felt the power coalesce in my hand in the form of a knife. As I had thousands of times before, I used the remainder of my strength and threw it with everything I had.

Time slowed. I could see the dagger rotating backwards, headed towards Maat. She lifted her right hand and I felt a magical shield forming. Asgardian runes erupted along the length of the dagger. It went through the shield like it wasn't even there. Maat's eyes were open as wide as they could be in shock. The dagger entered the palm of her outstretched hand like a hot knife through butter. It continued to pick up speed. The tip of the blade touched just underneath her right eye.

The world came back into real time. I heard the knife hit the back wall and clang as it hit the floor. Maat's expression was one of anger as she looked down at the hole in her right hand. She turned her hand over to look at the hole through her palm. Her expression turned to shock once blood started trickling to the floor from the hole in her face.

A voice that wasn't my own erupted from my throat in the form of laughter, "Haha!"

It was Loki.

Quickly after, my own screaming came through, "Fuck you! Fuck you! You took her from me." I was lost in rage as the whole room was shocked into silence.

She touched her hand to her bleeding cheek and she collapsed. I could feel the power coming through, as the rip scar formed at the back of the room. Ra stepped through to claim his prize. I remembered what a man said to me years ago. *Pick your battles and be able to live with the consequences.*

A blinding light came through the ceiling and landed in front of me. When it dissipated, there was what looked like a guardian angel. I blinked and there stood Thor. With one quick motion of Mjölnir, he dispatched the two vampires standing beside me. Wizards began sending fire and lightning from their staffs. Thor deflected them back into the crowd of wizards and vampires. Ra knocked half a dozen men out of the way. Thor began spinning Mjölnir until it appeared to be a solid shield in front of him. Ra sent beams of light from his eyes. The impact was deafening. It even pushed Thor back a few inches as his feet slid back across the marble floor. The bifrost slammed into the ground behind us, and with his free hand, he threw me back through it. The last thing I saw was Ra throwing something toward Thor.

I landed hard, rolling. I stopped at the feet of Loki. The bifrost ascended and there stood The Mighty Thor. When he turned around, there was a black spear that had impaled him through the left side of his chest. Mjölnir, as well as his right arm up to his elbow, was blackened by the beams from Ra. Baldr ran to him, and caught Thor before he fell.

You could see the frustration in Baldr's face when he

asked, "What did you do, brother?"

Thor was in obvious pain, grunting, "I saved the little warrior."

I don't think anyone who stood around understood the situation.

Baldr pleaded to his brother, "Why?"

Thor smiled as he looked at Loki and fought through the pain to say, "A room full of ancient vampires, wizards, and the god of Egypt himself, against Thor, Odin's Son. I wanted to know what it was like to be the underdog again."

And that's how I lost it all. I killed Maat, and I survived Ra, but I lost Lina. I'd give it all away for one more day with her.

Acknowledgements

I would like to thank my lovely wife Kelsea for allowing me the time it took to write this novel. I know it wasn't always easy. You helped to keep me focused on the finish line.

To my best friend and true brother: Nathan who always encouraged me. You kept my imagination sharp all these years.

To my editor, Erica Ellis, without you this book would be just a bunch of words thrown on the page. You turned it into a novel.

To my best beta readers: Jacqueline and Katie. Thank you for the support and help sharpening this story.

Last but certainly not least. To my son Alexander. I hope that when you hold this book in your hands over the years you'll see that dreams are worth pursuing and to never giveup.

Outro

Simon will return.....

Our next story in the More Than Human Universe takes
us to 1869. Izzy is the best sharpshooter on Earth.
She is hellbent on chasing down a robber
baron who is gobbling up the railroads.
She'll find out that there is more to this robber baron
and to the world around her than she could imagine.

He will find out she's More Than A Gunslinger.

About The Author

J. R. Carrel

I want to thank you for reading More Than A Vampire. If you enjoyed it please leave an honest review on Amazon. Every review brings The More Than Human Universe into reality.

JosephrCarrel.com - Website
@JosephCarrel87 - Twitter
J.R.CARREL - Facebook

Printed in Great Britain
by Amazon